The Rosary

The Rosary

Barbara L. Monahan

Rev. date: 11/03/2015

To order additional copies of this book, contact:
Xlibris
1-888-795-4274
www.Xlibris.com
Orders@Xlibris.com
715478

This book is for

Jim,
my second husband and soul mate;

Mary Kay, Jimmy, Danny, Kim, Thom, Steve and Rob,
my children;

my grandchildren and great-grandchildren;

my parents;

Pat and Kathy,
my brother and sister;

and

Carolyn and Pat,
my best friends.

We learn many things as we grow older;
loving more deeply and unconditionally is one of them.

CHAPTER ONE
Richard

Richard Lawton walked down to the deck at the edge of his property after dinner to smoke his last cigar of the day. The deck overlooked the St. Joe River and was built across the rear of his property adjacent to the river. He had the deck built shortly after buying the four-bedroom house three years ago. His wife Betty was against buying such a large home from the start and wanted to downsize, since all of their four children were married and on their own, but the river won out.

Richard always wanted to live on the water and justified his decision in buying the property by telling himself there would be ample room for everyone when their children and grandchildren came to visit. He also purchased a pontoon boat, so they could enjoy the benefits of the river and later added an indoor swimming pool and a tennis court.

On this particular inlet called River's Edge in South Bend, Indiana, there were eight homes built on oversized lots. All of them had showcase gardens and lawns of velvet and some with swimming pools. Luxurious cars were driven by many of the residents that included Land Rovers, BMWs and classy convertibles. During the weekdays, domestic and maintenance workers could be seen coming and going, tending to the lifestyle of the homeowners and the upkeep of their property—a haven of new money and upper crust living.

A two-tiered deck spanned the width of the lot. Building it was his idea. Betty was against the idea from the start, because she knew she would never derive pleasure from it. Her temperament was not compatible with the outdoors. She preferred to be pampered by air conditioning in the warm weather rather than experience any discomfort due to the heat. In the colder months, the benefits of a deck were hardly worth considering to her way of thinking. Betty's home improvement agenda had only one purpose—enhancing her wants. Any changes or additions Richard might want to make had to benefit her well-being, and the deck wasn't one of them.

The lower deck was divided in the middle by steps, leading down to the river. White wicker chaise lounges and rockers were arranged in seating groups on both sides of the steps. An umbrella table with four chairs and Richard's favorite chair, an old beach chair that had seen its better days, were placed on the upper deck. He headed toward it.

The part of the day Richard liked the most was the time he stole for himself while smoking his evening cigar on the deck when the sun was setting. The deck was a place for temporary escape. The sounds of the river and the incredible sunsets never failed to calm his spirit regardless of the season.

He took his favorite cigar out of his shirt pocket, an Arturo Fuente, unwrapped the cellophane around it, sniffed the aroma of the tobacco and moistened the cigar in his mouth. He lit it, drawing in the pleasure of a good smoke, needing this respite to face the remaining hours that lay ahead.

As for smoking, he had tried to break the habit time and time again, but only for a short period was he able to abstain before starting up again. He rationalized his inability to stop by telling himself cigar smoking was his earthly reward for the life he now had.

His life with Betty had become a pattern of repetitive actions almost to the point of being robotic, and nothing amazed him concerning her needs. It was easier for him to cope when he thought of himself as a robot—no thinking, no questioning, no feeling, nothing. He simply went through the motions doing a series of tasks that needed to be done day in and day out. If there was a solution to break away from this routine he could live with, it eluded him.

It was a cool evening with a gentle breeze. The tulips were pushing out from the ground in the beds on each side of the deck, announcing the coming of spring. The repetitive lapping of the water against the side of his pontoon boat, which was moored close to where he sat, was the only sound to be heard. After the first two or three puffs of the cigar, he began to feel his body relax. There was an agreement he had made with himself. Betty was not allowed to mentally claim any of his thoughts during this private time of his, and he tried hard to stick to it.

In his solitude he felt the emptiness that filled his soul. He often wondered if God would grant him an honorable escape through death. He was ready for it should that be His will. The next thought cancelled the previous one. Should he die, what would become of Betty?

As Richard tapped the ash from his cigar, a memory from the early days of their marriage invaded his reverie. After Betty and he made love, on those rare occasions when short term pleasure won over hardcore reality, he would often have a cigar, calling them victory cigars. He couldn't afford a good cigar then, only those cheap ones that came five in a box, which he usually bought at a drugstore. How crazy it all seemed now. There were no victories, and he certainly never won anything—not her love, nor her concern or even her appreciation for the many things he had given to her during their married life.

He became angry with himself. No more thinking about Betty tonight, which was easier said than done. She demanded so much. He never could determine whether she was the bigger thief of his hours or his way of life. Trying to figure out where it had all started to go downhill was senseless and dragging up the yesterdays and rehashing them again and again gained him nothing.

To those who did not know much about his private life, he appeared to be one lucky guy on the surface. He had four great kids all grown and leading good lives on their own, a wonderful home with many amenities, his share of toys, a membership in a prestigious country club and more than a handful of close friends. He also had a profitable business that provided for all of his family's needs over time, a brand new car every other year, a sizeable retirement account and a community that respected him.

Buried under all the outward signs of success was the one failure he found hard to accept—a loveless marriage from almost the very beginning, and it was much too late for an honorable dissolution of it. Time and circumstances had taken care of that exit years ago. His marriage to Betty was a mistake.

He felt old and used up. Despite all the signs of outward success, he felt cheated of the one thing he craved. No one knew how deeply he yearned to have a woman love him for himself.

As the dusk turned into early evening, he looked at his watch, stood up and put his cigar butt into a nearby coffee can. It was time for him to tend to duties.

The uphill climb to the house always winded him a bit. As he approached the patio, he stumbled over a loose flagstone and cursed. Not so much over the wobbly stone, but what awaited him. He opened the backdoor, went in and locked it.

Climbing the stairs to the bedrooms on the upper floor, he heard Betty call his name. "Richard, hurry up. Why does it take you so long to smoke one of those disgusting cigars? You are so inconsiderate, always thinking of yourself first."

As he walked across the room to her bed, he mentally corrected himself. There was something in his life that was amazing after all. Outwardly, he was functioning as a normal human being, but inwardly, he felt dead.

CHAPTER TWO
Kate

The alarm on the bedside table sounded. Kate turned reluctantly to shut it off. In the process it fell to the floor. She bent down to pick it up and returned it to its rightful place. Oh, how she wanted to curl up under the covers rather than get out of bed. Watching those late night movies were beginning to take their toll.

Sunlight streamed into the room through the white lace curtains. Looking out the window from her position in the bed, she could see three birds perched on a tree limb in the side yard. Their heads were close together as if they were discussing what they would do today.

Kate knew only too well what was on her agenda for the day. She was due in court to finalize the dissolution of her thirty-year marriage to Michael Francis Flannigan. During the two years they had been separated, she had tried everything she knew to get Mike to come back, but nothing worked. Actually, their relationship had begun to deteriorate prior to his leaving home. During this time, and after he finally moved out, she had shed plenty of tears over their relationship and the hopelessness of a reconciliation. She was more than ready mentally and spiritually to finally get on with her life.

The telephone rang.

"Hello," she said cheerfully, as she picked up the phone on the nightstand.

"Hey, it's me. Today is THE day," Jackie said.

Jackie Williams was Kate's only sister, and she was very close to Kate. She was the same height as Kate and thin, had an afro hairdo, big brown eyes that didn't miss a thing and could be counted on to do the unexpected. Kate was older by ten years, but Jackie was older by other standards. Jackie had been divorced from Steve Williams for five years. No children and no regrets. Steve was a state cop and had been an abusive husband. There were scars, but Jackie hid them well. Her life was better without Steve.

With her share of the divorce settlement Jackie bought a carryout pizza place in Springfield, Illinois, where she lived ever since she had been born.

Kate and Mike were also born and raised in Springfield, but after Kate and Mike married, they left Springfield and moved to another state due to his job. Over the years, a series of relocations followed for the same reason. The last move brought the family to St. Louis, Missouri, bringing Kate much closer to Jackie, and only 110 miles separated them.

For awhile there were hard times for Jackie and a lot of hard work, learning the pizza business, but it was paying off for her now. She had found her niche, and her bank account reflected it. Jackie thought with her head first. With Kate it was the other way around. Her heart always led the way.

"Thought I would call to see if you changed your mind about having company today," Jackie said, giving her sister one last chance to have someone by her side in the courtroom.

"No, I can handle this on my own, really. Gosh knows I've had ample time to come to grips with my marriage ending in divorce. Believe it or not, I'm ready for it to officially end. Today, I get my maiden name back. If mom and dad were alive, I wonder if they would approve?"

"I think they definitely would approve of their oldest daughter saying enough is enough and be done with it," Jackie said forcefully.

"You always seem to say the right thing at the right time, sis. Listen, I got to get going. I'll touch base with you later to let you know how it all went down. Okay? In the meantime, stop worrying about me. I'm fine. I really am."

"I'll be thinking of you," Jackie said before disconnecting.

Quickly, Kate got out of bed and headed for the bathroom. She brushed her teeth and then entered the shower. The water was hot and steamy just the way she liked it. It felt good on her skin. She toweled herself off and reached for her under things. Lace today, definitely lace. She wanted to look and feel as good inside as she did on the outside. Getting divorced after living with the same man for thirty years was a big deal to her. She wanted to look her very best.

Taking a package of panty hose out of the dresser, she sat down on the unmade bed and began to pull them on carefully. She didn't want to snag them. Her legs were slim and well shaped. Many times Mike told her they were her best asset.

Mike. Who would have guessed their marriage would be turning out this way? Surely, not any of their seven children who were now all grown, making their own way. Her mind drifted back to the scene she had with Mike the night he told her he was leaving her. He had come back from another one of his many weekend trips—trips without her. He told her he needed time to find himself. She never knew where he went nor did he ever leave her a phone number where he could be reached. Gathering her courage, this time, she decided to confront him. It was then he told her he didn't love her anymore. He only loved her as the mother of his children and he was leaving her. She pleaded with him to reconsider, losing her self-respect in the process. That night would forever remain in her memory—the beginning of the end.

She later learned he was seeing another woman. His affair and his all too frequent bouts of drunkenness had led to the destruction of their Catholic union. His neglect and disrespect of her hadn't helped either. In her head she knew her marriage was over, but her heart fought hard to accept it.

There had been one failed attempt to get their marriage back on track. Maybe she loved him too much, and Mike didn't love her enough, and toward the end not at all. After she accepted Mike's unwillingness to change during their separation period, see a counselor or talk to a priest, she no longer wanted to be his receptacle for any further mental punishment and filed for divorce.

Opening the closet door, she looked carefully at her suits. Not the black one. No dark colors today or a dress. No frills, all business. Her outward appearance needed to reflect how she felt inwardly. Like Jackie, there were scars, but she was more than ready to let go. She selected the red suit, a tailored white silk blouse and laid them on the bed. Out of a shoe box, she took a pair of black patent sling pumps. She then selected a matching black handbag with a shoulder strap. Taking her time, she began to dress.

Make-up was something Kate had never mastered as a young girl. It had never really interested her, taking more time than she wanted to give to it. She was five feet, three inches in height and slim. Her eyes were blue. Her brown hair was naturally curly, short and attractively styled, and her skin tone had a healthy, natural look. When she smiled, it was genuine, coming from within. Everything you wanted to know about Kate O'Connor Flannigan could always be learned from the expression on her face. What you saw is what you got. Her openness and honesty made her very vulnerable, but was magnetic.

Her optimism was high, especially in situations where she knew things may not turn out the way she hoped. The worse the odds, the better she liked it, although she did not think of herself as a risk taker. However, today, she was more than ready to legally get her maiden name back and get on with her life.

One last touch. She opened her jewelry box and selected her mother's pearls and matching earrings.

It was time for assessment. The suit hugged her body in all the right places. She was pleased by what she had chosen to wear. Not bad, not bad at all, she mused. There were still a few womanly weapons she could count on to keep a member of the opposite sex interested—at least if the right one ever waltzed into her life. She smiled and felt good about herself. Soon, she would be free. She picked up her handbag and car keys off the dresser, locked the house and got into her car.

Kate had been driving around for a good fifteen minutes before she finally nabbed a parking space three blocks away from the courthouse in Clayton. Not knowing how long the procedure would take, she loaded the parking meter with plenty of quarters. She crossed the street, bought a cup of coffee at McDonald's and walked toward the south entrance of the St. Louis County Court Building. After going through the check-in process, she asked one of the security guards where Court Room #9 was located.

"Take the escalator to the second floor, then the elevator to the fifth floor. Turn left after getting off. Court Room #9 is the second door on the right," the guard said.

Kate nodded her thanks and got on the escalator. As she rode up, she looked over the rail at the lobby below and saw two policemen guarding a group of four men in orange jumpsuits with hands and legs shackled. *Their freedom is being taken away, and I'm getting mine back today,* she thought as she sipped her coffee. Her incarceration period had been served. Her children, family and close friends had witnessed her pain at being betrayed and then rejected. With their love and help and her faith, she had managed to get past the hurdles of bitterness and resentment. Now, her entire motivation was geared toward moving on and starting over. As she got off the elevator, she was more than ready to begin the first day of the rest of her life.

Standing near the door of Court Room #9 was her sister Jackie, and she spoke first. "You didn't think I would let you have all this fun by yourself, did you?" she asked as she hugged Kate tightly. "I got up with the birds and drove down early."

"I should have known you would never let me go it alone. Thanks for coming to be at my side," Kate said, trying very hard to hold her emotions in check after seeing her sister.

"Every time I asked you if you wanted me to come you told me to stay put. I decided to quit asking permission and just get in the car and drive down this morning and seek forgiveness later. By the way, this court date is a little early for this old body of mine, when considering my prep time and the driving distance. I expect you to pay for lunch after you legally get undone from Mr. Wonderful to offset the pain of my early morning rising and subsequent traveling.

Of course, the price for my reassuring company will be discussed later, but it won't come cheap, you can count on that," Jackie said lightheartedly.

"I'm really glad you're here. Rest assured lunch will be on me and will definitely include dessert," Kate said.

As they entered the courtroom together, they found seats on the right side where Kate's lawyer, Brianna Ryan, was already arranging her paperwork on a table directly in front of her.

When Kate first contacted Brianna, who was recommended by a close church friend, she had a mountain of questions. The passage of time allowed Kate not only to take advantage of Brianna's legal savvy, but also to foster a genuine friendship with her. Kate knew Brianna liked her spirit and respected her for the choices she had made in dealing with Mike while he continued to live with her until everything was in place for his new life.

Kate reached over the balustrade that separated them and touched Brianna's shoulder.

"Hi, Brianna. Is everything okay?"

"Yes, it is. Any last minute questions, Kate?"

"No more questions, Brianna. I'm into answers now."

"Good. You're going to be fine, sweetie," Brianna said, and squeezed Kate's arm.

Within a few minutes, the bailiff made an announcement, "Hear ye, hear ye. The Honorable Judge Horace Burnett now presiding. All rise."

The sound of a door closing was heard. Kate looked around, but did not see Mike. She knew he would be sitting in the back of the room so he could make a fast exodus when the formality was over, the old easy-in and easy-out routine.

In the blink of an eye it was over, taking less than twenty minutes for the Honorable Horace Burnett and the legal system of Missouri to undo a married relationship of thirty years. She was now legally single again. Mrs. Kate Flannigan was now officially Ms. Kate O'Connor.

Kate thanked Brianna and both women wished each other well. Mike was nowhere to be seen as Kate and Jackie made their exit.

Kate breathed a sigh of relief. The last thing she wanted to do was exchange any words with her new ex-husband. Upon entering the hallway, both Kate and Jackie saw Mike in a phone booth with his back to them.

"Probably calling the Missing Persons Hot Line to see if his one friend has been found and if so, demanding an explanation why he didn't show up this morning," Jackie said. She had some of her own baggage to deal with concerning Mike. During the years Mike and Kate were married, she had refrained from making an issue over his patronizing behavior and his rude remarks to her.

"Whatever made me think I could do this without you?" Kate asked.

"Beats me. You would think the bell would have gone off in that head of yours. Forget it. Fortunately, I know just what both of us need right now—a greasy bowl of chili and a piece of pecan pie," Jackie said happily.

"You thinking of O'Brien's?" Kate asked, glancing at her sister with raised eyebrows.

"You bet I am. Let's hurry and beat the noon crowd," Jackie replied, taking her sister by her arm as they headed toward the elevator.

O'Brien's was not far from the courthouse, so they decided to walk. When they entered, it was noisy as usual. After waiting a few minutes, the waitress seated them and took their order. Jackie was full of questions, but Kate made little verbal effort to respond, only nodding or giving a yes or no answer.

"Okay, let's have it. What are you thinking? Get it on the table. Then, we'll dissect it for what it's worth," Jackie said, taking command of the situation.

"I don't know if I am up for one of our go-arounds," Kate responded with a sigh.

"My foot! You know as well as I do when you are on the brink of deciding something you usually make a survey of any living thing that has two feet and a head to find out if you just might be on the right track. As a case in point: remember when you were thinking of putting shutters on the house a couple of years ago, and you couldn't make up your mind? Well, I remember. You asked the mailman what he thought, your neighbor, Mrs. Bishop, what she thought and probably any delivery person who rang your doorbell that day. So, try me. I have opinions, too."

Their food had been brought to their table and between bites, their conversation continued. "If you must know, I have been thinking about the house," Kate said. "Maybe I should sell it. After all, what do I need with a four bedroom, three bath home now that I'm all alone?"

"I give up. Don't tell me only one hour after getting the house in the divorce settlement, you've decided to get rid of it, especially after telling me many times your greatest fear was not getting it?"

"I know, I know. But, the house has a five-year balloon note coming due in two months, and interest rates are certainly not the best right now," Kate said. "Besides, I found something that might work better for me, and I really don't need to maintain a big house anymore."

"Sounds like I'm hearing a germ of an idea here, Kate," Jackie said. "It's about time you are finally going to do something for yourself."

It was sometimes difficult for Jackie to understand her sister's perspective on family matters, maybe because she never had any children. She liked kids but knew motherhood was not for her. Despite their closeness, this subject had never been discussed between them even after Jackie divorced Steve Williams. She lived by herself for some time until Cole Jacobs entered her life many years ago and moved in with her. Neither of them was interested in getting married. They didn't seem to need a marriage certificate to prove they loved each other and continued to live happily together ever since they became a couple.

After they finished their lunch, Kate paid the bill. As they were leaving the restaurant, Kate said, "Are you staying over at my place or heading home, Jackie?"

"Don't take this wrong, but I think I've had enough excitement for today, so I'll pass," Jackie answered.

"I am so very grateful you drove down today. I really mean that."

"No big deal. What's a sister for anyway? I'll take a rain check on the idea you've got under your bonnet, though. Tell me about whatever is on your mind later when we have more time to talk," Jackie said.

"What makes you think I have something under my bonnet?" Kate asked.

"Oh, come on. I can smell one of your surveys a mile away," Jackie replied.

"Okay. I plead guilty. I'll clue you in soon. Call me when you get home, so I know you got there in one piece," Kate said, giving her sister a parting hug.

As Kate watched her sister walk away, she thought they now had something new in common. Both of them were divorced. However, her sister had a man in her life. Kate did not.

CHAPTER THREE
Richard

The smell of coffee woke Richard. He turned over in his twin bed and saw Betty was still asleep. Quietly, he gathered his bathrobe and slippers and headed downstairs. Louise Elmore, their housekeeper, was having a cup of coffee at the table and reading the newspaper when her employer came into the kitchen.

"Good morning, Louise. How goes it?"

"Can't complain, Mr. L. Sun is in the right place, and I'm vertical," Louise said.

Richard liked Louise and was lucky to have found her. She had been recommended by one of Richard's close friends who had employed her. When he and his family moved to another state, Richard wasted no time in hiring her. She lived only a few blocks from the Lawton home. She was pleasant, compassionate and capable. Her husband George was a postal worker. The couple was childless, enhancing her availability. Initially, she was hired to come twice a week to do the laundry and cleaning.

On the first day of Louise's employment, Richard had a conversation with her about his wife's excessive abuse of alcohol. Although discussing this subject with Louise was embarrassing for him, he wanted to prepare Louise for what he knew would be the norm, such as finding vodka bottles hidden in the various rooms she would be cleaning and Betty's abusive nature when she became intoxicated. He also asked Louise to inform him when a delivery was made to their home from a nearby liquor store, which was Betty's way of replenishing her supply of vodka behind his back. Most importantly, Louise was never to challenge Betty concerning any of these issues, because Betty would insist on her dismissal, the very last thing Richard wanted to happen. After his talk with her, she said she understood and would comply with his wishes.

With the passage of time, Betty developed multiple sclerosis, and the progression of the disease made it difficult for her to do many of the household duties that required physical effort. It was then that Louise came every weekday to care for her, taking over the running of the household completely and preparing meals for both of the Lawtons. On the weekends Richard took over the care of his wife unless other plans were made.

Richard knew Betty made certain Louise understood who was in command by tolerating and belittling her often. He also knew Louise's strengths. She was no novice in caring for someone with multiple sclerosis, taking Betty's verbal assaults and mood swings in her stride and overlooking them for what they were. At one point she told Richard caring for Betty was no picnic, and he appreciated her honesty. Louise was a keeper as far as Richard was concerned. He sensed the empathy she felt for both of the Lawtons was what motivated her to return each day.

"RJ called and wants to meet you for lunch today, Mr. L."

"Today?"

"Yes," Louise said.

"Did he say where and what time?"

"The Stadium, of course. He said between noon and 12:15."

Richard's only son, Richard James Lawton II, was known to family and friends as RJ. He was the image of his father, handsome, blond hair, expressive blue eyes, an overactive sense of humor and a personality that drew people to him. He wanted to become a coach, but fell in love with Sarah Winslow his senior year of college and married her. Her father talked him into joining his business after he graduated. The couple had three children, a girl and twin boys, and lived within a short driving distance from his parents' house.

"I'll call RJ while you fix me a ham and cheese omelet. Okay?"

"Deal, Mr. L. Give me five minutes. I'll call you when it's ready."

Richard heard the banging of pots and pans as he went into the library to phone his son. RJ answered on the first ring and said, "Hello."

"Good morning, RJ," Richard said.

"Hi, Dad. I'm running late. How about lunch at The Stadium around noon?"

"Works for me. See you soon and slow down," Richard replied and hung up the phone.

Shortly before noon, Richard pulled into The Stadium's parking lot. Within minutes RJ drove into the lot and spotted his dad's car, honking and waving as he passed him by. He had to circle the lot twice before he found an empty space. Locking his door, he grabbed his suit coat and started walking toward his father who was waiting for him.

Richard was proud of his son. His wife Sarah was a wonderful mother and homemaker. The couple's children were all good students, everybody was healthy and the family was a happy one. They were a church-going family who lived their faith and were really active in their church. Several times the whole family had been to third-world countries to do their share of rebuilding or whatever else was needed. RJ was everything a father could ask for in a son and genuinely enjoyed his son's company.

"Hi, Dad. Good to see you. How's it going?" RJ asked, as he caught up with his father.

"It's been one of those weeks. The parking lot is jammed. Let's hope we don't have a problem getting a booth," Richard replied, as they entered the restaurant.

"Not to worry, Pop. Old Vinita will take care of us. She knows better than to make us wait too long. Besides, she likes us. Here she comes now."

The waitress approached the two men and greeted them with her usual brand of witty humor. "Hello, do I know you two? You must be movie stars, right? How about a booth in the corner so you won't be bothered by photographers?"

RJ nudged his father. "See, I told you she likes us."

"We'll take a booth," Richard said without making a comeback to Vinita's last remark.

Vinita shrugged and led them to a corner booth and left them with menus.

"I'm having the Firehouse. How about you, Dad? Can that stomach of yours stand the assault?" RJ asked, as he folded his jacket and placed it on the seat in the corner of the booth.

The Stadium was known for its homemade chili. The grease covered the chili in the bowl like a blanket covers a baby. When the oyster crackers made contact with the chili, they turned orange.

Vinita returned to take their order, bringing two glasses of water. "What's it to be, men? The usual?"

RJ smiled. "Vinita, Vinita. Okay, just to keep you from becoming too much of a know-it-all, I'll have a Coke instead of a Pepsi."

Vinita raised her eyebrows and said, "I know you're doing that just to confuse me, but I'm on it. What about you, Mr. Lawton?"

"Make that two of the same, Vinita," Richard said.

"You'll be at risk, but it's your call. Don't worry, I'll bring extra crackers and keep watch on those water glasses to put out the fire," Vinita replied, gathering up the menus.

After she left, RJ immediately asked, "How's Mom?" He noticed how his father's shoulders sagged and how preoccupied he seemed to be. He was looking at a man he didn't recognize anymore—someone going through the motions of life without any personal participation.

Richard sighed. "She had a bad night. At one point, I thought I might have to take her to the hospital. This morning I talked with Dr. Norton. He said I need to really think about putting her in a nursing home soon. He made it pretty clear at this stage of her disease, I would not be able to give her the care she would receive in a nursing facility. I haven't mentioned this to Louise yet, but I know this news will not come as a surprise. I don't know what I would have done without her help these past months."

"Listen, Dad." RJ paused before he continued, wanting to be certain his father was really listening. "You've done everything you possibly can and more to keep Mom at home and comfortable this long. Frankly, you look like you could stand some rest yourself."

"I'm fine, really. Just things on my mind."

RJ's next words were chosen carefully before he spoke them. "It's time to let go, Dad, and let God take care of her."

Richard heard RJ's words, but was wrestling with his own inner demons, recalling a memory his son's words had triggered. Several years ago he was fed up with Betty's drinking and insisted she enter a treatment center. As he put it to her, she was going or else. The else was never defined out loud, but Betty sensed she had no choice but to comply. She went all right, screaming and cursing him every mile to Indianapolis, where the treatment center was located and far enough away for discretion. It came as no surprise to Richard when Betty told him it would be thirty days of imprisonment for her without the aid of any liquid crutch to get her through the countless hours of boredom.

The alcohol abuse education she received produced nothing in the way of change in her or her habits. The day she was released, Richard drove her home. After she was settled, he returned to work. Later, Louise told him as soon as she saw him drive away, Betty began frantically looking for the bottles where she had previously hid them. When she realized all of the liquor in the house had been disposed of before her homecoming, she then called the local liquor store and made arrangements for a delivery.

When he returned home at the end of the day, Louise met him at the door, shaking her head. He found Betty passed out on the chaise lounge in the bedroom with a bottle of empty vodka on the floor nearby.

Due to the progression of the disease, it became obvious Betty's condition would demand around-the-clock care. Richard made a pact with himself. He would be her caretaker—not her caregiver. There was a profound difference in motivation between the two, according to Richard. A caretaker assisted because of duty; a caregiver assisted because of love. With Louise's help, he had been able to care for Betty at home, but all of the family knew she would eventually have to be left in the hands of professionals.

He never knew if it was the booze or the disease that made Betty the way she was. When she was rational, she was a hateful, vindictive person, striking out at Richard as if to punish him for her condition. Often, she would exhibit much of the same behavior with her grown children as she had with him, driving them all away with her verbal attacks. None of them escaped her abuse.

RJ sensed his dad was taking a trip down memory lane and wanted to bring him back to the present, so he asked, "How's business these days?"

"Fine. Two new accounts came on board last week. I'm thinking of hiring a part-time designer."

Richard was the senior partner at Lawton and McBride Advertising Agency, the leading advertising and graphic arts agency in the South Bend, Indiana, area. Richard and Stan McBride had worked hard to make it so. Next year they would celebrate the company's thirtieth year in business with a client list that reflected some of the region's top companies.

The last couple of months, Richard had been leaning on his partner more heavily due to his personal demands at home. He waited for Louise to arrive in the morning so he could leave for work, and she waited for him to return in the evening to take over Betty's care. The routine had become his life, and because of the stress this generated, he had little peace of mind while earning his living.

Although Stan and Richard did not see each other socially, they respected each other and made a good team. Richard knew he would have to do something soon to get back on track with his business responsibilities. He wasn't being fair to Stan, and it laid heavily on his mind.

Vinita brought their food and said, "Enjoy," as she served the chili to the two men. Both of them picked up a spoon and began eating, smiling at each other as the crackers turned orange.

RJ grinned. "I'm addicted to this greasy mess like a gambler is to a slot machine. I think if Sarah had the recipe and made it, I'd be tempted to eat it for breakfast."

Richard laughed. His mood always brightened in the company of his son and looked forward to the luncheons with him.

Noting the two men had finished eating, Vinita approached their table, began clearing it and asked, "Would either of you like dessert? The cook made pecan pie today."

"I pass," RJ said, patting his stomach. "I would like a cup of coffee though."

"Same for me, Vinita," Richard said.

Waiting for the coffee to arrive, RJ looked at his father and decided to speak his mind. "Listen, Dad, you need a life. All you do is see that Mom is taken care of and go to work during the week. On the weekends when most people are out having fun, you take care of Mom yourself. Your daughters are worried about you as much as I am. You can't make a life sitting by a bedside."

"I know that, son. I also know it's time to put her in a nursing facility. I've already checked out the one Dr. Norton recommended. He said he would get back to me very soon."

RJ blurted out what was also on his mind, "Dad, we all know you'll take care of Mom, but what about yourself? I'm just going to say it. You need a woman in your life!"

Richard was somewhat taken back by his son's suggestion. Months ago Dr. Norton told Richard that Betty was destined to spend the rest of her life in a nursing facility, and he should prepare for this inevitability.

One of the first things he did was to consult his lawyer about his financial position. After hearing the facts of the situation, his lawyer advised Richard to obtain a divorce. Richard fought him hard on this advice. It seemed a cruel and heartless thing to put Betty through, considering the circumstances. After his lawyer explained the reasoning behind it, he complied, realizing monies would be needed to pay for Betty's care, the duration of which was not known. Their assets were divided fairly based upon each of their circumstances. Betty's share was put into trust funds for their four children.

At that time Betty also understood the reason for the divorce and agreed to it. It was handled quietly. Few people knew about it, although Richard told all of his children, and they also understood the reason for it.

"Listen to me, son. I am not interested in female companionship. I do have a woman in my life, and I am trying my best to deal with the cards that have been dealt to me. If things ever change, I could never take up with someone whose earlier life I know nothing about. Today's dating game is not what it was when I was in my twenties. Too many hidden mine fields for this old man. Let's drop it, shall we?"

RJ had one last arrow in his quiver and shot it. "I know this sounds sort of crazy, but just for grins, is there someone out there from your past who would interest you?" He did not want the conversation to end without getting some response from him, because this particular subject was one his father never wanted to talk about.

Richard put his coffee cup down and said nothing, looking out into space. Minutes passed. Then in a very low voice, Richard said, "There would be only one, RJ. I took her to the senior prom and dated her after graduation. I haven't seen her since art school, and I know nothing about her or her life. We never ran into each other at any of the class reunions."

"What's her name?" RJ asked.

"Mary Katherine Flannigan is her married name. Her maiden name is O'Connor."

"What was she like?"

"She went by the name of Kate and being with her was an adventure. She was a girl who knew the value of a day and lived each one like a celebration. When I was with her, she made me feel I was the reason for the celebration. I wanted to make her my wife after I finished art school."

"What happened?"

"She married someone else, and so did I," Richard said.

"And?" RJ asked, wanting more information.

"That's it. Like I said, we both married other people."

RJ wasn't satisfied with his father's response. There had to be more than his father was telling him. He pursued the subject by asking, "Have you ever thought about getting in touch with her, you know, finding out about things?"

Richard didn't want to admit the truth to his son. There had been times in the past when he thought about calling Kate.

"The answer to your question is no. My life is what it is. Right now, I have to get going. I'm late for a meeting with Stan. He's probably chewing at the bit wondering what's holding me up. I'll take care of the check. Leave Vinita a good tip. I'll call you about the nursing facility as soon as I hear from Dr. Norton. Good to see you, son."

He got up from the booth and quickly walked to the nearest exit.

CHAPTER FOUR
Kate

Kate woke up early Saturday morning and could hardly wait to telephone Jackie. She knew better than to phone her sister before mid-morning. Jackie always slept in Saturday and Sunday mornings because of the late weekend hours at her pizza place.

Breakfast was a cinnamon roll and coffee with the morning newspaper. Kate was now on the third cup and could not contain herself any longer. Glancing at her watch, she dialed her sister's phone number and prayed silently Jackie would be awake.

"Good morning. I hope I did not wake you," Kate said apprehensively.

At first there was no reply, and Kate thought she might have dialed the wrong number. Then she heard a muffled response from her sister. "It better be at least 10 a.m. for your sake," Jackie mumbled.

"I'm sorry if I woke you, but I can't wait to share my news."

"Yeah, okay, okay. So, what's your news?" Jackie asked.

"I sold the house and got my asking price. Your idea of putting the listing on the bulletin board at work paid off," Kate said.

Kate worked at Missouri Life Insurance Company in the Marketing Department. She liked her job and also the people with whom she worked, who looked upon her as a team player.

Although she had nothing to do with the actual selling of the various healthcare plans to companies, she was responsible for assisting a vice-president, a sales manager and eight sales associates in the Marketing Department. She provided the sales associates with the informational packets that went to the movers and shakers of the more than 500 plus employee groups who contacted them for possible health coverage for their employees.

"An employee in Human Resources saw the posting and came to see the house with his wife. They liked everything about it and even wanted to buy some of the furniture. We dickered a little over the money thing, but in the end I got what I wanted. Another plus is they want to take possession within the next thirty days and assured me financing would not be a problem."

"That's really great news, Kate. On the other end of that happy stick, have you found anything yet? Finding a house in thirty days might be tough. Tying all the knots connected with new home ownership and moving are going to be hard to pull off in that short of time, and I don't mean to be negative, either."

"I know. It is what it is. There is another reason I phoned besides telling you I sold the house. Remember when you accused me of having something in my bonnet? I did, but there was no time to go into details, then. What I really would like is for you to come to St. Louis this Monday since the pizza place is closed and help me decide between two houses I have been considering.

"One is a fixer-upper only two blocks from my old house, and I so love that area out by Grant's Farm. The other one is a surprise I am saving until you see it for yourself. Please tell me you can come. I know how busy the weekends make Monday a day of catch-up for you, but I really need your input," Kate begged, just a little.

Kate had almost made up her mind but needed someone to tell her it was the right choice and who better, than her sister Jackie.

"Count me in. I like looking at fixer-uppers just like you do, because we both can visualize potential. And, a mystery house... I can't wait. You've tickled my curiosity. I'll be there around noon so you can set up appointments if necessary, and I'll stay the night. But, I really have to leave early Tuesday morning. Will that work for you?"

"It will. I'll get right on the appointment thing as soon as we hang up. Thank Cole for me, will you? He's probably going to get double duty Monday, isn't he?"

"Forget it. He doesn't mind or keep score. Pacify your guilt by thinking about all the times I fill in for him during deer season, quail season, turkey season, etc. Cole is truly a man of all seasons," and they both giggled. "Now, can I hang up and get at least another hour of sleep?"

"You bet. See you Monday," Kate said and hung up the phone.

* * * * *

Monday, Kate took off a day from work. She had looked at many houses and condos but finally narrowed it down to two possibilities. Today, she was determined to decide which house would be the one.

From the front window of her house, she saw her sister's truck coming down the street. Jackie waved and parked her truck on the driveway. Kate met her at the door and gave her a hug. "Hey, you made it. This has to be a first. You must have gotten up pretty early to get here," Kate said, knowing Jackie never liked getting up early for much of anything.

"You got that right," Jackie admitted.

"Come on in, and I'll pour you a cold Pepsi. That should revive you somewhat, while I fill in the blanks about today's agenda," Kate said, as she took her sister's tote bag from her.

They sat at the kitchen table that was covered with pictures and real estate papers concerning the two properties. Kate placed the cold beverage in front of Jackie and said, "This first one is only two blocks away. It has two bedrooms, a sun porch that connects the house to the garage, a basement and a double lot. It's also on the corner. The home is all brick and an older one."

"Aha, now I get it. You said the magic words—older one. That means it needs work, right? It's a fixer-upper, isn't it? I have the feeling you are preparing me mentally to commit to something later," Jackie said with arched eyebrows and a big smile on her face.

"Well, I might need a little of your help and ideas, if this is the one I end up buying," Kate said, grinning all the while.

The sisters shared a similar trait. They liked projects, especially ones that involved painting walls, refinishing furniture and sewing. When a project did not present itself, they usually went looking for one.

"There's a story about this house," Kate said. "On my run in the mornings, this house is on my route. On the side of the garage facing the street, there are two ceramic pineapples. One is hung higher than the other between the two windows on the garage wall. They are about twelve inches in height and painted green.

"I could never understand why anyone would want to hang pineapples on the outside of a garage. I eventually found out a pineapple represents friendship and now, low and behold, those pineapples will be mine if I end up buying this place."

"Pardon me for making a point here, but I hope there is more to consider than buying a house based on pineapple ownership," Jackie commented, as she took a drink of her Pepsi.

Ignoring Jackie's humor, they headed out the door and got into Kate's car. Kate began telling Jackie more about the property while driving to it. They parked on the street in front of the house, and Sally Evans, the realtor, was waiting for them on the front porch.

"Hi, Sally. This is my sister, Jackie Williams. I brought her along so she could see the house and help me make a decision."

"No problem. Hi, Jackie, nice to meet you. There is no furniture in the house so you'll be able to visualize the fit of your furniture more easily," Sally said.

After Sally unlocked the door, the three of them began the house tour with Sally leading the way. There was a wood burning fireplace in the living room with custom built-in bookshelves on each side of it. The dining room was spacious and had an elegant crystal chandelier. The carpeting in both rooms needed to be replaced. Off to the side of the dining room was a hallway that led to a bedroom at each end of it. The bedrooms were in good shape with adequate closet space. A remodeled bathroom separated the bedrooms. Next to the bathroom was a door and when opened, steps led to the basement. At one end of the dining room, a butler's door opened into the kitchen. Although the appliances were up-to-date, the cabinets were outdated, but a coat of paint could easily transform them. The back door of the kitchen led to the sun porch, and Kate could visualize her old upright piano fitting nicely against one wall.

They checked out the basement where the laundry facilities were. The walls and floor were unpainted, and the ceiling was not finished. But, the entire area was dry. The old coal chute had been turned into a closet. The entire area was clean and had plenty of natural light.

After seeing the interior of the house, the three women walked around the entire outside of the property.

The back yard was small and ran the length of the house. Cyclone fencing enclosed this space. At the top of the driveway, there was a small concrete patio. Concrete steps at the end of the patio led down to the additional lot. White wooden fencing that needed repainting surrounded this space on three sides. A row of small evergreen bushes had been planted on the other side of the lot that butted up to the driveway from the top of it to the street.

After the women had toured the entire property inside and out, Kate turned to Sally and said, "Thanks for taking the time to show me the property again, Sally. I plan to make a decision within the next two days. There is one other property I am considering."

"You know where to contact me, Kate. I realize this house needs some updating and a women's touch, but you know what they say about real estate… location, location, location. The only reason this house is listed below market value is because of the work that is needed. Don't wait too much longer to decide. Another couple is also looking at the property."

"I hear you. Again, thanks. I'll be in touch," Kate said. She headed to her car where Jackie was waiting for her.

Getting into the car, Kate turned to her sister and asked, "Well, what do you think?"

"You won't run out of projects there for a spell, that's for sure. It appears to be sound, but really needs some work, which I am certain you are capable of doing. I like the floor plan, and the fact that it's on the corner is a plus. Quite a bit of yard to mow, though. I love the sun porch with the louvered windows and doors on each side of it, one facing the street and the other facing the back yard. All in all, I can see you living there, Kate. Certainly, the price is hard to beat, especially with the location in mind."

"I agree with everything you said. Now, I am going to take you to the other one and, between the two, I intend to make a decision before you leave and not on an empty stomach. After we see the other one, we'll weigh the pros and cons of both properties over lunch. Agreed?"

"Deal. Let's go," Jackie said.

Kate started the car and headed toward Summerset Boulevard, the street address of the two log model homes, giving Jackie details along the way. "Both models cannot be seen from the street and were built behind Kerth Properties, the building between Harry's Restaurant and Midland Tire. My curiosity got the best of me not too long ago, when I saw a banner across the front of the building occupied by Kerth Properties advertising log houses. So, I stopped and went inside to investigate. As it turned out, there is quite a parcel of undeveloped land in back of the three buildings, where two models are on display. I was really impressed with what I saw. To make a long story short, a salesman took me through the two models and sent me home with a ton of material to read. All together there are five models, and all of them are lovely. One of the models I went through and really liked is called the Missourian."

"I know the area you are talking about," Jackie said. "I, too, have passed by these businesses and never would have suspected there were model homes in the rear."

"You may not know this, but I have always dreamed of living in a log house," Kate said.

Jackie's eyebrows went up a notch. Her sister was full of surprises lately.

Kate parked her car in the parking lot in front of Kerth Properties. She locked the car, and they walked around a stone path that led to the model homes in back.

Kate opened the door to the log house she had visited before, and Jackie followed her.

"Oh, Kate. It is beautiful," Jackie exclaimed, as she quickly took in her surroundings. They were standing in the great room with a massive fireplace that dominated it. At the end was a small kitchen with a bar and three kitchen stools that served as the dining area. The master and guest bedrooms and a bath were also on the lower level.

"The furniture in the master bedroom is gorgeous. It's Amish made, isn't it?" Jackie asked.

"Yes. Such quality, beauty and craftsmanship. I've always dreamed of having a bedroom set like that one," Kate said.

Jackie climbed the stairs to the loft, which overlooked the great room. She walked down the hallway to a third bedroom and a second bathroom. She came back to the loft, leaned over the balcony rail and said, "Kate, it's perfect for you. Does it have a garage?"

"Yes, but the salesman said there wasn't enough land to build a garage on this site. And, of course, it's optional. I prefer a carport anyway, which is also available and would be cheaper."

Jackie joined Kate on the couch in the great room. "What are your thoughts on this one?" she asked her sister.

"If I did decide to go this route, finding a lot would mean I would have to go someplace where zoning would allow a log house to be built, which probably means someplace in the boonies. Commuting time to work would be longer. Right now, I'm kind of floating in a dream state, toying with the idea of living in a log house," Kate said.

Kate not only had a forty-five minute drive to work Monday through Friday, but she also attended Concordia University's accelerated program two nights a week after work from 6 to 10 p.m. To fill the hours when she became separated, she enrolled at Meramec Junior College as a night student, pursing a degree in liberal arts. She graduated from their two-year program, summa cum laude and enrolled at Concordia University to complete bachelor degree requirements. Her goal was to teach at the elementary level, the same goal she had when she graduated from high school, a goal that never got off the ground.

She received a scholarship when she graduated from high school. However, when she shared this honor with her father, he said he could not afford to send her to college. Although she was disappointed, she took the news in her stride. Instead, she took a job at Bell Telephone Company as a typist. Six weeks later, her typing teacher in high school called her. The attendance clerk job was open at the school from which she graduated, and her teacher thought Kate might be interested in interviewing. After her interview, Kate was offered the job and took it to the dismay of her father and never looked back. It was the first time she had ever stood up to him for something she wanted for herself.

"My reason for asking you to come with me today was to help me make a decision. So, what do you think, Jackie?"

Kate was a little scared. She had never bought a house by herself before and wanted someone else to tell her whichever one she decided upon was okay. She had yet to accept the fact she didn't need anyone's approval or permission one way or the other.

"Can you afford the log house?" Jackie asked.

"Yes, but I'll have to make payments. However, everything would be new. If I buy the fixer-upper, I can pay it off in full and have no monthly payment, which would be a big plus. On the other hand, many repairs need to be done. Bottom line is I would have a little left over if I bought the brick house and none if I bought the log house."

"Listen, Kate. Start thinking about what you want only for yourself. Buying a house is just like anything else, only a lot more money and more on the line. But, when the time comes to make your decision, if it's the brick house, I know you will be able to turn that house into something beautiful and have fun doing it. If the log house is your dream, then go for it, even if it does cost more money. My advice is to choose the one that will make you happy."

"I guess I have to convince myself it's okay to get new dreams, when the ones you have held onto for years have gone up in smoke. It's been a long time since I only had to think of myself," Kate said with a catch in her voice.

"That's the beauty of it all. You are capable of starting over, even if you might be having doubts right now. Good Irish stock and all that. Don't let your fears become your friend. You have a plan. Now, go work it. Buy the house you want, and don't look back. Just remember I get dibs on being the first one who sleeps in the guest room regardless of the one you choose."

"You always give me good advice. Let's go see if Mr. Simmons is on duty. He's the sales rep I talked with previously. I'd like to ask him a few more questions I've had since our last conversation."

"Would this Mr. Simmons happen to be athletic, intelligent, handsome, middle age and available?" Jackie asked.

"You're impossible. I am interested in a log house not in Mr. Simmons. I could care less about a man in my life right now. Okay?"

"Okay. I promised to behave myself, but one day you'll care all right. You may be divorced, but you're not dead," Jackie added with a mischievous grin on her face.

The two women walked the short distance to the sales office in search of Mr. Simmons.

CHAPTER FIVE
Richard

The clock in the kitchen chimed. Richard heard a car door slam. He pulled back the kitchen curtain. His friend Ken Patterson was walking up the driveway. Before he could ring the doorbell, Richard opened the door.

"Good morning, Richard. Where have you been hiding yourself? I've called you several times and left a message on your phone but didn't hear from you. I decided to take the chance you would be home this morning, hoping you might be up and around. As a peace offering, in case I said or did something that has triggered your silence, I brought doughnuts."

Ken and his wife Linda were neighbors of the Lawtons when both couples lived in Brighton Green subdivision. Their kids and the Lawton kids lived in each other houses while they were growing up. The two families saw each other socially at least once or twice a month, vacationed together several times and formed a closer bond than just being good neighbors. Both couples were within the same age bracket and had similar interests. As the friendship blossomed into a solid relationship, Richard thought of them as extended family.

When the Lawtons moved to the river, the friendship continued. Ken loved to fish and usually appeared early Saturday mornings now and then to shoot the breeze with Richard and go fishing.

Richard opened the door wider and Ken entered. The two of them went into the kitchen. Ken took a seat at the kitchen bar and took a really good look at Richard's face while he was pouring him a cup of coffee. There were circles under Richard's eyes more pronounced than before.

"I've tried several times to reach you, Richard, but I never was able to catch you at home and didn't want to leave a message. I hate to come home to a lot of phone messages at the end of the day, especially if they are trivial ones. However, if I didn't know you better, I might be inclined to think you have been purposely avoiding me for some reason and Linda, too. It bothers me to think about all those fish that are getting away," and he laughed, using a little humor to lighten the weight of his words.

"Well, rest assured you have done nothing wrong and neither has Linda. The fault is all mine. I have been avoiding both of you."

Ken was relieved and worried at the same time. Richard's tone was not only apologetic but also very forceful.

"Let's go sit on the sun porch. Bring your coffee and the box of donuts with you," Richard said.

The sun porch had windows on the side of the house that faced the river. Ken chose a chair away from the sun and put his cup on the table next to where he was sitting and got comfortable. Richard did not sit but paced back and forth, as if he was trying to decide what to say and do next.

"I am glad you came by today. I have been meaning to call you, really. I know you and Linda have made many efforts to see me this past month, and I have made innumerable excuses not to get together. Actually, most of the excuses were lies to avoid any contact, and for that I apologize."

Both he and Linda were well aware of Betty's physical condition and her excessive drinking. Her declining health curtailed many of their past social activities. Ken replied, "You don't owe me or Linda any apology or explanation. Caring for Betty and running a successful business must fill your twenty-four hours to the brim. Small wonder you have time to do anything for yourself. I understand."

"No, you do not. How could you? I've never shared what our life was like before we moved here. God must have known how badly I needed to talk to someone today, and here you show up at the door."

Ken did not reply to his friend's last statement and waited for him to continue.

"What I am about to tell you, I've never told anyone else, Ken, including my kids. Get comfortable. This is going to take awhile," and sat down in a chair next to him.

Ken shifted in his chair, as if giving Richard a sign he was ready to listen.

"When I lost my oldest brother to leukemia, I was fifteen years old. I never thought I would ever find someone I could relate to like I did with him. Nick was my hero—an ordinary guy with a heart as big as the Grand Canyon and a good listener. I use to pour out my innermost feelings to him whenever I had some kind of problem. When he died, I was devastated. Years later, when you and your family came into my life and our relationship took off and grew, I felt the same way with you as I did with my brother."

Ken nodded at Richard, his way of acknowledging Richard's compliment. He was a little uneasy, mainly due to the seriousness of Richard's tone and his tense body language. Whatever it was that Richard wanted to share with him, he now had his undivided attention.

Because of their close relationship, Ken was well aware of the Lawton's marital problems and Betty's excessive drinking and said, "Whatever is bothering you, personally or professionally, get it out in the open, Richard. I'm here to listen and help in any way I can."

Richard paused, as if he was thinking about how to begin. After he shifted his body to get comfortable, he began speaking, looking directly at Ken. "When I was a senior in high school, I pretty much knew I wanted to become a commercial artist. During my senior year, I fell head-over-heels in love with a classmate named Kate O'Connor. Kate was my date for the senior class play and prom. I dated many girls in high school, but Kate was special. She was attractive, smart and athletic.

"Kate's father did not allow her to date during her high school years, which was not known to the guys in our class. She always came to school events with a girlfriend or not at all. Due to the importance of the senior class play and prom, Kate was allowed to accept my invitation to both with the provision there would be no more dating until after she graduated. Her father believed high school was for learning, and Kate would have plenty of time to date after graduation. Then, she could accept callers on her own terms.

"The summer after we graduated, we dated doing the things most young kids did during the fifties. You know, movies, miniature golf, dancing, picnics, going to baseball games, things like that. I knew then I had found my life partner in Kate. I even shared my feelings with my mother.

"One night after a date with Kate, my mother was up when I got home, and we talked about her. She told me I would never marry her, because Kate and her family were Catholics. And, Kate's father would never allow her to marry a Methodist like myself or anyone else who was not a Catholic. I told mom not to count me out and was determined to prove her wrong.

"Shortly after graduation, Kate went to work as an attendance clerk at the high school we had attended. I got a job detasseling corn, a hot and dirty job, but the pay was good. I was saving it to pay for my tuition at the Chicago Academy of Fine Arts, where I had registered for the fall semester. I was looking forward to a summer of working and fun, especially with Kate.

"When I cashed my first paycheck, I wanted to buy Kate something that would sum up my feelings and leave no doubt as to my intentions, but not a ring. I never asked Kate to go steady after high school or gave her my class ring to wear as a sign of how much I cared. I guess I didn't want to scare her off.

"I wanted to give her a gift that would indicate I had taken some time thinking about it—a gift that would say something about me. A buddy of mine also worked with me detasseling corn. We took turns driving to save gas, and our pickup place was a small strip mall not too far from the pickup spot. My buddy was late one morning. I passed the time by doing some window shopping while I waited for my ride. As if God knew what I was looking for, I saw the perfect gift in a jewelry store window.

"Lying on a velvet cloth was a miniature Bible with a lovely Cross etched in the middle of it. The Bible was gold finished and shaped like a book no more than an inch in width and a little longer in length. Along the spine were the words, *Gems of Prayer*. The other three sides had grooves of equal width resembling pages. A knob with a ring through it was on the top, allowing the wearer to thread a chain or ribbon through the ring so it could be worn as a necklace. When the knob was pulled downward, the grooved part revealed a delicate gold rosary in the opening. In the lower right hand corner the designer's name was engraved.

"That evening I took Kate to a baseball game at Lincoln Park. After the game ended, we continued to sit there until we were the only ones sitting in the bleachers. I told her I wanted to give her something before I left for art school. I handed her the gift box with the rosary inside, hardly able to contain myself, as I waited for her reaction to what I thought was the perfect gift.

"She took the box from my hand and opened it and after looking at my gift, she said it was beautiful. I told her to pull the knob downward, which she did. Then she said she had never seen such a tiny and exquisite rosary and asked me if the rosary had been blessed.

"Let me tell you I certainly wasn't ready for that response. I had no idea what she was referring to. I told her I didn't understand and asked her what she meant by her question. She informed me all rosaries had to be blessed by a priest before they are used. Not being of the Catholic faith, how was I supposed to know that? This was not going the way I hoped. I felt like a jerk."

Richard stopped for a moment in his story, thinking of what he had just described. He did not miss Ken's big smile.

"Yeah... go ahead and laugh. You might be interested to know the kiss I got that night at her door was well worth any prior embarrassment on my part due to not knowing about the blessing thing."

"Young love. I've been there myself. Okay, so you were rewarded. Then what?" Ken asked.

"I need more coffee," Richard said and also picked up Ken's cup. He wanted Ken to truly understand how all this past history with Kate was connected to his marrying Betty and also his present state of mind. After refilling both cups, he sat down and continued his story.

"The summer passed quickly. We had a few more dates, and then it was time for me to leave for school. The last evening Kate and I spent together was at her house. In my mind, Kate would always be on a pedestal. She was the girl I intended to share my dreams and future with and could do no wrong.

"We were sitting very close on the couch in the living room. I told her I would not be coming home until Christmas break. Money was tight and any extra expenses such as bus or train fare for visits home were out of the question. Asking Kate to wait seemed selfish to me. I had nothing to offer her but months of separation, but I was in love, and I believed she felt the same way toward me. She even asked me not to go. I told her where I was going was for our future. Seems to me I relayed my feelings pretty clear to her. We clung together like Velcro when we finally had to say goodbye."

Richard paused, as if he was mentally recapturing the moment he had just described to his friend. After holding eye contact with Ken for several seconds, he pushed back his chair and walked toward the windows, as if he needed time to gather this thoughts for what he was about to say next. When he turned around, his voice and body language were anything but passive.

"Mail call was the highlight of my day then, Ken. Being away from Kate for such a long stretch of time was the hardest part for me despite the written correspondence that was exchanged and more so on my part than hers. There were days when I wanted only to hear her voice, but there was no money in my budget for long distance phone calls.

"When I came home at Christmas time, life was good between us. I missed her more than I knew possible and over the holidays, I told her how much I loved her and wanted her to be a part of my life.

Our last night together was spent talking about our future. She was excited as I was about the days ahead. Thinking back, it was I who did most of the talking; Kate did the listening.

"I returned to school and Kate to her routine. My bank account had grown healthy due to the added wages from a part-time job parking cars at a garage. I got the job through one of the guys I knew at school shortly after I returned from Christmas break. When the chance came to enroll in the summer session, I signed up rather than wait until the fall semester. Finishing quicker was better to my way of thinking. I could get home sooner to Kate.

"One night coming home from the parking lot, I ran into some of the guys from high school who graduated with me. They were working for the phone company. After talking with them about my end of things, they invited me to move in with the four of them. We were close buddies in high school, and I missed home, my family and Kate. Hitching up with them would be a good deal for me, and I said I would do it. Their apartment was also much closer to the art school. And, a bunch of guys living together in a big city like Chicago reeked of the promise of good times. I packed my things and within the week had a new address.

"Often on the weekends, the four of them went home. Three of the guys had a car so transportation was no big deal. They liked to party at the bars they previously hung around in before they moved to Chicago, and home is where they headed at the end of the working week three Fridays out of the month.

"Letters from Kate became less frequent. Those I did receive could have been from one of my sisters. It is difficult to challenge a paper relationship when time and distance are factors. I wanted to know the reason why her letters to me were so impersonal, but I was not a paper fighter. If there was a problem, and obviously that was pretty evident, I wanted to look into her eyes for my answers, not tear open another piece of correspondence and guess what was really being said between the lines. In a few months I would be finished with school. Until then, my love life would have to take its chances until Kate and I were face to face.

"I didn't have to wait long for the other shoe to drop. The couriers of bad news were my roomies. When the guys came back one Sunday night from their weekend visit home, they told me they had seen Kate at the Fireside, a bar the young crowd frequented because of the great dance band that played there on the weekends. She was with some Catholic guy she met at Dorothy Blake's wedding, another girl in our graduating class. This scuttlebutt came from a close friend of Kate's who was at the Fireside the same night as my buddies were. According to this girl, Kate had been seeing this Catholic kid for several weeks. It appeared to be serious from what she had heard from the grapevine.

"I stood there dumfounded. My first reaction was the information had to be incorrect. Not Kate. Not betrayal. The *whys* were tumbling around in my brain, while trying to hide my emotions in front of my friends. I was determined not to let them know how deep or how much this news had yanked my heart out of my chest, but I was hurt bad. I resigned myself to silently tolerate what I had just learned until I heard the facts from Kate.

"Within a short interval, her letters to me stopped with no explanation offered. Oddly enough, she never got around to sending me a *Dear John* letter for closure. She just stopped writing. Maybe between the lines in her letters, she had been telling me things had changed between us, but I neglected to acknowledge them. Certainly, the infrequency should have been a red flag that something was not right, plus she had returned the rosary to me.

"Bouncing back was a horrendous process for me. As the weeks passed, I had no choice but to accept the fact Kate and I would be nothing more than a memory. I resigned myself to my circumstances concerning Kate. There would be no letter from me asking her for an explanation. The return of the rosary was explanation enough. It was over. Live with it and learn from it was the balm I applied to my broken heart. If I wasn't the man for her, I was not going to try and convince her differently. There wasn't going to be a Kate O'Connor in my life, and that was that.

"I began…"

"Time out," Ken interrupted, making a gesture with his hands indicating a break. "Are you telling me as much as you loved this young woman, you made no effort at all to see what the score was between the two of you? You let her go without so much of a letter or phone call from you? This behavior does not reflect the Richard I know."

"Well, back then I only saw black and white. There was no gray. That was my philosophy. If she didn't know the kind of man I was or had the potential to become, that was her problem. We Lawtons were raised that way. My mother always told all of us we were special, and she told us often. If Kate wanted to get serious with someone of her own religion or whatever other reasons that prompted her to put me out to pasture, then so be it. Although I was torn to pieces, I wasn't going to give her the satisfaction of knowing how much she had hurt me."

"I must say your reaction was admirable and manly," Ken said. But, it cost you something, didn't it?"

"Yes, it did. The loss of Kate was hard to bear, especially when the relationship crumbled without any explanation on her part, and I kept my feelings hidden from everybody, Ken. She had hurt me big time."

Richard began pacing back and forth in front of Ken and in a voice filled with emotion said, "So much for the Kate/Richard relationship. I began seeing a student at school, Elizabeth 'Betty' Rhodes. Betty was a blonde with a terrific body and somewhat of a flirt. There was a great physical attraction between us that soon led to sex. Two months before graduation she told me she was pregnant and said we would have to get married. This news hit me in the face full force, but I was raised to do the right thing. After the shock wore off, I did some heavy reflection. Because of my belief in Christ and marriage, I felt we should make the best of the situation by trying to make the marriage work. Betty agreed. And, in the depth of my heart and soul, I made peace with the fact I was going to marry a woman I hardly knew and did not love.

"Betty called her parents to inform them we were going to marry. She told them she would be bringing me home to meet them as soon as we could make arrangements. They lived in a small town three hours away from school. We borrowed a car from one of Betty's girlfriends to make the trip. Facing her parents was not easy for either one of us. Betty was their only child, and I'm certain they were disappointed. But, they accepted the situation and me along with it.

"Betty told me earlier her mother was a heavy drinker. The short time I spent with her mother during that weekend confirmed the fact Betty's mother definitely had a drinking problem.

"The following weekend I brought Betty home to meet my family. My mother was suspicious of the many hastily made arrangements and came right out and asked me if Betty was in a family way. For the first time in my life I lied to her, figuring the lie would take care of itself later.

"Two weeks before the wedding, Betty informed me the pregnancy was a false alarm. We decided to go ahead with the wedding, because neither one of us wanted to deal with the family issues, meaning explanations that were sure to follow had we decided to do otherwise. I did not have the maturity to call it off and put my family through the anguish and embarrassment. Certainly not a great way to start a life together, almost strangers, but we were two young people with different agendas, willing to make a go of it.

"We were married on a sunny afternoon in June at the Methodist Church down the street from my parents' home, where all my family and I were members. I stood before God and said my vows and promised myself I would do whatever it took to make the marriage work, but I knew it was a mistake.

"After the ceremony, a small reception was held at my parent's house in the backyard with the family and a few close friends of mine. Betty's parents didn't attend either the church ceremony or the reception. I don't think even Betty knew the reason why they didn't attend the wedding, and we both knew it had nothing to do with the driving distance. Sadly to say, they were not there to see how their only child looked as a bride on her wedding day."

"How awful for Betty," Ken said.

"Yes, it was," Richard replied.

Recalling this time in his life brought back a multitude of painful memories for Richard. He covered his emotions by lighting up a cigar and after several puffs continued his narrative.

"That evening, Betty and I got in my old green Packard, which I left at home when I went away to art school. We drove to Chicago where I had accepted a job in an established graphic arts agency. Our honeymoon was spent in a small one bedroom apartment we had rented the week before.

"Betty got a job as a receptionist, and money was no longer as tight due to the two paychecks. Within a short time we were able to trade in my old Packard for a new red and white Ford convertible. On the weekends we partied with friends from school or the guys I had roomed with previously and their girlfriends. Betty was definitely a party girl and liked going to the clubs to drink and dance. As the months rolled along, she started going out with her new girlfriends from work at night, which I did not like. I didn't rag her about it, because many nights I had to work late to keep up with the workload at the office, leaving her with time on her hands.

"Betty often came home from these evenings woozy from too much drinking. When the alarm went off in the morning on a workday, she would call in sick. We were young, and I understood the way she felt about her job. Marking time is how she defined it. Betty's art degree had yet to open any doors for her, and she did little or nothing to make that happen, and I let it ride.

"Our first child, Laura Lee, was born nine months later. Once again, money became a problem. Betty did not return to work after our daughter was born, and I changed jobs for more income. I was the assistant advertising manager of the Belmont Company, a leader in the field of fishing tackle. To supplement the loss of Betty's earnings, in the evenings I designed paper products such as plates, napkins, cups and tablecloths for a local graphic arts agency. Between the two jobs, I was working day and night. True to the promise I made to myself, I accepted the responsibility of husband, lover, provider and father and felt things were going along okay. Not great, but okay.

"The Belmont Company came out with a hot new fishing line they wanted me to promote with a very substantial increase in base pay plus a bonus on initial sales. The job required me to attend fishing shows all over the United States, giving fly casting demonstrations. I became an expert at fly casting and did many fly casting tricks that included volunteers from the audience. I must admit, I enjoyed myself every bit as much as the audience did.

"Betty stayed in the apartment with Laura Lee, waiting for me to drop in for a quick visit during the weekday when the show was within driving distance of Chicago, only to leave again to rejoin the circuit's schedule.

"What happened next I guess was inevitable, and I do not care to share the details. Let me just say trouble knocked on our door, and Betty answered it. She wanted out of the marriage. I blamed myself, and all of the ifs ran through my brain. If I had not traveled as much… if I had not worked all those extra hours at the art board while I was home… if I had paid more attention to Betty, her needs and our home life... and so on and so on. My self-examination made me accept complete responsibility for the break-up of our marriage. Divorce was not acceptable to me or would be to my family back home. These things didn't happen to Lawtons, and it sure wasn't going to happen to my new family. I was simply not going to let this marriage go under and let our beautiful little girl down. In the interim, Betty moved in with a girlfriend, who was also going through a separation, and took Laura Lee with her.

"We went to counseling, and the next year was spent trying to regain lost ground. I made up my mind to turn things around with Betty. When I did something thoughtful like giving her flowers, she showed no signs of appreciation or interest. If I took her out to dinner, it was not for my company but for another opportunity to drink. When I did something wrong, I was heavily chastised. Nothing I did pleased her. My emotions were like an elevator, and Betty knew just the right buttons to press.

"She, however, made no changes to her lifestyle when I was away. She continued going out with her girlfriends to the clubs, drinking and having a good time, and leaving Laura Lee with a babysitter. It was obvious the marriage counseling had failed.

"I finally came to the conclusion my marriage was over. I decided to quit my job, file for divorce and move to South Bend to start a new life. There had never been a divorce in my family. I was ashamed to tell my parents, let alone see them, so I shut them out, staying silent and away.

"Betty and Laura Lee moved in with her folks. If I thought I had hit bottom before, the days that followed were filled with remorse so great that I would have given anything to make it right. We were only twenty-two years old and headed for the divorce court. Laura Lee would never know me, and that is all I thought about morning, noon and night. At best, all I would get would be visitation rights. Kids were not given full custody to fathers back then. I felt so defeated. Every morning when I shaved, I was forced to look at the man in the mirror who had come to realize that no amount of success at the office can compensate for failure in the home. Despite my efforts to hold our marriage together, I had lost the battle.

"My lawyer called me to let me know the divorce papers had been sent to Betty. Two weeks later, someone rang the doorbell at my apartment. When I opened the door, Betty was standing there and asked if she could come in.

"I was more than surprised to see her, I was stunned. No effort had been made on her part to contact me after I was told she received the divorce papers, so I assumed she was in agreement about ending the misery both of us were living. I had no idea where this was going, and, as I opened the door wider to allow her to enter, I wondered if I might be making a mistake.

"She looked around before taking a seat on the couch and told me she got the divorce papers and thought it might be a good thing if we talked about the situation before either one of us did something we would regret. She begged me to listen to her and said she wanted to give our marriage another try, fully realizing she had disappointed and hurt me. But, she also had been disappointed and hurt. We were parents now, and there was a third person we had to think about, meaning Laura Lee.

"Her coming to my apartment that night caught me completely off guard. I had already thought long and hard on what would be best for Laura Lee before I went to see a lawyer. The thought of Laura Lee being shuffled back and forth between us for the rest of her life turned my stomach every time I thought about it. It also turned my stomach to have Laura Lee exposed to Betty's excessive and continued drinking.

"Then she told me, maybe she needed to receive divorce papers in order to wake up to reality and concluded the reasons the marriage had failed were due to long stretches away from each other, boredom, immaturity, too much freedom or whatever, and she pleaded guilty to all counts. She felt the one good thing we did together was Laura Lee and knew I would fight her for custody of our child. She was not asking for a miracle, just another chance, and her reason for coming to my apartment wasn't primarily because of Laura Lee, either. She admitted she didn't want to become a divorcee and really wanted our marriage to work. The whole time she was baring her soul, her remarks were delivered in a trembling voice and humble attitude.

"I was pretty shaken up myself, when I told her how much her showing up unannounced pulled the rug right out from under me. And, I told her I would have to think about what she had proposed. I then made it quite clear the love and trust I once had for her was gone. I believed then, once you have gone through a marital travesty such as we did, neither partner ever again regains what has been destroyed. She was asking a lot.

"As she got up from the couch and opened the door to leave, she turned and faced me. I'll never forget her parting words. With her cheeks wet with tears, she admitted what she was really asking for was forgiveness, and, if I could do that, maybe I might be able to give her another chance."

Bringing up these past events was not easy for Richard. He surprised Ken by saying, "Everybody has baggage, but you've probably really underestimated mine."

Ken let that one pass by asking, "Do you need to take a break?"

"No. I'm okay. It isn't easy going back. Second guessing is just another way of torturing yourself. I've certainly done enough of that over the years. Recalling some of the past times now makes me wonder if I did the right thing."

Richard put out his cigar in the ashtray and sat down again but said nothing for several minutes. Ken patiently waited for him to go on, and, when he did, his voice betrayed his weariness.

"After the shock of seeing Betty wore off, I did some deep thinking. Because of my upbringing in the church and my belief in Christ and marriage, I did not see how I could refuse Betty, although I had many, many doubts as to a successful outcome. But, I was willing to try. Maybe we both had gone through a rite of passage called growing up, since the whole mess had started. If I couldn't forgive, when it came around to my turn, would I be forgiven? Then, of course, there was Laura Lee to think about, too. I loved her so, and children need both parents.

"After many long gut-wrenching discussions between the two of us, promises were made on both of our parts. I phoned my lawyer and informed him we had reconciled our differences. There would be no divorce at this time. I quit my job, and we moved to South Bend where I started an advertising agency with a former coworker. So, it began, leaving our past behind us. The wounds of our marriage had left scars. But, new friends were made, and life went on. In the years that followed, Diane, RJ and Rachel were born.

"We functioned as a family doing all the things normal families do while raising kids. Then at the age of thirty-one, Betty got a bad break and was diagnosed with multiple sclerosis. The many doctors we consulted told us no two cases are alike and symptoms can be varied. A person may have symptoms that worsen over time while another person may not have symptoms for years. Betty started out in the first group. She was a fighter and was determined not to let the disease control her life.

"As my business grew and entertaining clients increased, so did Betty's drinking. She not only drank socially, she drank during the day while I was at work and the kids were at school and had several cocktails before and after dinner. If there is truth in alcoholism being inherited, it was certainly true in Betty's case. Like mother, like daughter.

"The number of times I had to apologize to clients and friends when we socialized because of the scenes Betty made was unbelievable, and, when we came home, I had to sneak her into the house so the kids would not know how drunk she was. I didn't want the children to see her in a drunken state, but I was only fooling myself. They knew, Ken. Kids are not immune just because they are kids. The stress that had invaded my life had also invaded theirs.

"It was during these alcoholic episodes that I thought if only I did this or that Betty would change or see the damage she was causing, not only to herself, but to our family. And, oddly enough, with all the problems I had at home, my business prospered, the children continued to grow up whole, and we all survived. I think this was also about the same time your family became more heavily connected with mine due to our kids being involved in many of the same activities at school. So much of the best parts of their growing up years were stolen from them because of their mother's addiction to alcohol. All of us had become experts at walking on eggs.

"Betty's drinking escalated, and, when the last child left the nest, it became a part of her daily routine. One vodka cocktail after another. She was by herself all day with no one to tell tales about her habits. Bottles of vodka were hidden everywhere and when she ran out, all she had to do was to call the liquor store and have more delivered. Many times I would come home from work and find her passed out. When she came around and tried to talk to me, I could never tell if her slurred speech was due to the disease or the vodka, and many trips were made to the emergency room from falls at home, cuts and broken bones. You and Linda should remember some of those times, because you were the ones who helped me more than once in dealing with them.

"I knew something had to be done to ensure her safety and quickly, after her last binge. I called all my daughters and son and told them I was placing their mother in a thirty-day alcoholic treatment center in Indianapolis, far away so her friends would not know, and they agreed with me. Unfortunately, this action failed to produce any positive results. Betty fought the doctors, the program and the whole concept of rehabilitation every day she was at the facility. It turned out to be a total waste of effort and money. The one thing it did produce was more animosity in Betty.

"Weeks turned into months, and Betty continued to abuse alcohol. RJ advised me to divorce her and start a new life, but there was no way I could leave Betty. Her parents were deceased by this time. I was her husband, and she was my wife, for better or worse, in sickness and in health, till death do us part. I agreed to those terms when I stood before God and married her, and I couldn't deny my own beliefs.

"Don't think I did not want to jump on a plane and disappear from the cards I had been dealt. I was a prisoner every bit as much as Betty was but in a different way. Maybe Betty wanted to jump on a plane and disappear, too. I'll never know, because to this day she has never revealed this to me drunk or sober in all the years we have lived together. Whatever demons she has, she has kept them to herself.

"Now you know all of it. As I said before, no one else knows what I've just told you. I have tried very hard to protect Betty and the family from all of this past misery and keep my public affairs and business image above reproach. Men don't want to admit to other men that things are bad at home, and for years I have been smiling on the outside and hurting like hell on the inside. I'm tired, Ken; I'm so tired, and I feel all used up."

Ken felt there was more to come, so he remained sitting, waiting for Richard to go on.

Richard pulled himself together, got up from his chair and said, "As you know, during the last few months, Betty's memory and bodily functions have become tremendously impaired. Sometimes even now, she doesn't know who I am. The drugs are making her comfortable, but they will never cure her, because there is no cure. With each passing day the disease takes more and more from her, and Louise, bless her heart, is at the end of her rope, too. I have been advised by her doctor to place Betty in a nursing home, immediately. You happened along this morning and like the crack in the dam, it all came pouring out of me."

Neither man moved or spoke, both wrapped in a silence that defied any speech or movement. It was Ken who broke the spell. He got up from the chair, walked over to where Richard was standing and put his arms around him, hugging him tightly. It was not a time for words, but a time for the sharing of understood sorrow.

CHAPTER SIX
Kate

Kate took off from work Wednesday, Thursday and Friday to move. She hired a moving company, and all was set for a Thursday start. The closing on her house was scheduled for Wednesday morning. The new owners were taking possession the following Monday. This schedule would give her more than enough time to clean up, after all of the furniture and the things in the garage were moved to her new place.

It was raining Wednesday morning, when Kate drove to Sally Evans' office to sign the necessary papers. The couple who purchased her home, the Stewarts, were already there and sitting in the lobby. She greeted them and said, "Are you as anxious as I am to get the paperwork part of this house buying over with today so we can both get on with it?"

Paul Stewart replied, "Probably more so than you. Our kids are driving us nuts. We've been living out of boxes for the last week. What about you?"

"My new place will definitely be an adjustment due to less square footage, but I'm hoping, once all of my furniture is arranged and the rest of my stuff is put away, it will be fine. I had a big garage sale a couple of weeks ago, which helped to get rid of a lot of things."

Kate had mentally placed the furniture in the rooms, when she first looked at the bungalow she had finally purchased, which was only a few blocks away from where she lived previously with Mike. She decided to put her desk and computer in her bedroom rather than the spare bedroom, which she wanted to have ready for any family members, when they came to visit and stayed overnight.

Due to the placement of the double windows in her bedroom, her bed would have to go in front of them and her desk to the side of it. Having a work space in her bedroom was certainly not romantic, but so what? There was no romance in her life anyway. Besides, one more adjustment more or less was no big deal. She was getting use to coping with a great many things.

Within a short time, she and the Stewarts were called into Sally's office. "Good morning, everyone," Sally said. "This is a big day for all of you. Please have a seat, and we'll get started with the paperwork."

Kate and the Stewarts spent the next hour completing the needed paperwork. The last piece of business was giving the keys to the home she once shared with Mike and their children to the Stewarts. It was a bittersweet moment for her, buying a home on her own. While she was married, she and Mike had purchased a number of other homes together, due to his job that required relocation to other states. This time, the name at the bottom of the contract would only be hers.

She said her goodbyes, left Sally's office and walked to her car. The house with the pineapples on the garage now belonged to her.

CHAPTER SEVEN
Richard

More than a year had passed. Somehow Richard managed to get through each month as if marking time, living the same routine day in and day out. He tried hard not to think of the future and was so grateful his business occupied his mind completely during the workday. When the business day ended, he had to take care of Betty, after Louise left for the day and on the weekends. His personal life had no luster, no highs or lows, just a routine that rarely varied.

Betty's condition continued to decline. She lost the ability to walk and became wheelchair bound. Richard had the bedroom furniture taken to the sun room on the main floor of the house, thinking she would have some enjoyment of at least looking out the big window in the room, while she stayed in bed or sat in her wheelchair. However, getting her up and about in the wheelchair was also a chore. Between the dementia and impaired attention, bladder dysfunction, muscle spasms and now the leg paralysis, it was getting harder and harder for Louise and him to care for her at home.

He now realized the decisions he had put off making could no longer be postponed. Every time he talked with Dr. Norton and was asked if he had started to look into a nursing facility for Betty, he became evasive. From the discussions Richard had with Betty before the disease really took hold, she told him she wanted to stay at home rather than the alternative. Richard was bound and determined to do everything he could to make this happen for her until there were no longer any options left.

Richard saw the mailman walk by through the living room window and went to get the mail. It was a gorgeous sunny day. The leaves had begun to gracefully float from the trees, as if on cue from the gentle wind that was responsible for their journey to the front lawn. Autumn was Richard's favorite time of the year. He scooped the envelopes from the mailbox and noticed there was a white envelope with an address he did not recognize in the upper left hand corner. Someone named Andrews was sending him something. It probably had something to do with a contribution. Then, he remembered. Jerry Andrews was the class president during his senior year in high school.

He went to his desk and sat down, going through the rest of his mail. The advertisements went into the wastebasket. The bills were put into the middle desk drawer for payment later. The white envelope was saved for last. He sliced the envelope open with his letter opener and inside was an invitation to attend his fortieth high school reunion and a RSVP form.

The reunion was to be held Saturday, October 8, 1993, at the Lakeside Motor Boat Club, where all of the others had been celebrated in the past, with a cocktail hour at 6 p.m. and dinner at 7 p.m. The following Sunday morning, a breakfast was also scheduled for 9 a.m. at Sullivan's Bowling Center.

As he was checking his appointment calendar, the phone rang.

"Hi, Richard. It's Connie."

"Hey, sis, good to hear from you."

Richard had three sisters and Connie McFarland was the middle one. Of the three, he was the closest to her. They were only two years apart in age and inseparable growing up. Where Richard went, Connie was not far behind. During their high school years, it was her big brother who looked after her, especially when she became old enough to date.

Shortly after she graduated, she married a classmate of Richard's, Lenny McFarland, who owned and operated the Cadillac dealership in Springfield. They had two sons, and when they finished college, both of them also worked at the dealership.

He did not hear often from his sister due to their lifestyle and Connie's involvement in it. Between entertaining clients, keeping up their home on Lake Springfield and spending several winter months in Florida, she called only when she had reason to do so.

After asking about Betty and exchanging news of both families, Connie asked, "Did you get the invitation to the class reunion?"

"As a matter of fact, I got it today and was just reading it. Are you and Lenny going?"

"Yes, that's the reason I called. I guess it's too early to ask if you plan to go. Should you decide to do so, you know you are always more than welcome to stay overnight with us rather than get a motel or drive back home at such a late hour," Connie said.

"Thanks for the offer. Right before you called, I was checking my calendar. I haven't been home for awhile and would really like to see some of my old crowd. The last reunion Betty and I went to was the tenth. Hard to believe forty years have slipped away. Let me get some things cleared from my end and get back to you. Should I come, I'll leave early Saturday and stop by the house so we can have some time to visit, how's that?"

"I'd like that, and so would Lenny. I hope you can stay overnight. We don't see enough of each other. Should it not work out, I understand," Connie said.

"Oh, don't forget to send in your reservation to Kathy Middleton if you plan on attending. Her address is on the form," Connie added.

"Will do. Tell Lenny I said hello, and I'll call you in a couple of days."

Richard hung up the phone and looked for the reservation form. He found it and put it in his desk drawer to fill out later, pending his decision.

He sat there and thought about the reunion, seeing old friends and such. And, of course, old friends included Kate Flannigan. He wondered about her and her life. Did she still look as good as she did in high school only older? Had the last forty years been good ones for her? Was she happy? Most importantly, would she be attending, too?

He wasn't ready to admit to himself or anyone else the possibility of seeing and talking to her was the real reason why he wanted to go.

CHAPTER EIGHT
Kate

Kate took a week's vacation from work to move, and the move went well. After all the boxes had been unpacked, the furniture arranged and order had reasonably been established, especially in the kitchen and bathroom, she felt at home. There was still much to be done, but for now, she was more than pleased with her pineapple house as she had come to call it.

There was only the weekend left before she had to return to work Monday and decided to spend it working outside. Since the weather was ideal, she decided to paint the mailbox at the end of the driveway, so she could plant some flowers around the base of it that she had purchased the day before. There would be plenty of time for the paint to dry before her mail was delivered around noon.

After she painted the mailbox and planted the flowers, she went to work in the garage. She was looking out the garage window when she saw the mailman's truck stop in front of her mailbox and went to get the mail.

As she walked up the driveway, she rifled through the various pieces of mail and stopped dead in her tracks when she saw an envelope with a return address from the Metropolitan Tribunal

Archdiocese of St. Louis. She quickly tore open the envelope and began reading.

Your former spouse has submitted a petition to this office, requesting an investigation into the validity of his marriage to you. It is the Law of the Church that you be informed of this petition and that you be provided with the opportunity to participate in this investigation. It is for this purpose this letter is being sent to you.

The more she read, the more shocked she became. Mike was petitioning the Catholic Church for a declaration of nullity, which meant there was some defect present at the time of their marriage, making it invalid from the very beginning. Looking at the date on the letter, he also wasted no time in applying for an annulment. They had only been divorced for a short time.

Forms were also enclosed for her to return, indicating her intentions concerning participation in the investigation. And, if she did not choose to participate, the investigation would proceed without her.

Her hands were shaking as she put the letter back into the envelope and walked back into the house. She sat down at the kitchen table and read the letter again. By the time she came to the end of it, tears were streaming down her face, and she was sobbing. Why was Mike wanting an annulment? There had to be a reason. Knowing Mike as she did, he didn't do anything unless he gained something from it. Then, it hit her. He wanted to remarry, and he couldn't do that in the Catholic Church without an annulment.

Knowing about a friend's annulment experience who had gone through the process, Kate was aware that a Tribunal does not attempt in any way to assess blame or impose guilt with regard to the process, but it simply attempts to obtain as much factual information as possible from both husband and wife to determine the validity of the marriage from its inception.

Regardless of the length of a marriage and the number of children that may have been born out of a marriage, Church Law considers the marriage is either valid or invalid at the moment it was contracted. When the Church finds some defect present at the time of the marriage, it is able to declare the marriage invalid from the beginning. However, the Church cannot annul a valid marriage.

Even with all of this prior knowledge, Kate had some problems coming to terms with the procedure. The divorce for her was bad enough, but an annulment would be the end. If she needed any proof there was no hope of a reconciliation, she now had it.

What about their children? Would they find out and, if they did, would they understand the annulment process and the reason for it? Most importantly, would they be affected by it emotionally?

All the happiness Kate experienced during the past week had been obliterated, after she read the letter from the Tribunal.

Right then and there, she decided she would not participate. She immediately went to her computer and typed a letter to the Tribunal, stating she had no intention of participating and asked to be notified of the results. She folded her reply, placed it in an envelope and went looking for a stamp. She would say nothing about the matter to her sister nor her best friend, Ruth, and especially, not to any of her children.

She took a wooden box from the top shelf of her closet where other private letters were kept and added the Tribunal letter and her reply to it, and returned the box to its place on the shelf.

She sat down on her bed. The letter's implications had hit her hard emotionally. She was totally devastated.

* * * * *

The year past quickly for Kate. Between working, going to school twice a week, all that degree completion required and fixing up her pineapple house, she had little time left for much of anything else, including a social life, however sparse.

Sometimes she would go to a movie Saturday evening with her friend from work, Ruth Dennison. Ruth was two years older than Kate and lived only a couple of miles from her and was also recently divorced. Their friendship blossomed through a mutual interest in writing and the desire to earn a college degree. Twice a week they attended evening classes at their respective universities; Kate at Concordia University and Ruth at Washington University. Kate wanted to teach; Ruth's interest was marketing.

Night school hadn't presented any eligible men for either one of them. Kate was usually always the oldest student in her classes and so was Ruth in hers. Starting college late in life was not the usual run-of-the-mill thing most women did.

Being divorced wasn't all it was cracked up to be in the sense of meeting the opposite sex, either. Kate was not the kind of person comfortable in making the bar scene to meet a man nor answering personal ads. Neither was Ruth. They both agreed being a late bloomer was a drawback in more ways than one.

Kate overslept Sunday. The sound of rain against her bedroom window woke her up. She glanced at the alarm clock, which she had failed to set, realizing it was too late to make the early Mass. She would now have to go to the last one at 10 a.m., which was the longer Mass due to the singing of the choir.

She laid there looking at the ceiling, thinking of all the things she wanted to get done today. Ruth was waiting for Kate's decision on the trip she wanted to take to Oxford, Mississippi, to visit Faulkner's home next weekend. Although Kate had never been to Oxford, let alone the state of Mississippi, she couldn't drum up enough enthusiasm to make the trip. She wasn't looking forward to telling Ruth, especially since Ruth had really pitched in and helped her during the move. She had even taken a day off from work and also showed up on the weekend to lend a hand.

Kate rose, putting her feet in the house slippers beside the bed. It was this gesture that reminded her of Mike. He, too, always hunted around for his bedroom slippers before he left the bed. She didn't miss Mike, but she did miss the intimacy, the witnessing of the repeated insignificant acts of the other person over the course of many years of living together that become embedded in the memory.

There were no bedroom slippers belonging to a man in her present life. Mike had found someone else. Why hadn't she? Stop it, she said to herself. I have a lot to be thankful for—a home I can call my own, an interesting job that pays more than an adequate salary and grown kids and grandchildren who are all healthy and great company. I've also been blessed with two close friends who would come after me in the wee small hour of the morning without reservations, a good mind and body and many more positives. So what if there is no man in my life? There may never be, and I will be just fine. One is a whole number, too.

Enough. It was time for her to get ready for Mass and tell God how very grateful she was for what she did have.

Kate rose and went to the kitchen to make coffee. While the coffee was brewing, she brushed her teeth and made the bed. She returned to the kitchen and decided to leisurely read the Sunday newspaper while eating her breakfast. After reading several sections, she suddenly looked at the kitchen clock. She didn't want to be late for Mass. Gathering the dishes, she put them into the dishwasher and hastened to dress for church.

She grabbed her purse and car keys, locked the house, got into her car and backed out of the driveway, heading for Holy Cross Catholic Church, the church she and Mike had joined when they moved to St. Louis. The drive there was only a five-minute one from her house, but Kate liked to get there before the service started to have her own personal time with God. Looking at her watch, there would be time to do that before Mass began.

The church was built in the round with a main aisle and two side aisles. Kate liked sitting on the left side and not in any of the front pews. She genuflected and took a seat in the middle before she knelt down to pray on the kneeler. No one had come into the section where she was sitting. After praying, she rose and sat quietly, waiting for the service to begin.

She thought about her failed marriage. It still bothered her. Failing was not something she took lightly, especially in a relationship that she vowed before God she would honor according to His will. On top of that, there were also her conflicting feelings toward Mike's annulment.

Overcome with emotion, she felt the tears run down her cheeks. Never before had she lost control of herself in public, but she was not ashamed to allow God to see her pain and offered a silent prayer to the One who knew her better than she knew herself. The prayer she offered was more of a request. She asked God for mental freedom from her failed marriage and to send her someone to love who would love her back.

Kate went home after church. After lunch, she decided to go shopping at the mall. But, first she planned to go through the stack of mail that had been piling up on the kitchen table all week. She changed her clothes, took a cold Pepsi from the fridge and sat down at the table and began sorting the mail—first the junk stuff, then the bills and lastly the letters. As she was going through the pile, a white envelope caught her eye. She recognized the return address. It belonged to Jerry Andrews, a classmate of hers from high school. Putting the rest of the mail aside, she opened the envelope. Inside was an invitation to her fortieth class reunion and a response form.

Kate and Mike missed only one of her reunions over the years, the tenth one, due to the death of Kate's father. She always enjoyed going to her reunions, and Mike did, too. Mike attended St. Patrick Boys High School and knew many of the Northeast High School guys, because he was on the basketball and baseball teams and played against them.

Her next thought caused her concern. If she decided to go, she would be going alone. Bummer! Why is it harder for a woman to go stag than it is for a man, she wondered? She decided to fill out the reservation form later and placed it on top of the bills she intended to pay. The rest of the mail went into the trash can.

Taking the shopping list she had made from under the magnet on her refrigerator, she glanced through it. New drapes needed to be purchased for the guest room. There would be no problem making a decision for new drapes. She could handle that one. Going to her class reunion alone was something else.

CHAPTER NINE
Richard

The past few weeks had been busy ones for Richard and had passed exceedingly fast. Between moving Betty into the nursing home and his work load at the office, he had little time to think of anything else.

The vacancy Richard was waiting for at Sunrise Manor had finally come through, and RJ helped him move Betty and her things into her new environment. She was now in the hands of professionals, which made both men rest a little easier.

He was also swamped at the office with deadlines to meet, finishing up projects that had been pending for his final approval and making arrangements to meet with a new client in Chicago Heights.

Shortly after talking to his sister Connie, he sent in his RSVP to Kathy Middleton. Connie was disappointed he would not be spending the night at their home, but at least she and Lenny would have a chance to visit with him at the reunion. Tomorrow he would be leaving for Springfield, and he still had lots of loose ends to tie up before he left.

Tonight, Richard was having dinner with Ken. Linda had been out of town for several days, visiting her folks, who lived in Milwaukee, and was due back late this evening.

Both men had a yen for pizza and agreed to meet at Leo's Italian Restaurant, their favorite pizza place. After parking his car, Richard entered the restaurant and immediately spotted his friend and walked over to where he was sitting at a table near the salad bar.

"You're on time for a change. I might even pick up the tab out of sheer wonderment of your timely arrival," Ken said, grinning at Richard.

Richard sat down and said, "September and October are my busiest months, and I am up to my armpits in deadlines. If I wasn't going out of town tomorrow, I would still be at the office burning the midnight oil or stuffing the files into my briefcase to work on at home over the weekend. He changed the subject and asked, "Have you ordered yet?"

"No, but here comes the waitress."

A young girl in a red polo shirt and black shorts with a pony tail approached their table. "Hi, my name is Molly. What would you like to drink?"

"We'll have two Coors Light and an extra large pizza. Make it half sausage, pepperoni and mushroom and the other half just pepperoni," Richard replied.

"Say, I know who you are," the waitress said. "Aren't you the fellow who designed Leo's logo and came up with the saying on the back of my shirt, 'You've tried the rest, now have the best?'" she asked.

"I'm the one. Does that mean I get extra pepperoni on my half of the pizza?" Richard asked.

"Probably not, but no harm in trying," she said as she wrote down their order, gave them a big smile and walked toward the kitchen.

"When is Linda coming home?" Richard asked.

"Late tonight around 10 p.m. When are you leaving for Springfield?" Ken asked. He knew Richard's reunion was this weekend.

"No later than 8 a.m. tomorrow morning. On the way down, I plan to see a client in Chicago Heights. I'll have some time to visit Connie and Lenny before the reunion. I also have some shopping to do this evening before I leave tomorrow."

"Maybe a new tie?" Ken asked, raising his eyebrows.

"Maybe," Richard replied nonchalantly.

Ken wanted in the worst way to ask Richard if he thought Kate might be at the reunion, but he kept his silence.

"Go ahead and ask," Richard said, as if reading Ken's mind. "I know you well enough that when you start fidgeting and acting like there is an ice cube down your shorts you want to know something.

"Okay, I'll make it easy for you. No, I do not know if Kate is coming to the reunion. I don't know anything about her life. I told you before all I do know is she lives in St. Louis, and I haven't seen her for forty years. When her mother died in the early sixties from cancer, I called her to tell her how sorry I was to hear her mother had passed. It was a very brief exchange. Since then I have had no contact with her or information about her. There will always be a part of my heart reserved for Mary Katherine O'Connor Flannigan regardless of where life has taken both of us."

"I'm surprised. I would have thought you would have made inquiries to find out if she would be coming," Ken said.

"You have a devious nature I was not aware of, ole buddy. No, I made no inquiries and furthermore, I'm not going to this reunion to rekindle a romance from the past, especially since I have no clue about her life's history all these years since high school."

"I'm not buying what you're trying to sell, but, whatever the weekend brings, I hope you find some answers. And, I promise I won't say a word to Linda about the reunion. You know how she is. She'd hound you with questions before and after," Ken said.

Their conversation ceased, as Molly approached their table with more beers and the pizza. Richard had not been totally honest with his friend. He was very much interested in the life and times of Mary Katherine O'Connor Flannigan, and, to his way of thinking, a new tie certainly couldn't hurt.

CHAPTER TEN
Kate

Kate planned to repaint the walls in the guest bedroom. Ruth helped her pick out a color, after seeing the new drapes she had purchased, and was coming over later to help. She was on the ladder with paint roller in hand, when she heard the telephone ring and nearly tipped over the paint pan as she descended from the ladder.

"Hello," Kate said breathlessly, as she answered the phone.

"Hi, Kate. It's Carolyn. I just wanted to tell you Kathy Middleton called me and asked if I would call you. She got your reservation, but you forgot to mail your check for the dinner."

"Oh, land of mercy. I'm so sorry. These past few weeks my mind has been going full speed with little direction. I'll put it in the mail today."

"No big deal. Since I'm reservation chairman, send it to me instead of Kathy."

"I will, and again, I apologize," Kate replied.

Carolyn Sommers was Kate's best friend. Their friendship began when they were freshmen in high school and continued after graduation and marriage. Carolyn married Tom Sommers, shortly after both of them graduated from college, and remained in Springfield. Tom taught math and was the baseball coach at Northeast High School, the same high school from which all of them had graduated.

Although Kate had moved up and down the map while married to Mike due to his jobs, she and Carolyn kept in touch. When Kate and Mike came home to visit, the visit always included getting together with Carolyn and Tom to share news of family and friends.

Tom had passed away two years ago, and Carolyn had recently started dating Bob Martin, another classmate whose wife was also deceased.

"How's the house coming along?" Carolyn asked.

"I have two more rooms to paint upstairs and the basement walls and floor. My weekends are busier than my weekdays. I look forward going to work these days to get away from the manual labor," Kate replied.

"You can't fool me. I know how much you like to paint and have projects."

"Speaking of projects, you must be pretty busy yourself as reservation chairman of the reunion. Will there be a good crowd attending the reunion this time?" Kate asked.

"Reservations are looking good. There were over a hundred and forty students in our class and twenty-one in the January class when both groups graduated, and so far with only one week to go, one hundred and ten have sent in their reservations. The committee decided to included the January class with ours due to its small size."

"Not bad. I am looking forward to coming, even though I will be coming alone."

There wasn't a great deal Carolyn didn't know about Kate's private life. They had been best friends for a long, long time. Going alone to the reunion would be hard for her, and Carolyn was well aware of it. To ease her mind, she said, "Kate, don't worry about coming by yourself. You can sit with Bob and me. You know you could always bring a date."

"Very funny, Carolyn. I think my last date was with my ex, and we all know how that worked out," Kate said.

"I know someone who would be happy to have your company," her friend replied.

"Yeah, who?"

"You know who. Richard Lawton, that's who. He would come after you in a New York second, if he knew you were free."

"Now, you're a soothsayer, huh? Would he be bringing his wife along or have you had a vision about that, too?"

"I don't know anything about his marital circumstances, but he sent in his reservation form, indicating only he would be attending."

Kate did not reply immediately. Richard Lawton, her old beau. She hadn't seen him since they split up years and years ago, right after he went to art school. She remembered, however, he had called her when her mother passed away to express his condolences. Thoughts of Richard and their yesterdays flooded her mind. Her silence prompted Carolyn to ask, "Are you still there, Kate?"

"I'm still here, just woolgathering. There's the doorbell. It must be Ruth. She's coming over to help me paint. I got to run. I'll put the check in the mail today. See you soon. Take care."

Kate was relieved when the doorbell rang, which allowed her an excuse to cut the conversation with Carolyn short. She did not want to take a trip down memory lane with her friend concerning Richard Lawton. Knowing he was coming to the reunion made her feel somewhat apprehensive and more so, especially since he was also coming alone.

Kate knew nothing about his life, only that he was still married and wondered if he knew she was not. If the subject of divorce was brought up while visiting with classmates at the reunion, she did not want to discuss it. She did not want to admit her marriage had failed, especially to Richard Lawton.

CHAPTER ELEVEN
Richard

Richard heard a car pull up in the driveway. He saw RJ getting out of his truck. He called out to him, from the opened kitchen window, and then went out the back door to meet his son.

"I thought you were going camping with the family this weekend," Richard said.

"Maybe. According to the weather report, it looks like it might turn into a rainy weekend. We weren't planning to hit the road until after lunch anyway, so we'll see what it looks like then. I just wanted to run over before you left and tell you to enjoy yourself at the reunion. Please do not worry about Mom. If we don't go camping, I'll probably take the family to visit her."

"I already called the nursing home earlier. Nothing has changed. I guess that is good news. At least your mother is comfortable and getting the best care there is, which gives me some measure of peace."

"Dad, promise me one thing," RJ said. "Forget about your worries and just have a great time. I am so happy you decided to go. Knowing you as I do, I figured you might back out at the last minute and not go."

Instead of trying to read into RJ's last remark, he smiled and said, "We'll have lunch next week, and I'll tell you all about what it's like to meet up with your former classmates after forty years have passed. Oh, to have hair on top again," Richard said, as he patted his bald head.

"Dad, you're something else. One more thing, the weatherman predicted big time rain later in the morning in the direction you are headed. If it turns sour, promise me you will stop until it's safe to drive again. A slick pavement can be just as bad as an icy one, and night driving in the rain can be dangerous."

"What's with the promises? Of course, I'll stop if it gets rough. You're getting to be as bad as me, giving out free advice all the time."

"Like father, like son," RJ said.

"By the way, I plan to make a stop in Chicago Heights to see Bill Myers, Auto Unlimited's advertising manager. Auto Unlimited is one of our new clients. We're doing their catalog this year. The company manufactures automobile parts and specializes in windshield wipers. Since it's on the way, and I gain an hour when I hit Illinois, I plan to drop off the preliminary layouts for his review, which will also give me an opportunity to meet him personally again. When I talked to Bill earlier in the week, he told he would be working at the plant Saturday anyway, so I made arrangements to meet him before I go to Springfield."

"Why is it you can't just go have a day to yourself? Promise me..."

"There you go again with the promise thing," Richard said.

RJ shrugged his shoulders and moved toward his father to give him a big bear hug. "Have a good trip, and remember to be cool at the reunion."

Watching his son drive off, Richard thanked God for his one and only son and went back into the house. RJ had helped him tremendously in Betty's transition to the nursing home.

A strong wind was snapping the flag around the flag pole in the back yard, and it began to rain. Noting the time, he needed to get moving and went upstairs to shave. It was a good two hours to Chicago Heights, and he always prided himself on being early rather than late.

He took a good look at his reflection in the mirror. He was not going bald on top; he *was* bald on top, and so what if he needed reading glasses? Thanks to his interest in tennis and the convenience of a tennis court on his property, he was in good shape for a man of his years. Recently, he also received a good report from his physician regarding his latest physical. All in all, as he looked at his six-foot-one-inch image, he felt upbeat and good about himself.

Maybe the anticipation of seeing Kate again was responsible for his frame of mind. He wasn't kidding himself. That was exactly the reason for his optimistic mood.

He finished shaving and headed for the shower. After toweling off and dressing in casual clothes, he packed for the reunion event, taking great care in selecting what he would wear. His gray suit went into a hang-up; his shoes, socks, underwear, toiletries and shirts were then packed in a small suitcase. The last thing he placed on top of his shirts was the new tie he bought, which was still wrapped in tissue paper. The tie made him think of his good buddy Ken. Remembering what Ken implied subtly, concerning the tie purchase, brought a smile to Richard's face.

He loaded his car, backed out of the garage and began driving to Chicago Heights. The rain was only moderate, and the traffic moved along at a good pace. After he exited the highway, it was only a short distance to Auto Unlimited's warehouse. He saw Bill Myers standing and waving to him on the loading dock. He parked his car by the loading dock steps and got out.

"Hi, Bill," Richard said, extending his arm to shake hands with his client. "Good to see you. I made pretty good time despite the rain. Traffic wasn't that bad, either."

Bill took his hand. "Hello, Richard. I'm sorry to be the bearer of bad news, but your son called about twenty minutes ago. He wants you to phone him at his home immediately. There's been an accident. You can use the phone in my office."

Richard's first thought was something had happened to Betty. He followed Bill to his office.

"Sit here at my desk and make your calls. Don't worry about any long distance charges; just dial the number you want." On his way out, he shut the door to give Richard privacy.

Richard dialed RJ's home number. He picked it up on the first ring. "Dad, it's Ken. He's been in an accident. Linda called from the hospital. She tried to get you at home and when she didn't, she called me and asked if I could track you down. I told her you were making a business call in Chicago Heights. It's a good thing I remembered the name of the company and Bill Myers' name. After getting the company's phone number from the operator, Bill Myers answered the phone when I called.

"Linda did not have all the complete information about Ken when she phoned me, but according to what the police told her, Ken's car was hit by a truck that ran a stoplight. The impact was on Ken's side of the car. Linda wasn't with him. He had been on his way to get an oil change. The ambulance took him to Mother of Mercy Hospital.

"Linda didn't want to call any of the family before she got a chance to talk to the doctor. She only got to speak with Ken briefly before they took him into surgery. She sounded really shook up over the phone and asked me to get word to you as soon as I could. Her parents are out of town. She's by herself at the hospital and asked if you would come."

"Of course, I'll come. Call the hospital and have them get word to her. Let her know I am coming from Chicago Heights. With the time change and traffic I don't know exactly when I will get there, but assure her I'm on the way."

"Do you want me to go over there?" RJ asked.

"No, just make sure she gets the message. Go ahead with your plans. I'll call you later tonight."

Richard then called his sister. Luckily, Connie was home and picked up the phone immediately and said, "Hello."

"Connie, it's Richard. I'm in Chicago Heights. I just got a message from RJ. There's been an accident involving Ken Patterson. RJ called my client and was able to reach me. Remember, I told you I was going to call on a client before coming to your place. When I phoned RJ back, he told me Ken was in an accident and was being taken by ambulance to the hospital. Linda is by herself and asked if I would come. Their two kids, Susan and Peter, live in California, and her parents are out of town."

"Oh, Richard. How awful. You must be in a hurry. Call me later, and let me know about Ken."

Richard hung up the phone, picked up his briefcase and went looking for Bill. He found him on the loading dock, waiting for him. "Make all the calls you need to make?" Bill asked.

"Yes, and thanks for all your help. A close friend of mine, Ken Patterson, has been in a car accident. I was going to Springfield from here, but I'm heading back to be with his wife, who is alone right now at the hospital. Both of their kids live in California and the other family members who live in South Bend are out of town. No hospital vigil is easy, especially if you are alone."

He opened his briefcase and pulled out the material he was going to go over with Bill. "Here are the preliminary layouts, Bill. I planned to spend some time with you today to see if we are on the right track, but..."

Bill interrupted him. "No need for explanations, Richard. I understand. I'll look over the layouts and call you the first of next week. We'll talk then."

The two men said their goodbyes. Richard walked down the loading dock steps and got into his car. In minutes he was on the highway again, driving back to South Bend, hoping his friend would be all right.

Richard made good time on the way back to South Bend. After arriving at the hospital, he made inquiries at the main desk and was told to go to the eighth floor waiting room. When he entered the waiting room, he saw Linda was alone and sitting in a chair. When she saw Richard approaching, she stood and faced him. The look on her face was one of relief as she said, "I cannot tell you how glad I am to see you, Richard."

"It's okay. How is Ken?"

"The police called me at the site of the accident and said Ken was in a car accident and nothing more. I found out later the paramedics came and took him to Mother of Mercy Hospital. I jumped in the car and got here as fast as I could. I didn't get to see Ken, because they were prepping him for surgery. I only got to talk briefly to the doctor, who was on duty, a Dr. Ashcroft. He told me Ken's left leg was broken, and he had lost a good deal of blood due to a deep cut on his arm. He thought he might have to remove his spleen, too. I haven't called any of the family yet, because I wanted to wait until I talked with Dr. Ashcroft again. The nurse told me Ken is in recovery now, and Dr. Ashcroft should be coming down soon to talk to me."

Linda's composure was about to crumble. She wanted answers. Waiting alone she had ample time to think, and not knowing Ken's outcome was wearing on her nerves.

"You look like you could use a cup of coffee, Linda. You stay here and wait for the doctor. I'll find the coffee shop and bring you back one. Okay?"

"Thanks, Richard. I could use a cup of coffee."

Richard found the coffee shop and purchased two coffees. While waiting for the elevator in the lobby to take him back to Linda's side, he prayed silently for his friend.

When he returned to the waiting room, Linda was talking to the doctor. Not wanting to interrupt, Richard stood by, listening closely to what was being said.

"Your husband has a broken leg. He lost quite a bit of blood, but a transfusion was given to him to replace the blood he lost. He's going to have a nice scar on his arm but no impairment. He also suffered a concussion. In addition, I had to take out his spleen. He's in recovery and is not awake yet, but he has been assigned a room. As soon as he wakes up, you can see him. All in all, Mrs. Patterson, your husband is a very lucky man. With medication and rest, he'll return to health within a very short time. But, he will need to be hospitalized for a couple of days. I want to run some more tests, routine ones."

"I understand, and thank you, Dr. Ashcroft. She turned toward Richard to acknowledge him and said, "Dr. Ashcroft, this is Ken's best friend, Richard Lawton."

Looking directly at Richard, he said, "Nice to meet you."

Dr. Ashcroft then resumed his conversation with his patient's wife, "I'll check on your husband again this evening. If you have any questions, Mrs. Patterson, you can reach me by calling the hospital," and touched her arm as he turned and walked away.

Linda looked at Richard and said, "I apologize for taking you away from your business, Richard, but I was frantic. When I got hold of RJ, he told me you were on your way to Chicago Heights to see a client. I hope I didn't..."

Richard interrupted her. "Don't concern yourself. You did the right thing. It was just a courtesy call anyway. No big deal. Forget it."

Ken had kept his word. Linda knew nothing about his class reunion, or she would have mentioned it.

"I can't thank you enough, Richard."

"Let's check with the nurse and find out the number of Ken's room," Richard suggested.

"That's a good idea. We can wait for him there," Linda replied. "Now that I have been assured by Dr. Ashcroft Ken is going to be all right, I'm fine, I really am. I'm going to stay until Ken is brought down from recovery. Possibly, he'll be awake enough to talk to me then. If you have to be some place, go on and go. I'll call you later," Linda said.

"If you don't mind, I'll wait with you. I want to be here when he wakes up, too," Richard said. He looked at his watch. He was going to miss the class reunion. So much for possibly seeing Kate O'Connor Flannigan.

CHAPTER TWELVE
Kate

Kate drove into the parking lot of the Lakeside Motor Boat Club and looked for a place to park her convertible. The weatherman had predicted rain for the early evening, and it was coming down forcefully. The spaces closest to the clubhouse were already taken. She ended up parking a good distance from the front door. The road leading to the clubhouse was a dirt road and muddy. She decided to wait awhile before making a run for it.

As she sat there watching the wipers making half circles as they cleared away the rain from the windows of her car, her thoughts drifted. She found it difficult to believe forty years had passed since she was in high school. Then, she thought about the absence of Mike Flannigan, the young man who at nineteen had captured her heart from the minute she had been introduced to him. Had he been with her tonight, he would have left her off under the clubhouse portico, so she wouldn't have to worry about ruining the new Italian dress scandals she was wearing for the reunion event.

There were times when circumstances would rekindle memories of Mike at the unlikeliest times, like tonight. Since his leaving, she developed ways of dealing with the random thoughts of him that surfaced when she had to cope with some mundane problem like muddied and possibly ruined Italian footwear. Being on her own had taught her the difference between being lonely and being alone. In truth, she had been introduced to loneliness long before Mike had left her.

The rain had momentarily stopped. She decided to make a dash for the door. She turned off the ignition, gathered her things, including her umbrella, locked the car and ran toward the clubhouse. Her new scandals would have to survive just like she had learned to do.

After depositing her umbrella with all the others that took up one corner of the foyer, Kate used the ladies room to freshen up. She checked herself over. The hem of her navy blue dress was a little wet, and her shoes were caked with mud, especially the heels. Wetting a paper towel she dabbed at them and with a little light rubbing, they were damp, but good as new.

Forget about your appearance, she said to herself. Think only about having a good time with old friends. Now that she had a plan, she opened the door and walked toward the registration desk. Carolyn Sommers was handing out a name badge to someone Kate did not recognize.

"Hi, Carolyn. Have you one of those for me?"

"I sure do," Carolyn said, and she came around the table to give Kate a hug and pin the badge on her dress. "I have you sitting at our table on the right side of the podium. You won't have far to walk to give the invocation."

Kate had been asked to give the invocation at all the reunions except the tenth one, which she had missed due to the death of her father. Why she had been chosen for this duty had always been a mystery to her, but she enjoyed doing it and spent considerable time in developing a meaningful prayer.

"Get yourself a drink at the bar and mingle. I'll join you at our table shortly," Carolyn said. "Almost everyone has arrived who sent in a reservation. You follow Jerry after he gives his opening remarks. It's good to see you, Kate, and those shoes of yours are beautiful."

Leave it to my best friend to say just the right thing at the right time, Kate thought, as she walked toward where she would be sitting, saying hello and chatting with former classmates along the way. For the most part she recognized everyone despite the obvious changes since their twenty-fifth class reunion.

Someone rang a bell. Jerry stepped behind the podium. It was time for everyone to be seated. He began his welcoming speech.

Kate looked around the room hardly listening to what he was saying. She spotted Richard's sister Connie and her husband Lenny, but did not see Richard and wondered if he was here somewhere. The room was crowded, making it difficult to see everyone. Kate was grateful she was sharing a table with Carolyn and Bob. The other two couples at their table were high school friends of both her and Carolyn, so conversation would not be awkward. Hopefully, no one would bring up the subject of her divorce through the guise of small talk.

Kate heard her name being called. Pushing back her chair, she rose to deliver the invocation. The words she had written came from her heart, and she delivered a message of thankfulness without a flaw. Now, she could really enjoy dinner and the rest of the evening. Speaking in public always made her nervous.

After everyone had gone through the buffet and finished eating, people began circulating again. Kate and Carolyn were the only ones who remained at their table. The others had headed for the bar or outside for a quick smoke.

"He's not here," Carolyn said.

"Who?" Kate asked.

"Please, no games. You know I am talking about Richard. He sent in his reservation a couple of weeks ago and then left me a phone message this morning to tell me a close friend of his had been in an automobile accident. He was needed by his friend's family and would not be able to make the reunion."

In some ways, Kate was relieved to hear she would not be seeing Richard after all and said, "I'm sorry about his friend. Honestly, Carolyn, just because Richard and I dated a little after high school, it doesn't amount to a hill of beans."

Carolyn wouldn't let the subject drop and said, "I know I've said this to you before, but he would come after you if he knew you were divorced. Have you ever thought of calling him?"

"Now, why would I do that? Has it slipped your mind? He happens to be married." Kate hoped her face would not betray her. She felt herself blushing and certainly did not want to admit she had thought of Richard, especially after she became divorced, wondering how his life had turned out. But calling him, no way.

"I talked to Connie when she picked up her name badge. She told me Richard had to place his wife in a nursing home several weeks ago," Carolyn said.

"What is the point of this conversation?" Kate asked.

"I just want to see you happy," her friend said.

"I am happy. What you really mean is you want to see me involved with someone," Kate replied.

"I want to see you sharing your life with someone who appreciates you for who and what you are," Carolyn said.

"You sure know how to hit the nail on the head, don't you? I guess Mike never did much of that, did he?"

"You know the answer to that question whether you want to admit it or not. You were a threat to him, Kate. He stifled you so he wouldn't have to compete, making him look like so much more than what he actually was, and it worked. As an outsider looking in, I never could understand why you never figured that out for yourself."

"Notions of love and good old 1950 upbringing, I guess. Not to change the subject, but isn't that Richard's sister Connie heading toward us?" Kate asked.

"That's Connie all right," Carolyn replied.

Connie walked toward their table with a smile on her face and stood to the side of Carolyn and said, "Hi, ladies. I have a favor to ask. Since Richard couldn't make it to the reunion, I would like to send him the program. He was on his way here, but received word that his best friend was in a car accident and returned to South Bend to be with his friend's wife at the hospital. I thought it would be great if everyone could sign the program and write something so he could have a momentum of our fortieth reunion celebration. After all, forty years is somewhat of a milestone, and I know he would really appreciate it."

Bob had returned to the table at the same time Connie began talking and replied, "Sure, that's a good idea. It would have been great to see Richard and bat the breeze. Next time you talk to him tell him he was missed." He picked up the program and pen that Connie handed him and began writing.

He passed the program to his wife and after Carolyn finished writing her note, she passed it to Kate. It was Kate's turn to write something. Without giving it a great deal of thought, she picked up the pen and wrote, *Do you remember taking me to the senior class prom?* and signed her name, Kate O'Connor. Kate handed the program back to Connie, who thanked everyone and moved on to the next table.

The evening began to wind down. People began to leave. Hugs and handshakes were given with promises to stay in touch. Kate went to get her umbrella and was fumbling for her car keys when Carolyn came to say goodbye.

"Call me when you get home. I worry about you being alone and on your own, especially driving home at night," Carolyn said.

Kate gave Carolyn a hug and after releasing her looked her straight in the eye and said, "I am alone and on my own, Carolyn. It's okay, really. Maybe Mr. Right will never find me, and that's okay, too. Don't worry about me. I'm stronger than you think. If it will make you feel any better, I'll call you when I get home."

On her way out to where she had parked her car, Kate said goodbye to several other classmates. The rain had stopped, but the road was still very muddy and filled with puddles. She made no effort to sidestep any of them. Her mood had changed. She no longer cared about her beautiful Italian dress scandals.

CHAPTER THIRTEEN
Richard

Ken was still groggy after the nurse brought him to his room. Linda leaned over the bed and kissed her husband on his cheek and held his hand. He opened his eyes briefly and smiled at her and nodded off again.

"He'll wake up and fall asleep again until the anesthesia wears off," the nurse said. "That's normal, and he's fine. He came through the operation with flying colors, and his blood pressure is good and so is his heart rate. That broken nose and his bruises make him look in worse shape than he really is. His left leg has to remain elevated to eliminate the possibility of a blood clot. He's going to be uncomfortable for awhile with his leg in a cast. It's also going to itch, and he'll find it difficult to get at the itch.

"I'll be in now and then to check his vitals. If you have any questions, don't hesitate to ask," the nurse added, as she turned and left the room.

Ken was coming around again. "Is that Richard over there, Linda?" he asked.

"Yes, he's here. He stayed with me the whole time they were trying to put you back together," Linda replied.

Richard walked closer to the bed. "Hey, good buddy. How do you feel? The doctor and nurses say you're going to be up and around in no time."

Ken nodded his head and gave Richard a thumbs-up.

"I'm going to head out and leave you two alone," Richard said. "Ken, get some rest, and I'll see you tomorrow."

Richard picked up his jacket and left the room. As he waited for the elevator, he said a prayer of thanks to God. With a little time to mend, his friend was going to be all right.

When he got home, he was exhausted. He showered and got into his pajamas. As tired as he was, he knew RJ and Connie would want to know about Ken's situation, so he called both of them, but neither answered. He left a message on their recorders about Ken's condition. Then he made himself a ham and cheese sandwich, grabbed a cold Diet Coke from the fridge and ate at the kitchen table.

It was too early to go to bed. He went into the den and turned on the television. Within twenty minutes he was fast asleep in the recliner. The sun woke him up the next morning, because he had forgotten to close the curtains in the den the night before.

He went to the kitchen to make a pot of coffee and have a bowl of cereal. The ringing of the phone interrupted his coffee making.

"Hello," Richard mumbled. He was not fully awake yet.

"Hi, it's Linda. I hope I didn't get you out of bed?"

"No, not at all. How's Ken?"

"That's the reason I'm calling. He's doing great. I stayed the night, and he slept soundly. Right now, I am waiting for the doctor."

"That's great news. I plan to look in on him sometime this evening," Richard said.

"Would it be too much to ask if you could relieve me for an hour or so this afternoon? I don't like leaving him alone during the day when he is awake, but I have to pick up Susan and Peter at the airport. After I called them when I got home from the hospital last night, I brought them up-to-date on their father's condition. Both of them insisted on coming. Their flight gets in at 2:30 p.m."

"No problem," Richard said.

"Thanks, Richard. I cannot tell you…"

"Linda, it's okay. I'll be at the hospital in plenty of time to see you before you have to leave for the airport."

They said their goodbyes. Richard thought about Ken's wife and how much her actions reflected her love for her husband in both good and bad times. Betty had never shown that kind of love to him even in the good times. Ken was, indeed, a lucky man, even though he was laying in a hospital bed, and he envied him.

CHAPTER FOURTEEN
Kate

Kate heard the telephone ringing as she put her key in the kitchen door. She hurriedly opened it and grabbed the wall phone.

"Hello."

"Hey, it's Jackie. I've been calling for the last hour. By rights, I should be still sawing logs, but I am dying to know how the reunion went. Did you have a good time?"

"I just got back from church," Kate said.

"Hope you said a few prayers for me," Jackie said. Although Jackie, like her sister, was raised a Catholic, she was not a church goer.

"Of course, I did," Kate replied.

Kate's sharp tone set off a bell in Jackie's head. Normally, when she called her sister, Kate was always ready to have a conversation. Not so today. Something was not right. Jackie decided to give it another try and came right to the point. "Was Richard Lawton at the reunion?"

"Not you, too. He is a married man and has nothing to do with my life, and I have nothing to do with his. Last night Carolyn couldn't wait to tell me he was not there, as if my only reason for going to the reunion was to see him."

Jackie knew Carolyn from the time her sister and Carolyn were in high school. Later on when both of them married, the two couples often came to play cards with Kate and Jackie's parents.

"Sorry, Kate. Even though I was ten years younger when you dated him, I always thought he was going to be the one. I guess I will always think of him as the fish you threw back in the water."

Jackie had a way of cutting right to the chase and not mincing words. By all accounts, it was true. Kate had thrown Richard Lawton back into the water many years ago. Now Mike had done the same thing to her after thirty years of marriage. Although the comparison was unbalanced, she couldn't help but think what goes around, comes around. She, too, knew about rejection. The wound left scars.

"I'm sorry I barked at you, Jackie. To be perfectly honest, I was hoping to see Richard. I admit I was curious to know how his life turned out after all this time. In a way, I was saved being embarrassed by his absence. Had he been there, and if the subject had been brought up, I was relieved I didn't have to admit I was divorced. Having a marriage end in divorce after being together for thirty years and seven children from that marriage is not something to write home about. It's failure spelled with a capital F."

"Kate, do yourself a favor. I know about rejection, too. It can leave ugly marks, but over time the pain of failure will lessen as you come to grips with it. Let it go. Stop beating yourself up over Mike Flannigan. Pardon me for saying so, but he isn't worth it. You've moved on and full speed ahead, sis. You've got seven great kids who love and appreciate you, a nice place to live, a great job, a convertible, good health and you're a size eight. It doesn't get much better than that. Trust me."

"Oh, Jackie, you always make me feel so much better when I am down in the dumps by reminding me of what I do have. I do have a good life, and maybe I don't have a man in my life right now, but so what?"

"That's more like it. I have to get going. Cole is waving his arms at me to get off this phone. However, I want to leave you with one thought before I hang up. Your life ain't over yet, kiddo."

CHAPTER FIFTEEN
Richard

Monday morning Richard returned to work. He had another busy week ahead. He visited with Susan and Peter at the hospital and was told Ken would be released Tuesday, if there were no new complications. That news alone gave him great relief.

Richard didn't have a secretary, only a receptionist, who took care of the business mail but not his personal mail. He decided to take time out and address the pile that had accumulated on his desk. He picked up a large envelope with a return address he recognized. It was from Hathaway Pioneer Homes, a company he had contacted, regarding log house building.

When the doctor advised him to put Betty in a nursing home, he had made up his mind then to sell the big house, knowing she would never be able to come home again. In time, he wanted to build a log house for himself somewhere. Having a log house in the woods on a good fishing lake had always been at the back of his mind every time he had his back to the wall with a deadline to meet.

With the sale of his business almost wrapped up, he had started looking for a place to settle, as well as a builder of log houses. He made a note to call Hathaway Pioneer Homes and jotted down their phone number.

An oversized envelope on the pile caught his attention. His sister's return address was in the upper left-hand corner and spiked his curiosity. Unusual, he thought. Connie did not mention she was mailing him something. She was a phone person, not a letter writer.

He slit the end of the envelope with a letter opener. Inside was the program from the recent class reunion. On the cover was a picture of Dufflemeyer's, a hamburger and ice cream place where the Northeast High School kids hung out. Duff's, as the high school crowd referred to it, was on Northside Avenue, within walking distance of the high school. It was known for its milkshakes served with a shortbread cookie, chocolate cokes, greasy hamburgers and the best caramel apples he had ever eaten. He remembered it was just about this same time of year the apples, individually wrapped in waxed paper, would be displayed on trays in their front window.

The establishment was next to the Olympia, which was the north end's movie theatre. A nearby parking lot served both businesses. There were three parking spaces in front of Duff's, usually taken by the high school guys who had cars. The guys would stand in front of the parked cars, leaning against them, so they could look over the girls either going in or coming out of Duff's or the movie theatre.

Many a night Richard's 1942 green Packard was parked in one of the spaces. Not the most sporty or current of cars, but he had paid for it himself by working at Farmers' Dairy after school and on the weekends as a short order delivery person. Occupying one of the parking spaces was one way he could look at Kate without her knowing it, while she sat in the booth selling movie tickets during the weekday and weekend evenings. She was a part-time cashier at the Olympia during her junior and senior years.

Thinking of the Packard brought back memories, especially the one that happened the Monday after he had taken Kate to the prom. He remembered the incident and conversation with her as if it were yesterday.

Several weeks before the prom he had asked Kate for a date, but she refused and did not give a reason why. However, when he asked her to be his prom date, she agreed to go with him. After the event, Richard assumed other dates would be forthcoming, since both of them had a good time. He couldn't have been more wrong.

Kate lived as far away from the high school as he did but in another direction, and she walked to school each day, which was more than a mile from her house. Monday following the prom weekend, he got up a little earlier and drove out her way with the intention of giving her a ride to school. He spotted her about a block away from her house and made a u-turn, driving up alongside of her.

"Hi, Kate. Hop in," he called out through the open passenger window.

Kate looked at him and kept right on walking.

Richard was confused by her manner. He called out to her again. "Hey, Kate. Get in. I'll give you a ride to school."

Without looking at him, she said, "I can't. My dad told me not to get in a car with boys."

Richard burst out laughing, but the look on her face told him she was dead serious. He called out again to her and said, "The car isn't filled with guys. It's only me. Come on, get in."

She gave him a look that indicated she was not going to be a passenger and continued walking as if Richard and his 1942 green Packard were invisible.

Richard remembered his utter frustration concerning the car thing. Her refusal to get in really ignited his temper. Girls did not give him a hard time, and here was the girl of his dreams, giving him the brush off. Why would her father tell her such a thing? It was beyond his understanding. He gunned the motor and took off down the street for school with the tires squealing.

When he got to school, he made a beeline for her locker and waited for her to appear. He wanted to know why she had given him the cold shoulder. When Kate finally arrived at her locker, it took some prodding to get the truth out of her why she refused to ride with him. He realized how much it was costing her to tell him.

"This is so embarrassing to admit, especially face-to-face, but my father meant what he said when he told me I would have to wait until after I graduated to date. It's a small wonder he allowed me to go to the class play and senior prom with you."

Knowing what kind of girl Kate was, it became obvious to him she intended to obey her father's wish. Now that he understood, he loved her even more for being true to what her father asked of her, regardless of her own feelings on the subject.

Graduation was in three weeks. Then, he would make his move. He intended to ask Kate O'Connor to be his steady girlfriend.

Enough of the yesterdays. He got up and went into the employees' lounge and poured himself a cup of coffee, returned to his office and picked up the reunion program again. He began reading the various messages his classmates had written on the inside of the front and back pages. On the inside of the back page, he came across Kate's message; *Do you remember taking me to the senior class prom?* It was not the text of the message, but the signature under it that caused him to spill his coffee. She had signed Kate O'Connor. That was her maiden name. Her married name was Flannigan. Why had she signed Kate O'Connor?

The ring of the telephone on his desk broke his concentration.

"Richard Lawton."

"Hi, Richard. It's Connie. Did you get the program I sent?"

"Actually, I am sitting here at this very moment thumbing through the pages. Thanks for sending it. By the way, Ken is doing fine and is coming home tomorrow if there are no new complications. I really wanted to come to the reunion and visit with some of the guys I once ran around with. The sending of a yearly Christmas card doesn't really hit the mark like a good old-fashioned person-to-person conversation."

"You're so right. This was the first time Lenny's class consolidated with yours, and it worked out well," Connie said.

"Apparently, Herb Tobin hasn't lost his touch for comedy, Richard. Did you notice what he wrote?" she asked.

Herb Tobin also lived in the same neighborhood as Richard and Connie when they were kids. Even in grade school, Herb liked to play tricks, earning him the reputation of class clown, which escalated during his high school years at Northeast.

Richard read Herb's entry again. *Hey, dude, put down the paint brush. Get a life. Miss ya.* Herb's message was right above what Kate had written, which is why he remembered it.

"Far from me to defend Herb Tobin, but it seems to me he hit the nail on the head even though he hasn't seen you in a blue moon," Connie said.

"Let's not go there. Okay, Connie? It's a worn out subject as far as I'm concerned."

She knew she had touched a nerve and changed the subject, launching into a description of the event itself.

Richard didn't care about what Herb Tobin had written nor was he interested in Connie's small talk about the reunion. What he wanted was to get right to the point about the way Kate had signed her name, but didn't want to seem anxious in asking his sister why. He also didn't want his sister to jump to any wild conclusions of her own in posing the question. Connie knew about Richard's feelings for Kate and also how much he had been hurt by her abrupt ending of their relationship many, many years ago.

After his sister had finally related all the details of the reunion to him, Richard gathered up his nerve to ask about Kate.

"I noticed Kate Flannigan signed her name rather strangely. What's that all about?"

"What do you mean, strangely?" Connie asked.

"She signed her name Kate O'Connor, after what she wrote. Why would she sign her maiden name rather than her married name?" Richard asked.

"Because she wanted her maiden name returned to her when she became divorced, according to Carolyn Sommers. She and I spent some time at the reunion talking about Kate."

This news hit Richard like a bolt of lightning. Kate divorced! His mind was racing. He didn't know much about Mike Flannigan, but Kate was a Catholic to the core. This had to be a big setback for her.

"Well, that news is certainly a shock," Richard said.

"Maybe to you and me, Richard, but keep in mind Kate moved away right after she married and has lived in several states since then. Rarely, do I run into anybody who knows anything about her or her life. I'll say this much—she looked stunning. She is still as slender as she was in high school and appears to be the same old Kate. Age has grayed her hair, but she has acquired a sense of grace and presence. She has moved on to another level of beauty.

"I didn't get much of a chance to talk to her personally, but in the few minutes we did have together, she told me she had been living in St. Louis for over twenty years and just recently bought a bungalow in South County not far from where she previously lived with Mike and their family before she became divorced. Three of her sons live in St. Louis, too. Two of them are single and the youngest son is married. She also has a married son and daughter living in Dallas, Texas, and another married son, who lives in Indianapolis, Indiana. I made a point to remember all of this, because I knew you would ask me about her and her family. By the way, her dad passed away a year after her mother.

"I also talked with her sister Jackie. I didn't know she was the owner and operator of Prime Pizza in Springfield. She does a tremendous pizza carryout business, and although I have never had one of her pizzas, the word on the street is her pizza is second to none in Springfield.

"The doorbell is ringing, Richard. I got to go. Keep in touch. I'll talk to you soon, and give Ken my best," Connie said.

Before she hung up the phone, she remembered one last thing to tell her brother and hurriedly added, "Oh, I almost forgot. Kate came without a date."

The line went dead, and Richard was trying to digest all of Connie's news. He remembered the only time he contacted Kate was when her mother passed away. Connie had sent the obituary from the *Springfield Journal and Register* newspaper to him. Kate was living in Springfield then, and the conversation had been very brief. She thanked him for calling. That was the last time he had talked to her.

He hung up the phone and stared out the window, letting his mind absorb the news he had just heard. Kate O'Connor Flannigan was divorced. That thought filled his being with a tremendous urge to find out more about the woman he had always intended to marry. But, how and from whom?

CHAPTER SIXTEEN
Kate

The phone on Ruth Dennison's desk rang. She picked it up on the first ring. "Actuary Department, this is Ruth Dennison."

"How about lunch today?" Kate asked.

"Sounds good to me, Kate. You want to eat in the cafeteria, or do you want to go elsewhere?"

"I have something to tell you and would rather go someplace with some privacy and not as noisy as the company cafeteria. How about across the street at Union Station?" Kate asked.

"I have a yen today for some Mexican food. How about Maria's Mexican Grill? I got a coupon we can use," Ruth replied.

"Fine, I'll meet you in the lobby at noon."

"Is everything all right?" Ruth asked. "You sound stressed out."

"I definitely am," Kate said.

Ruth hadn't talked to Kate over the weekend. Usually, the two of them went out to dinner at the end of the work week, but last Friday Ruth had driven to see her daughter in Mount Vernon and hadn't come home until late Sunday night. Something was up.

The morning passed quickly for Kate with routine duties, which was good because her concentration was not on company business.

She could not quit thinking about the telephone call she received last night from her youngest daughter Abby and the bomb she had dropped. She needed to tell someone about what she had been told, and why not Ruth? She knew as much about her life as Jackie did. She could get what was bothering her off her chest immediately rather than wait until tonight when she intended to call her sister and discuss Abby's news with her.

When it was time for lunch, Ruth took the elevator and headed toward the front entrance of the lobby where she could see Kate waiting for her. When she caught up with her, Kate said nothing. She quickly entered the revolving door and walked down the steps to the street. Ruth had to hurry to keep up with her.

After the two women were seated in the restaurant and their orders were taken, Ruth decided to take the plunge. "Okay. Let's have it."

Without any preamble, Kate said, "Mike got married over the weekend in Jamaica."

Ruth let that bit of news float in the air for a minute, giving Kate the opportunity to continue. When she didn't, Ruth felt she had to say something and asked, "How did you find out?"

"Abby called me last night," Kate answered.

"Did she give you any details?"

"No, and I didn't want to hear any."

"It is obvious you're upset, Kate. I wish I knew what to say to comfort you, but Mike isn't in your life anymore. Is there more to this than what you're telling me?" Ruth asked.

Kate played with her silverware, moving it around. Then, her words spilled out as if she couldn't say them fast enough. "Learning about an affair is so devastating to the one who is the injured party, but people do make mistakes," Kate said.

Ruth was confused. Who was Kate referring to? Was she now doubting her decision to divorce Mike after all this time, thinking about what might have been had she given him a second chance? And, had he asked for one?

Kate didn't give Ruth a chance to speak. She immediately started telling Ruth about the past.

"Mike started dating Natalie, shortly after the breakup of his relationship with the woman he was seeing, while he was married to me. Natalie is a good friend of Mike's younger sister. She's a single woman and a practicing Catholic and lives with her parents. When they decided to marry, Mike needed an annulment, so they could marry in the Catholic Church.

"As you know, I did not participate in the annulment process, because I didn't want to be blamed if he did not get it. I knew in the back of my mind the fact I was pregnant when we married would one day come back to haunt me. I figured he would use this as a means to get the annulment so he could marry Natalie. The annulment was denied, and the relationship between him and Natalie ended."

"Yes, yes, I remember you telling me all of this," Ruth said. She was trying hard not to convey her exasperation, because this subject had been beaten to death by the two of them ages ago. "Why are you so upset? I don't get it. Somebody has to pick up his shirts from the cleaners. You should thank your lucky stars it isn't your job anymore."

Kate ignored Ruth's sarcastic comment and continued telling Ruth her feelings. "The news of his marriage triggered my memory of the responses Mike gave on the petition he submitted to the Tribunal when he wanted an annulment in order to marry Natalie. Being a Catholic, yourself, you probably know each spouse is allowed to read the responses the other spouse submitted. They're called the Acts of the Case. Since I did not participate, all I wrote down was I believed I was a good wife and mother."

"Yes, I also remember you telling me this, too. Again, what is it that has you in such a state?" Ruth asked.

Kate continued. "Since neither the petitioner or the respondent is allowed a copy of the submitted material, I wrote some of his answers on a piece of paper, which is allowed, and I saved the paper. I put it in a locked portfolio where I keep all my other important documents. After Abby called, I got out the paper and reread what he had written. His answers came crashing down on me again."

Ruth asked, "Is all of this past history troubling you again? Are you still upset over his annulment responses that he submitted to the Tribunal?"

"I've never told anybody else what he had written, but I need to get pass this somehow. I can't seem to do it on my own."

Ruth could feel her friend's anguish. Obviously, Kate was reaching out to her. "Okay, I'm listening," Ruth said.

"I didn't write down all of the answers he gave. That would have been impossible. What I did write down were his answers to a few of the questions that overwhelmed me when I read them. If he really felt that way about me and our marriage from the start, he was like a prisoner serving time without parole."

Kate pulled out the paper from her purse, unfolded it and in a voice that quivered said, "He wrote he had lived a lie all the years he was married to me and from day one never felt close to me. There was never a doubt in his mind our marriage would not be a permanent situation for him. If I had not been in a family way, there would have been no marriage at all. The reason he married me was due to the way he was brought up—to make the best of things and do the right thing no matter if you believed in it or not. He gave me everything I asked for in the divorce settlement, because all he wanted was out. I failed to make him happy."

Ruth said, "Although all of this past business with Mike has been an ordeal for you, I cannot hold back my thoughts any longer. Kate, do you honestly believe what he wrote is true? He was after a document which would allow him to receive an annulment. He wasn't interested in telling the truth, only getting what he wanted.

"Do you really believe he was unhappy for all the years you two were together, fathered seven children in eight years and then decided to leave after thirty years, because you couldn't make him happy? Come on, you are a smart cookie.

"The reason he didn't get the annulment seems pretty obvious to me. He couldn't sell what he had written. Some people will go to great measures to get what they want, and painting a new picture is one of them. Another word comes to mind—lying. Now, tell me what does all of this have to do with the present, and why you're so upset?" Ruth asked.

"Don't you see, Ruth? What does all of this say about me? I was there for those years, too. It shook my being to the bone, when I read his annulment responses years ago. Even to this day, I have always wondered whether his answers were truth or fiction. All kinds of doubts flood my mind every time I think about them or read them again.

"The phone call last night from Abby brought all those memories back. It's the one chapter in my life I would like to close for good. I want to know the truth, and I've certainly earned it. If what he wrote is true, it indicates I'm a very poor judge of character in choosing a life partner. If someone came into my life now, what chance would I have for a successful relationship? Sure, I'd be starting over, but obviously with…"

"Stop it, Kate," Ruth interrupted. "You're beating yourself up. Those years with Mike are behind you. Learn from them and bury them as lessons learned, regardless if you ever find out the truth. You may never find out what you want to know.

"Do you really think Mike was going to say or write down anything that might hinder him from getting an annulment? That was what he was after. Furthermore, he doesn't care about your piece of mind past or present.

"He apparently is looking to begin again with someone else, hence the new marriage. If he had been granted an annulment somewhere along the way, would you have been notified?"

"Yes," Kate answered.

"Then since you haven't received any notification confirming an annulment, Mike must not have been married in a Catholic Church. Therefore, obviously, getting married in a Catholic Church is not as important now as it once was for him.

"Let it go, Kate, all of it. Make a new beginning for yourself by closing those chapters in your life. Let God take over, starting now. Think instead of those seven kids you have from your marriage. And, be thankful you're not the one who has to answer to Mike's roll call anymore. Throw away the paper with those answers, too."

Kate looked at her friend's face and saw only empathy. She took Ruth's hand in hers and asked, "Why is it you always have the right advice, where I am concerned, at the very right time I need right advice?"

"I might have to start charging you for my words of wisdom if this keeps up. Here comes the waitress with our orders." She picked up her glass of water and held it out to Kate. "I propose a toast to new beginnings."

Kate picked up her glass of water and said, "Amen."

CHAPTER SEVENTEEN
Richard

After digesting all of Connie's news, Richard knew he had to see Kate, but how could he accomplish this? He subconsciously began tapping his pencil on his desktop, while his brain was trying to come up with a plan of some sort. Of course, Carolyn Sommers' wedding. She was Kate's best friend in high school, and he knew their relationship had flourished through the years, according to his sister. Kate would most probably be at the wedding and reception. The big plus was Carolyn knew the history between Kate and him, during their high school years, and also liked Richard.

He picked up the phone, called the operator and gave her his request.

"I have a Carolyn Sommers living at 2141 Oak Dale Drive. Would that be the correct address?" the operator asked.

"Yes, I think it is," Richard responded, tapping his pencil even more insistently as he waited.

"Please hold for the number," the operator said.

Richard carefully wrote down the number. Thankfully, it was not an unlisted one. He hung up the phone and immediately dialed Carolyn's number, while thoughts of what he would say to her gathered in his mind. He also hoped he wouldn't have to offer an explanation as to why he wanted to be invited to her wedding.

After several rings, no one answered. There was no recorder, so he wasn't able to leave a message. He hung up the phone and was frustrated but determined to try again later.

The waiting was not easy for him. He got up from his desk and began pacing the floor. Maybe a cigar would help. Opening the middle drawer of his desk, he pulled out a cigar and lit it and resumed his pacing, mentally practicing what he was going to say.

Hi, Carolyn. This is a voice from your past. Good old Richard Lawton calling. I just found out Kate Flannigan is now Kate O'Connor. I need to check her out. Since she will probably be coming to your wedding, I need an invitation. I promise I'll send a nice gift.

He couldn't believe he was doing this. He couldn't remember the last time he had talked to Carolyn. She might think he was some kind of mental case, but he didn't care. All he knew was he had to see Kate, and he couldn't think of any better way than to show up at her best friend's wedding.

The clock on the wall indicated thirty minutes had passed. Richard could wait no longer. He dialed Carolyn's number and after three rings the phone was picked up.

"Hello."

"Hi, Carolyn. This is Richard Lawton."

"Oh, my gosh. Talk about a voice from the past. It's been awhile. For the life of me, I can't remember the last time we talked," she said.

Richard immediately felt guilty. It was true; he hadn't talked to Carolyn for some time. He did not use people to get what he wanted. But, his desire to see Kate was so overwhelming that he pushed his guilt to the far corner of his mind and said, "This is somewhat embarrassing, but I hope you'll understand, Carolyn. I'll come right to the point. My sister told me you were getting remarried in a couple of weeks. I would like very much to be invited to your wedding."

Not only was she surprised by his call, she was also puzzled by his request. He had definitely caught her off guard. She wanted desperately to ask why he wanted to attend the wedding but instead said, "Of course, you can come to my wedding, and please don't be embarrassed by asking to be invited. Bob and I would be happy to have you come.

"The wedding is going to be a small one—second time around for both of us, you know. We are getting married at Wesley Methodist Church. Didn't you attend that church when you were growing up?" Carolyn asked.

The reference brought back a memory for Richard. "You're right. I did." He also attended the funeral service of his older brother Nick and got married there, too, but did not share this information with her.

"Give me your address, and I'll put an invitation in the mail tomorrow. And, don't think another thing about it," Carolyn said.

No sooner had these words been conveyed when the light went on in her head. He was asking to be invited, because he knew Kate would be coming to her wedding. What better chance to see her without raising any questions as to his personal motives!

He gave Carolyn his address, and she repeated it back to him. She said nothing further as if waiting for him to say something. When he did not, the lull in the conversation made him feel uncomfortable. He sensed she was waiting for an explanation concerning his request. The quicker he got off the phone, the better, before he gave in and admitted his real reason for wanting to attend her wedding.

"Thank you for being so kind. I really appreciate it." Feeling guilty, he blurted out, "I guess you are wondering why..."

"I think I know why, Richard. See you soon. Goodbye."

She hung up the telephone, picked up the paper on which she had written Richard's address. Intrigue...yes, definitely intrigue, she mused. Beyond a doubt, whatever Richard Lawton was cooking up, it was going down at her upcoming wedding.

CHAPTER EIGHTEEN
Kate

Jackie and Kate sat together in a pew in the middle of the church, waiting like everyone else for the wedding to begin. Jackie turned to Kate and whispered, "See anyone you know?"

"Sitting two pews up on the same side as us are two couples I recognize from school and across the aisle are a girl and her mother who are Carolyn's neighbors. There may be others I know sitting behind us. I can never decide if it's better to sit in the front of the church or the back at a wedding," Kate said.

"You could be in a wedding party yourself, Kate. You look gorgeous," Jackie said.

"Thanks for the compliment. A week ago I rummaged through my closet and discovered I had nothing appropriate to wear to a wedding, so I went shopping at the mall and came up empty. You know the dress shop next to Dawson's Market where I go grocery shopping? I went there in desperation and got lucky. It's a little too fancy for me, but I love the colors."

Kate's chiffon skirt was magenta in color with a polyester and rayon jacket patterned with assorted flowers in pink, green and silver against a magenta background. Dainty magenta buttons fastened the jacket. The neckline was trimmed in brocade and continued down the front of the jacket on both sides and all around the bottom, and the keyhole neckline gave way to just the right amount of cleavage.

"You must have splurged, too," Kate said to her sister. "Is that a new outfit you are wearing?"

"Sort of. The blouse and jacket are not new, but the skirt is. I ended up getting the skirt on sale and then splurged on a pair of new leather boots."

"Aren't we a couple of swells?" Kate asked. "Truthfully, I rather be in a pair of jeans."

"Now, that's my kind of wedding," Jackie replied.

Both women fell silent as the organist began playing, and the wedding began. Bob Martin and his two brothers, all dressed handsomely in black tuxedos, took their places in front of Pastor Kline. All heads in the audience turned as the traditional wedding march was heard, signaling it was time for the bridesmaids and the bride to make their entrance.

Carolyn had two attendants, both of whom were Bob's married sisters, wearing long dresses of dark green chiffon and carrying white roses. As Carolyn passed the pew where Kate was standing, she turned her head and gave her friend a smile that brought tears to Kate's eyes. Kate was so very happy for her.

Carolyn's first husband Tom had not been true to her, either. Her marriage also ended in divorce, but divorce did not keep Tom from appearing and disappearing in her life, depending on his current state of affairs. Six months after their divorce, Tom died. When Bob Martin entered her life, Carolyn had once told Kate that Tom's death brought her closure, allowing her to begin again without any loose strings from the past holding her back.

Richard had taken the aisle seat that was several rows from the back of the church and was sitting next to his niece, Joyce Logan. The Logans were neighbors and good friends of the Martin family.

"See that woman in the floral jacket about midway up, sitting next to the woman in the beige jacket?" Richard whispered to Joyce.

"Yes, the one with the short hair?" Joyce asked.

"That's the girl I was going to marry, when I graduated from art school."

"What happened?"

"My ego got in the way, and I let her go," Richard answered.

"Wow, that doesn't sound like you."

"It was me all right back then. All puffed up about myself."

Joyce said nothing in reply. Richard was obviously lost in his thoughts from the past, and it was not the proper time or place to delve deeper into his words.

The ceremony concluded with the kiss at the altar, and the couple proceeded down the aisle to welcome everyone in the vestibule.

As the pews were emptying in front of them, Joyce turned to Richard and said, "Go on. Go up there and talk to her. Don't be such a wimp. All through the ceremony the only person you looked at was your old heart throb. Go on. I'll wait for you in the parking lot."

He smiled at his niece and left the pew by way of the side aisle and walked toward Kate. Richard did not recognize the woman who was with her.

Kate was getting ready to enter the main aisle, but dropped her car keys and went searching for them. Jackie waited for her to find them, sitting patiently in the pew. The people in the pew behind them didn't wait and proceeded to leave. After Kate found her keys, she sat back down, put them in her handbag, turned to her sister and said, "Sorry to be so clumsy."

When she turned her head the other way, Richard Lawton had taken a seat next to her in the pew and was smiling at her.

"Hi, Kate."

It took a few seconds for her to respond. "Richard. What a surprise! I certainly didn't expect to see you here today."

"It's a long story. My niece's family are neighbors of the Martins, and I came with that crowd," Richard said. He hoped his explanation would not raise any questions on Kate's part. He was certainly not going to divulge how he had instigated an invitation.

Kate was still trying to recover from the shock of seeing Richard. She noticed how handsome and trim he looked in his navy blue suit and how relaxed he was. Richard had always been a take-charge kind of guy back in the days when she was dating him, and with maturity this trait was still noticeable by the way he presented himself. His blue eyes focused on Kate as if he were absorbing her.

It took a few more seconds before she said, "Richard, do you remember my sister Jackie?"

"I remember Jackie the ten-year old who liked to jump off the brick stoops on each side of the front steps of your house rather than walk down the steps," Richard said.

"I quit making that exit years ago, when I started wearing high heels," Jackie replied, giving Richard a big smile.

Their conversation was interrupted when an older woman, apparently a friend of Kate's, approached her, asking for directions to the reception. While Kate was giving her directions, the woman was writing them down on a piece of paper. Kate had to repeat them several times before the woman felt she had them right.

While Kate was occupied, Jackie leaned closer to Richard and said, "It's good to see you again, Richard. If you have a minute later, I'd like to talk to you."

He was puzzled and wanted to ask why, but there was no time. Kate had rejoined them and said, "I'm back." Kate smiled at him, and Richard forgot all about Jackie's request.

"I'm sure the two of you can continue your stroll down memory lane without me," Jackie said. "I need a cigarette. I'll meet you by the car, Kate. Good to see you again, Richard."

Kate watched her sister as she walked toward the rear of the church. She was soon lost in the group waiting to congratulate the newlyweds.

After Jackie left, Richard and Kate remained sitting alone in the pew. Richard could not keep his eyes off of Kate. His sister Connie was right. She was older, of course, but the years that had passed had changed the girl he once loved into a beautiful and confident woman.

"It was a beautiful wedding, wasn't it?" Kate asked.

"Yes, it was. It has been a long time since I have been in this church," Richard replied. "And, some of my memories are not happy ones. Services for my brother Nick were held here, when he passed away."

Kate remembered Richard telling her about his brother and knew how deep the bond was between the two of them.

"This is my first time here and unlike some of your memories, Carolyn's wedding will remain in mine as a happy one. She deserves happiness after what she has been through," Kate said.

"Isn't that the way it goes? One person has good feelings about something, and another has negative ones," Richard replied.

Kate wondered if they were still talking about the same thing and made no response to his comment. She changed the subject and said, "You missed the reunion. It was a good time. I went alone." That last part slipped out. Did she subconsciously want him to know that?

He made no reference to her last remark. Instead, he said, "Connie sent me the reunion program. You bet I remember taking you to the prom. Do you remember the jacket I wore?" Richard asked.

"How could I forget? It was plaid with black satin lapels. Your sister made it for you. Somewhere in a box of old photos, I still have a picture taken that night of you and me."

Kate looked around and noticed the church was almost empty. "We better high tail it out of here before we are the last ones to make our congratulations to the newly wedded couple." She gathered her purse and rose, and Richard followed her.

People were still waiting in line to speak to the newlyweds, and Richard and Kate became separated. Kate went ahead to give her happy wishes to Carolyn and Bob, and Richard walked over to where his niece and her family were waiting for him to join them.

Kate hugged Carolyn and whispered in her ear. "You failed to tell me he was coming, you little stinker."

Carolyn whispered back, "Intrigue… intrigue."

Giving Bob a kiss on his cheek, Kate left the church and walked toward her car. Jackie was waiting for her.

Kate unlocked the door and got situated in the driver's seat. She turned to Jackie and said, "I'm not sure how to get to the Lakeside Motor Boat Club. Do you know the way?"

"Not to worry. I do," Jackie replied. "However, we have to make a stop first. I'm out of cigarettes."

By the time Kate and Jackie arrived at the reception, many people were standing around the bar, and some were already seated at various tables. Carolyn and Bob were nowhere to be seen. Kate assumed the wedding party was closeted in another room with the photographer for wedding pictures. Kate didn't recognize anyone she knew, and the two couples from school, who were at the church, either had not yet arrived or were not coming.

"Want something from the bar, Jackie?"

"No thanks. If you want to mingle, go ahead," Jackie responded.

"You are a good sport to come with me today. I'm not one to mingle, either. Let's just get a cold Pepsi and sit down at one of the tables. What do you say?" Kate asked, walking toward a table that had not been taken.

"Works for me. Making small talk with strangers has never been my thing. You stay put. I'll go get our drinks," Jackie said and left Kate, sitting by herself.

Apparently, the picture taking was over as the members of the wedding party made their entrance and began taking their places at the head table. Carolyn spotted Kate sitting alone and walked toward her.

"You look lovely, Kate. That dinner suit is stunning," Carolyn said.

"Thank you, and you are a beautiful bride. I am so happy for you."

"Did Jackie come with you to the reception, or are you alone?" Carolyn asked.

There was that word again. *Alone.* Kate did not like the assumption the word implied in her case. It made her feel so vulnerable.

She quickly responded, "No, Jackie's here. She went to get us something to drink at the bar."

For a brief moment, the conversation hung out there in space. Carolyn was somewhat reluctant to bring up anything having to do with Richard's presence. Kate could possibly ask her to explain why he was invited, which would require an explanation on her part. She decided to cast caution aside and asked, "Did you get to talk with Richard?"

"Yes, I did," Kate answered.

Carolyn was waiting for more details, but, when they did not come, said, "In the receiving line, he told me he would not be able to come to the reception, but didn't say why."

When she heard this bit of news, Kate made no response. She was getting good at hiding her feelings. She was disappointed at his absence and relieved at the same time. Now, she could be herself and enjoy the rest of the evening with her sister Jackie. She had said goodbye to Richard Lawton a very long time ago anyway.

CHAPTER NINETEEN
Richard

After saying goodbye to his niece and her family, Richard took one last look at Kate. She was talking to someone in the receiving line, as she waited to congratulate the newlyweds. It took everything in him to turn away and leave to go home. As he pulled out of the parking lot, his mind was racing with thoughts of Kate and past memories of their relationship. Seeing her had made him feel alive, a reaction he had not experienced in a very long while.

The drive back to South Bend would provide him with time to think about what he would do next. He was definitely going to contact her. Despite the time and circumstances that had passed, his desire for her burned as brightly in his heart as it had forty years ago.

He pulled into his garage and went into the house. His tiredness overpowered his emotions. All he wanted was a hot shower and sleep. On the kitchen counter, the light on the telephone headset was blinking. He hit the button to replay his messages. It was the third message that brought him back to reality.

This is Dr. Norton. This is not an emergency. I need to talk to you about Betty. Please come to my office Monday morning at 9 a.m.

The recorder did not record the time of messages, so Richard had no way of knowing when Dr. Norton called. He had no idea what Dr. Norton wanted to discuss with him but felt relieved there was no emergency. He thought about calling the nursing home, but it was late. If there was a problem, someone on the staff would have called him and left a message.

Climbing the steps to his bedroom on the second floor, he marveled how a short telephone message could wipe out almost instantaneously his temporary feelings of happiness, however brief, and reminded him of his obligations, as if he had no right to think of his own needs.

He pulled back the covers and crawled into the empty bed.

The next morning Richard awoke to the sound of rain. From the bed he could see the day was starting out to be gloomy. Quickly, he showered, shaved and dressed. His agenda for today was full, giving him only a half-hour to grab a quick bite to eat before he was to see Dr. Norton.

He parked his car in the parking lot next to the building where Dr. Norton's office was located and walked across the street to the restaurant with umbrella in tow. He didn't feel like eating and only ordered a cup of coffee. After drinking it, he walked back toward the building.

Dr. Norton's receptionist acknowledged Richard with a bright smile and said, "The doctor will be with you in a moment," before ushering him into Dr. Norton's private office.

Richard took a chair opposite the desk and waited patiently. Within minutes Dr. Norton opened the door and greeted Richard with a firm handshake. "Sorry to bring you out in this weather, Richard. It's raining like nobody's business out there. Open up your umbrella so it can dry while we visit. Put it next to the door over there."

Richard did as he was asked and returned to his chair, waiting for the doctor to speak.

"I ordered some tests recently. The results of those tests have come back, and I wanted to share them with you in person."

Richard sensed the forthcoming news was not going to be good, by the look on the doctor's face and his manner.

Dr. Norton took a chair opposite Richard and began talking. "As you know, the experimental radiation treatments in the past did not help your wife. Currently, the MRSA infection alone is too powerful for her to overcome, and it is running rampart throughout her body. The dementia is getting worse, and this last bout of pneumonia has also taken its toll. All I am able to do is prescribe drugs that will keep her comfortable and pretty much pain free. I am very sorry, Richard, but I want to prepare you. Betty is failing."

Several minutes passed before Richard responded to what Dr. Norton said and then asked, "How long?"

"Maybe two or three months at the most, possibly even less. It's hard to say. Each case is different, Richard."

"Isn't there anything out there to help her? Some treatment or drug or something you haven't tried?" Richard asked.

"No. She simply has too many overwhelming conditions and complications to fight and very little left to fight with. They are all ravaging her body. She's on God's time now," Dr. Norton replied compassionately.

Dr. Norton came around from behind his desk. He put his hand on Richard's shoulder, squeezed it and left the room, closing the door to give Richard privacy to absorb what he had just been told.

Richard sat there, not quite knowing what to do or where to go. Memories of Betty and their life together flooded his mind as if he were watching a silent movie. The ringing of the telephone on Dr. Norton's desk brought him back to the present. He got up and left but forgot to take his umbrella with him.

CHAPTER TWENTY
Kate

Several weeks passed since the wedding. Kate was busy at work more than usual due to her part in preparing a presentation for a major St. Louis firm. Her assignments were placed in a basket on her desk every morning. When she arrived at work, the basket was full, and rarely was it empty at the end of the day, despite her best efforts to make it so. This was simply the nature of her job. She had grown accustomed to the workload, which made the day go faster. She truly liked her job, despite the heavy responsibilities she was given. She was more than good at what she did and was paid well for it. Even more importantly, she felt she belonged and was appreciated.

Her phone rang. "Marketing Department, Kate O'Connor."

"Good morning, Kate. Can you slip away for a cup of coffee?" Ruth asked.

"Give me five minutes. I'll meet you in the cafeteria," Kate replied.

The two women were seated by the window in the cafeteria. Ruth brought up the subject of Thanksgiving. "Can you believe Thanksgiving is almost here?"

"Yes, I know. Finals are always the week before the Thanksgiving break. Two term papers are also due then. When I'm not working, I'm either cramming, burning the lights at the library at night or finishing up a project on the house in order to start on another. I'm looking forward to the time off," Kate replied with a sigh.

Ruth nodded and pursed her lips. She understood perfectly Kate's position.

"It looks like I'll be spending another Thanksgiving without my children and grandchildren," Kate said. "Andy and Sean will probably go to their girlfriend's house for dinner, and Ryan always goes to Portageville with his wife and kids for the holiday. It's so expensive for Mary Rose, Mike Jr., Patrick and Abby to come home for Thanksgiving with all their children. I'd rather they come when they can spend more time."

"I'm in the same boat as you," Ruth said. "It's sometimes a problem when kids move away, especially at holiday time. It appears the two of us will be dining again at Miss Tillie's."

Miss Tillie's was a cafeteria near Kate's house and catered to the retirees, who resided in condos nearby. The two women ate there at least once a week. The food was good, the price was reasonable and close to where they both lived.

There was something depressing about eating at Miss Tillie's on Thanksgiving, but Kate did not want to verbalize her thoughts, because she didn't want to possibly hurt her friend's feelings.

"I better get back, Ruth. I have a ton of work to do. We'll talk later about Thanksgiving." Kate picked up her coffee container and took it with her.

* * * * *

The Sunday before the holiday, Kate went to early Mass, stopped after church to pick up some donuts and went home to put the finishing touches on her term paper for Tuesday's class.

She heard the telephone ring as she put her key in the kitchen door, hurriedly opened it and grabbed the wall phone.

"Hello."

"It's me, checking in," Jackie said.

"Hi, Jackie. I just got back from church. I stopped off at the Donut Hole and bought some donuts. I have a term paper to polish before Tuesday and figured a couple of donuts and several cups of coffee would help me get the job done," Kate said.

"Hoped you prayed for me," Jackie said.

"Of course, I always do. What's up?" Kate asked.

"Have I got a story to tell you. Better get yourself comfortable, Kate. I'll hold on until you do."

Kate took off her high heels, opened the box of donuts and took out an iced jelly donut. She pulled out a chair to sit on and propped her feet on another. "I'm all ears," Kate said, as she took a bite of the donut.

"Richard Lawton called me," Jackie blurted out without any preamble.

There was no immediate response from Kate. Jackie wondered if she had heard her and repeated, "Richard Lawton called me."

"I heard you the first time. Why would he be calling you?" Kate asked.

"You probably don't remember this, but at Carolyn's wedding while you were talking to that woman about directions, I was making small talk with Richard. Just before you turned around to rejoin us, I told him I wanted to talk to him."

"Pardon me for asking, but what for?" Kate asked.

"I wanted to thank him for the sign he drew for me when I had my lemonade stand, because I don't think I ever did," Jackie answered.

"Now, I've heard everything. My gosh, Jackie. Do you know how many years ago that was? What made you want to make a thing out of that?"

"I was only eight years old when he made it for me, and I don't think I thanked him then. Besides, I liked that sign and kept it for a very long time. I thought he was pretty cool to make me a sign in the first place," Jackie said.

"How did he get your number? It's still unlisted, isn't it?" Kate asked.

"Yes, it is. He said he called the operator and was told my number was unlisted. Finally, he called Prime Pizza and left his number for me to call him, which I did last night. I took the night off. Since it was still pretty early, I called him back. So, now you have it."

"Now I have what?" Kate asked.

"Use your head, Kate. He probably tried to phone you first only to find out you had an unlisted number. Calling me to get it was his next play. Believe me, I'm sure he was not at all interested in learning what it was I wanted to talk to him about. What he was really after was your phone number and figured I would give it to him.

"I bet he also tried calling Carolyn, too. When no one answered, he put two and two together. The Martins are probably still on their honeymoon. Apparently, he must want something if he went to all this trouble to find out how to get in touch with you.

"Anyway, we talked for quite awhile after I gushed about the sign thing. He told me a little about his life since moving away from Springfield. He has quite a story, let me assure you. Quite frankly, anyone who bares his soul like he did to me deserves some sort of response and not from me either. I guess the ball is in your court. So now what?" Jackie asked.

Since there was no reply from Kate, she asked, "Are you still there?"

"Yeah, I'm here. This is so out of the blue. Never in a million years did I ever think Richard Lawton would be calling you," Kate said.

"Come on, Kate. It's so obvious. It's you he wants to talk to." Jackie then began telling Kate briefly a few of the personal things Richard had shared with her. When she finished, she asked, "What are you thinking, sis?"

"I don't know what to think. What does he want from me?"

"He didn't say. All he asked me for was your phone number. I didn't want to give him your unlisted phone number without your permission, but I did give him your address. I hope that was okay."

"It's okay. Not to worry. I would, however, really like to know what this is all about."

"My guess is you'll have to wait to find out, but I do believe he is going to contact you. Kind of exciting, isn't it?" Jackie asked. "It's like getting a box as a surprise. You don't know what's inside until you open it. You know, anticipation."

"Honestly, Jackie. Keep in mind not all boxes contain good things."

"Think positive, sis. Think positive. I got to go. I think I am more excited than you are over all this."

Jackie said goodbye and hung up the phone. Maybe, maybe, maybe, Richard Lawton, whatever he was up to, might be just the right individual to put her sister together again—the way she was before Mike Flannigan broke her heart.

CHAPTER TWENTY-ONE
Richard

The restaurant was crowded when Richard arrived. Vinita saw him when he came in the door. She passed by him and said, "Good morning, Mr. Lawton. Your son is sitting in the corner booth, left side," before she hurried away with a tray full of food.

RJ watched his father making his way toward him. He could not help but notice how haggard he looked and wondered why his father wanted to meet with him today of all days, the Tuesday before the Thanksgiving holiday. He had tons of loose ends to tend to and had not planned on even eating lunch.

Richard took off his coat and sat down in the booth. "Hey, thanks for getting here early. This place is jammed. I had no idea it would be this packed," Richard said.

"Not to rush you, Dad, but I can't linger today. The morning has been hectic. There's a problem with one of our biggest clients in Kokomo, something to do with missing parts. I might have to do a last minute run to solve it. Sarah's on this church committee, and I promised her I would drop off some flyers for her at the printing company before they close today."

Before Richard could respond, Vinita was standing before them, ready to take their order.

"What's the soup for today?" RJ asked.

"Broccoli with cheese," she replied.

Richard nodded his head and RJ said, "Make that two with coffee. We're kind of pressed for time today, Vinita."

"I get it. Be back in a flash. Doesn't take much time to dish up two bowls of soup."

The restaurant was noisy due to the lunch crowd. Richard was not looking forward to bringing RJ up-to-date concerning his mother's condition. There was never a good time or place to share bad news.

As promised, Vinita returned with their orders quickly, served both of them and went off to wait on other customers. From the look on both of their faces, she sensed they wanted to be left alone.

Richard kept stirring his soup without eating it. Finally, he put down the spoon and looked directly into the eyes of his son and said, "My news isn't good news, RJ. It's about your mother. I was out of town over the weekend and went to a wedding in Springfield. When I got back, Dr. Norton left a message on my recorder, asking me to drop by his office yesterday, which I did. He said there was nothing more he could do for her. The drugs she is taking will keep her comfortable without any pain, but he wanted to prepare me for the inevitable outcome. I already called your sisters and brought them up to speed."

RJ sat there silently, looking out into space, as if he needed time to compose himself before he responded to his father's words. "It's hard, Dad, it really is. Just looking at Mom tears me up."

"I know, son, I know."

RJ was silent, lost in his own private thoughts, realizing the time had finally come for acceptance.

When RJ spoke, he changed the subject. "Where are you going for the Thanksgiving holiday, Dad?"

"Louise is going to cook a turkey dinner for me tomorrow, including all the trimmings. All I have to do is warm them up in the microwave. When I left this morning, she was busy making a pie.

I'll watch some of the football games, and I also have some letter writing to do."

"Sounds like Louise has come through one more time," RJ said. "What are your plans for Friday?"

"I plan to go to the office. The rest of the world can go Black Friday shopping, but I pass. I get a lot more done at work when I'm alone. I'll be fine, so don't worry about me."

After eating his soup hurriedly, RJ looked at his watch. "Dad, I got to run. We'll talk further after I get back. I'll call you. Okay?"

"Drive carefully. Enjoy Thanksgiving and the weekend with Sarah's parents, and give my best to everyone."

"You take care of yourself, too. I love you, Dad."

Richard watched his son leave the restaurant. He felt alone, just like the time when his brother Nick died.

CHAPTER TWENTY-TWO
Kate

Driving home from work Monday, all Kate could think of was a hot bath and curling up in bed with something good to read other than a textbook. She was tired.

She pulled into the garage and walked down to the mailbox to get the mail. Inside the mailbox were several letters and a catalog. As she looked through the letters, she noticed one of them had Richard Lawton's return address in the left hand corner and wondered why Richard Lawton was sending a letter to her. Closing the mailbox, she hugged the bulky catalog and letters to her chest, so she wouldn't drop them, and walked back toward the house.

After unlocking the door, she dumped all her belongings on the kitchen table, her gloves, purse, keys and the mail. Although Richard's letter spiked her curiosity, she took off her coat, hung it up and headed for the bedroom. Bath first, mail later.

Dressed in robe and slippers and a towel around her wet hair, she returned to the kitchen and put the tea kettle on the stove to heat. She wasn't hungry but wanted a cup of Earl Grey to warm her insides. After the water boiled, she made herself a cup of tea and took the mug over to the kitchen table. She sat down, propped her feet up on the seat of another kitchen chair and picked up Richard's letter to read first.

Dear Kate,

By now, receiving a letter from me should not catch you completely by surprise. I'm assuming your sister told you I called her, wanting to know how to contact you. She gave me your address, and I truly hope you are not angry. I also hope after you read my letter it will erase any doubts as to why I wanted to get in touch with you.

The reason I called your sister was to respond to what she said to me during our brief visit at Carolyn and Bob's wedding. She said she wanted to talk to me, but didn't get a chance to tell me why. What could a little girl from so many years ago want to talk to me about? I assumed it had to be about you. Well, to my surprise it was to thank me for a lemonade sign I must have made for her years ago, when we were dating in high school. Cripe! I wanted to talk about you. Later in the conversation, I opened a part of my life to her. Why, I don't really know.

Perhaps you are wondering why I have resurfaced after all these years of silence. I guess with age comes maturity and a wisdom that allows a person to address past feelings a young man, such as I once was, would have never shared with anyone. It's different, now. I'm too old for games, Kate. What follows is the truth.

I realize you never made a commitment to me way back when we were seeing each other, but you were the girl I wanted to be with for the rest of my life. I had, as you know, dated my share of girls, but in my heart you were the one. I put you on a pedestal and wanted you to share my dreams and future. Perhaps those feelings were in a young man's heart, but that's where my head was at that time! When I heard you had married, it hurt. But, a young handsome man, such as I thought of myself at that time, doesn't show that kind of hurt to others. Instead, I sought a new mate to help me conquer the world.

I met Betty at art school, and it was a great physical attraction, which soon led to intimacy and then the unexpected announcement she was in a family way. Wedding plans were made. Although she informed me before the wedding she was not pregnant, we went ahead with the marriage. My belief in Christ and marriage prevented me from choosing the alternative. I knew as I said my vows it was a mistake but couldn't bring myself to walk away in front of my family and the few friends who attended the ceremony.

After we were married, we went back to Chicago, where I got a job at an art studio. Betty became a receptionist at an insurance company. We worked and had fun in the evenings and on the weekends—too much fun that included a good deal of drinking in private clubs.

When our first child was born, money became tight. I changed jobs and went to work for the Belmont Company as an assistant advertising manager. This job, and designing milk cartons for a local advertising agency to supplement the loss of Betty's paycheck, kept me working day and night. When I was at home, I spent most of the time at the drawing board. Betty was bored and started going out with her girlfriends from work to the same clubs we once went to as a couple.

While I was doing artwork at night to pay the bills and babysitting our lovely little girl, Betty was out having a good time with her girlfriends.

Then, I got a promotion, which required me to travel extensively. I was gone for weeks at a time and blamed myself for the breakup of our marriage. I was hardly ever home. Betty wanted a divorce. She moved in with her parents who lived in Indianapolis and made arrangements with her mother to take care of our child.

I was overwhelmed! However, I was not about to let our marriage become just another statistic nor was I willing to let our beautiful little girl down. I went to see Betty to work things out, and we did.

The next two years Betty and I tried to regain lost ground, but it was useless. I filed for divorce and moved to South Bend and started an art agency with another guy.

Shortly after receiving the divorce papers, Betty came to my apartment one night. Her purpose in coming to see me was to tell me she wanted to give the marriage another try. Although I was asking for custody of our daughter, I knew I would not get it. At best, I would only get visitation rights, if I lost. That was unacceptable to me. It was then I faced the facts. I convinced myself it would be better for everyone concerned to try and make the marriage work, although my love and trust for Betty was over.

We had three more children, two girls and one boy. Betty continued to drink heavily, but we all survived and my business thrived. To outsiders we looked like the All-American family. When the children moved out, Betty's drinking escalated.

I forced Betty to enter a treatment center in Indianapolis, so her friends would not know. At that time all our children advised me to get a divorce and start a new life. Then Betty developed MS, an incurable disease which had its way with her brain and body. I couldn't tell if her actions were due to the disease or the drinking. That was five years ago.

Since the treatment she has not had a drink, but each day is a trial. And, the MS has steadily progressed. Her memory and bodily functions are impaired, and sometimes being with her is like being with a child.

I can't tell you how many days I wanted to escape and go somewhere, but somewhere is nowhere. I told myself I must do what needed to be done and that was to stay the course as painful and as loveless as it might be.

You might be wondering why you are hearing from me after these many years of silence. It started with the death of Carolyn's husband Tom. I called her to express my sorrow.

Over the next few months from time to time I called Carolyn and, during the conversation, I would ask about you, or she would talk about you. This started me thinking about my loneliness.

After Connie sent me the reunion program and told me you were divorced, I thought it might be a great time to contact you, thinking I would not be out of line to at least learn how you were doing and talk to an old friend—okay, an old flame. You are the reason I went to the wedding.

When I found out you were divorced, it seemed to just progress from there. Then, when the opportunity to contact you was presented by your sister's remark, I took it, and all the old memories came back. I've kept all my unhappiness inside hidden from everyone, including my children... like a crack in a dam, it all came flooding out. It may be crazy, but I don't care. In ways I can't explain, I thought now might be the time of do something for myself.

What do I want? My heart wants you to run away with me for the rest of our lives to a log house on a lake somewhere. You can do as you wish, and I'll paint to my heart's content. But, my brain and the real world we live in wants nothing more of you now than your friendship with any limitations you set. But, I want to make one thing perfectly clear. Should my situation change and you are free, I intend to court you. So, I'm giving you fair warning, Kate O'Connor. Prepare yourself for my re-entry into your life.

When I saw you at the wedding, there were still sparks inside me, which made me feel alive, something I haven't felt for a long time. You are still on that pedestal, Kate. I truly hope you don't think I have given up. God has been good to me, even in the bad times.

Should you respond to this letter, and I hope you will, please include your phone number, since it is unlisted.

Love,
Richard

She laid his letter on the table in front of her and sat there quietly, thinking about what she had just read. Richard knew about suffering, too, even more than she did. The letter became dampened by her tears, as she gathered the pages with trembling fingers and returned them to the envelope.

Sleep did not come easy to Kate that night. Her thoughts kept her tossing and turning and as a result, she overslept. Wasting no time, she went through her morning routine, dressed, brewed a pot of coffee, poured some into a travel cup and left the house for work.

Her thoughts of Richard Lawton were temporarily put on hold. Her business day began in full swing and never lost momentum. After a meeting with all of the sales associates, which took most of the day, she felt drained and was glad when it was time to call it quits. Closing down her computer, she gathered her things, put on her coat, left the building and walked toward the parking garage.

On the way home, she began thinking of Richard and decided she would answer his letter tonight. The school paper she was working on would have to wait. First, she would get into her sweats and have something to eat. Then, she would write her letter.

CHAPTER TWENTY-THREE
Richard

The days were numbered for Richard—one day after he mailed his letter, then two days after he mailed his letter, then another day and so on. His mail at home was delivered before noon. He could hardly wait for his lunch break at work, so he could drive home and check the mailbox. Each time he found it empty, he rationalized why he hadn't received any response from Kate. Maybe she was too busy. Maybe she was overwhelmed by what he had written to her. Maybe she was seeing someone. Maybe she was not interested. No reply was still a reply. The last possibility was unbearable to him.

All of these scenarios kept running around in his head, making it difficult for him to focus on business matters. Even his staff noticed how jumpy he was, which was so out of character for him.

After a week had passed, he called Ken from his office after everyone had left for the day. "How's it going, good buddy? Am I interrupting dinner?" Richard asked.

"Can't complain and no, you're not interrupting dinner. How did the wedding go?" Ken knew about his plan to check out Kate by attending the wedding. What Ken really wanted to know was if

Richard's ploy had produced any results. He came right to the point by asking, "Was she there?"

"Yeah, she was there all right," Richard replied. "She came with her sister Jackie."

"Well, did you get a chance to talk with her?" Ken asked.

"Yes."

"And?" Ken pushed.

"Since I didn't get much time to talk with her at the wedding, and I didn't attend the reception, I mailed her a letter pretty much telling her what I told you about my life with Betty. I even went a little farther than that."

"Meaning what?"

"Let's just say I declared myself, and I am waiting for her reply. It's been a week today, since I mailed the letter and still no response."

"Call her. You know the drill—High School 101," Ken said.

"Very funny. I can't. Her number is unlisted."

"I see. Maybe she's busy at her job or has some unexpected obligation that's taking up her time. When you think about it, a week isn't very long considering mail delivery," Ken offered in the hope of easing his friend's frustration.

"Ken, you're such an eternal optimist."

"Listen, Richard. Have a little faith. Hang up the phone and go home. Eat that nice dinner Louise has probably left in the oven for you and turn on the television. Get your mind off the subject of letters. Remember, tomorrow is another day."

"Okay, Scarlett. You've been a big help. Talk to you soon," Richard said.

When he got home he found a note on the table from Louise. *Had to leave a little early. Dinner is in the oven, and your mail is on the counter. See you tomorrow.*

He felt miserable. Perhaps he came on too strong and scared Kate. Thinking about what he had written, his letter must have been a big shock to her. This was *not* High School 101, and he was too old for games. He lived in the real world, the world of deadlines, where each job was needed the day before he got it. He was comfortable in making things happen fast, rationalizing his recent actions.

Several letters were lying on the kitchen island. He grabbed the pile, looking for an envelope with Kate's return address in the upper left hand corner. Yes! There it was. Hey, Ken, you old son-of-a- gun. Forget about tomorrow. Today is the day! Dropping the rest of the mail on the kitchen island, he sat down without even taking off his overcoat and began reading Kate's letter.

Dear Richard,

   I received your letter, and it made me feel very sad. You've had some painful times and have been sorely tested.

   There are many things I remember about our relationship. Looking back, I didn't have much concern for your feelings, when we parted company years ago. I would like to think it was due to immaturity on my part. It's a little late, but I'm sorry for my insensitivity.

   My marriage to Mike Flannigan also started out with me being pregnant. I did not set out to trap him; it just happened. We met at his cousin's wedding and were paired together as groomsman and bridesmaid. I knew, after spending time with Mike that day, I wanted to spend the rest of my life with him. I guess I got bitten by the old love at first sight bug. My sister repeatedly tells me how very lucky I have been to know love that deeply, although that depth was never returned to me.

   We had problems before we moved to St. Louis. I always thought they would go away, when Mike settled into his new job here. Things were okay for awhile, but he began to isolate himself from me and our three sons, who were still living at home.

   At the time, I did not know Mike was seeing someone. He explained his indifference toward me by blaming it on business pressures. People asked me, after he left, if there was another woman, and I defended him. I couldn't convince myself he was capable of such a thing. Much later I learned he was not only capable of that but a great deal more.

Yes, there were signs, but I suppose I chose to ignore them. Mike wasn't interested in me or anything I did. He was only interested in his freedom—freedom from me, freedom from his home responsibilities, freedom from being questioned about his actions and whereabouts. His need for freedom is the reason he gave me for leaving me.

I found his rationale difficult to believe, much less understand, because Mike never had to report to me or few others for that matter. This attitude carried over into his professional life, which eventually got him into trouble. At two of the companies he worked for, where he held an executive position, upper management asked for his resignation.

All of my family, including our children, said I needed to get on with my life. I decided to seek the counsel of my parish priest. After telling him about my martial situation, he told me if Mike was unwilling to return, after a reasonable length of waiting on my part, he advised me to get a divorce to settle legal matters, which I did.

Mike likes to drink, too. His abuse of alcohol not only caused him personal problems but also contributed significantly to the breakdown of our marriage.

He finally did admit there was another woman. My guess is he wanted to wipe his conscience clean by telling me. All that was left for me to do with our thirty-year marriage was for me to bury it, which I did by divorcing him.

It has taken many years to put myself back together. All things considered, I have a good life now. Like you, I've had my share of troubles, too. Neither one of us are unique, either. There are probably many others in the world, who have been dealt worse hands and have lived to tell about it, and maybe even laughed, eventually.

I wake up each morning now and try to look upon the day as an adventure—not knowing what's in store for me but enjoying the day for what it is. I guess peace and contentment come closest to describing it best. That is not to say I would *not like a special someone to share my days, but I am gun shy now and very reluctant to risk too much of myself for fear of failing again.*

If it's my friendship you are after, it's yours without any limitations. If I do nothing else with the rest of my life, I hope I never hurt anyone, because of something I said or did.

Just remember you are not alone. God hasn't forgotten about either one of us. Usually, things work out for the best. You have a friend in me and a much better one than you had in 1953. If there is anything you need, all you have to do is ask, and, if I am able to give it, I will. I have enclosed my business card and on the back of it I have written my unlisted telephone number.

Kate

Many thoughts were racing in his mind after reading Kate's letter, so he read it again. When he finished reading it for the second time, he particularly noticed she had closed her letter only with her name. He wondered if her feelings of failure would end something before it even got off the ground.

CHAPTER TWENTY-FOUR
Kate

Kate was running late. She usually did not try and come home after work before her class started, but she forgot one of her books. As she turned the corner to her house, she glanced at the front porch. A white mailing tube was leaning against the porch railing, and she wondered what could be in it.

She pulled into the driveway, parked and unlocked the back door before quickly going to her desk and grabbing the textbook she needed. With one foot out the back door, she remembered the parcel on the front porch, turned around and headed for the front door.

She hadn't sent away for anything and wondered who was sending her something. When she picked up the tube, she noticed the return address on the front of it, Lawton and McBride Advertising Agency. What could Richard be sending her? Her curiosity was getting the best of her and wanted desperately to find out what was inside of the tube Richard sent, but she glanced at her watch. She would barely have time to make it to class on time. She picked up the tube and went back into the house. On her way out the back door, she put it on the kitchen table and locked the door behind her. Whatever Richard was sending her would have to wait until she got home later than night.

Kate prided herself in being punctual for her Tuesday and Thursday evening classes. Concordia University's offsite campus was in Clayton, a good thirty-minute ride from her house. Occasionally, she picked up a cup of coffee and a hamburger at a drive-through on her way to class, but not tonight. The time she had taken to mull over Richard's package had taken care of that.

She drove into the school parking lot, picked up her books and ran all the way to the entrance of the building very much out of breath, arriving in the classroom only minutes before Professor Jacobs did. She no sooner placed her books and belongings under the desk chair when she heard her voice being called.

"Ah, Ms. O'Connor. We seem to be breathless about something tonight. I hope it concerns the homework I gave. Perhaps you can begin our discussion by giving your viewpoint on Ann Rand's philosophy?" All other thoughts vanished from Kate's mind as she made ready to respond to Professor Jacob's request.

Kate had a hard time concentrating. Even the fifteen-minute break didn't seem to rejuvenate her mentally or physically. She was looking forward to the end of the class. When the bell rang, she gathered her books, left the building and got into her car. She couldn't get home fast enough.

When she opened the back door, all she had on her mind was a hot shower and a good night's sleep. Then she saw the tube on the kitchen table. Save the best for last, she told herself, as she put away her books, undressed and got into the shower.

The shower had restored her energy. She loved surprises, too. After tearing away the tape from one end of the tube, she withdrew something wrapped in cellophane and unrolled it. It was a large print of Notre Dame's administration building, surrounded by pine trees covered in snow with Father Joyce and Knute Rockne ghosted in the sky. Printed in the middle of the bottom margin was the print's title, *Tradition of Excellence*. Before she had time to look at it further, the telephone rang. Calls at this time of night were usually emergency ones, and she hurried to pick up the phone.

"Hello," she answered cautiously.

"Hi, Kate. It's Richard. I've been trying to reach you all evening. Since you didn't answer the phone, I assumed you would eventually return and kept on trying. I hope I'm not calling too late."

"No, not at all. I go to school two nights a week and usually get home around this time." She was relieved it was not an emergency and apprehensive at the same time, because Richard was calling her.

"You go to school?" he asked incredulously.

"Yes. Count on me to do everything backwards," Kate said.

"Listen, you must be exhausted after working all day and then going to school. I don't want to keep you from sleep. Maybe I should call another time."

"No, it's okay. I'm wired after class. I usually read before I fall asleep anyway."

Richard got right to the point and said, "I got your letter today."

Before he could say anything else, Kate said, "And, I received a lovely print."

"That particular print has sold more copies at the Notre Dame bookstore than any other. I chalk up its popularity due to the subject matter."

"You may be right about the popular subject matter, but I think it's much more than that. How about the talent of the artist who painted it? Thank you for sending it to me."

"You're welcome," he replied without acknowledging her compliment and went on to say, "Since you said you were usually wired after class, do you mind if I call you at this time? Some nights I come down to my studio at the office to paint, and I, too, have a hard time getting to sleep when I get home."

"No, I don't mind at all. Quite frankly, on the other weeknights I don't attend class, I'm up either writing papers, studying or watching television," Kate replied.

She picked up on his reference to future calls he might be making at this hour, but for what purpose?

"Kate, I'll come right to the point. I would like very much for you to show me some residential areas that are near St. Louis. I've pretty much decided I'm going to relocate within driving distance of St. Louis within the next year. Plans are in the works to sell my half of the partnership to my partner. The sooner I can find what I'm looking for, my other plans will be put into play," Richard explained.

"I realize the Christmas holidays are around the corner, but I was thinking about next weekend. I'd like to fly in Friday morning and then rent a car. I'd have Friday afternoon and all day Saturday to explore any possibilities and head home early Sunday morning," Richard added.

"Is that something you could help me with? If you don't want to do this or are too busy, I completely understand. My thinking is you've lived in St. Louis for a good number of years and might know more about the kind of area I am looking for after I clue you in to my list of wants."

There was a lull, as if he was waiting for Kate to say something, but before she could respond, Richard broke the silence by saying, "And, I would like very much to see you and spend some time with you."

A bell went off in her head when Kate heard his last remark. She decided not to make any reference to it. Instead, she said, "I think I can help you. Let me put together a list of potential places that might be of interest to you. Can you call me tomorrow night? By then, I'll have the phone numbers of the possibilities, so you can make appointments for Friday and Saturday, which might save you some time. Will that work for you?" Kate asked.

"It will. I thought I'd make overnight reservations near your home to save traveling time. Can you recommend a motel or hotel near you?" Richard asked.

"Yes. The Leland is within a short distance of where I live. It's located on Berry Road. I'll also get the particulars on The Leland and have all the info for you tomorrow when you call."

"Great. Plan on dinner Friday and Saturday nights, that is if you'll allow me to take you to dinner," Richard said.

"Absolutely. Dinner is my usual weekend fee for assisting in any real estate matters," Kate said good-naturedly.

"Great. Your sense of humor sure hasn't changed, Kate. I'm glad. I better let you get some sleep. I'll call tomorrow night around the same time. Goodnight, Kate."

"Goodnight, Richard."

Richard Lawton seemed to be wasting no time in re-entering her life. Letters were one thing, physical presence was quite another. It had been a long time since she had dinner with a man and began thinking about what she would wear.

CHAPTER TWENTY-FIVE
Richard

Snow had fallen during the night, covering the ground like an untouched canvas. Winters in South Bend required a good pair of boots, a strong back for shoveling and a love for a cold climate that could last for weeks.

Louise had come early. Richard could smell the aroma of something being baked as he laid in bed. On the day she came to clean, she always fixed him breakfast before he left for work.

He had a great many things to do today and felt energized. His conversation with Kate last night was the reason for his exuberance. Mentally, he was already making plans for his trip to St. Louis and could hardly wait to get to his office to get the ball rolling. He went into the bathroom to take his morning shower, whistling as he got out of bed.

"Good morning, Mr. L. Sit down. Your breakfast is almost ready." Louise noticed how very cheerful he was, and so full of energy.

"Good morning to you, too," he replied as he sat down at the kitchen table and looked at the plate she set before him. "Wonderful, Louise, wonderful! You sure know how to cook up a darn good breakfast. Eggs, hash browns, bacon, fresh orange juice, an English muffin with your homemade strawberry jam and hot coffee for a chaser. I might have to walk to work after I eat this."

Louise beamed at his compliment. He thought she might be wondering what, or who, was responsible for the good spirits of her boss this morning. Little did she know it was not a *what* but a *who* and was not ashamed to admit it had she asked.

Leaving him to enjoy his breakfast, Louise went to the utility room closet and got out the vacuum. The work day was beginning for both of them.

The first thing he did, when he got to his office, was to make a reservation at the motel Kate had suggested. Then he booked his flights. He would arrive in St. Louis around 9 a.m. Friday and leave Sunday at 8 a.m. When he called Kate tonight, he would also ask her to make dinner reservations for Friday and Saturday nights.

Richard hung up the phone, intending to make another call, but saw Stan standing outside his door and asked, "Need to see me about something?"

"No, not really," Stan replied, entering Richard's office. "You're in a bit early this morning, aren't you? Anything going on that I should know about?"

Stan and Richard's relationship was strictly business from nine to five. Neither man invaded the other's business territory. This arrangement worked from the very start of the partnership. They respected one another for their individual contributions toward making their business prosper and grow over the years. Rarely, did they see each other socially.

"I came in early to make some reservations. Friday, I'm going to St. Louis for the weekend again, but I'll be back in the office Monday."

"Nothing has changed in our agreement, has it?" Stan asked.

"No, no. The takeover is all set as we agreed. I intend to remain on board until April 1 as we discussed. Over the past couple of weeks I have been reviewing the brochures I sent away for earlier. I've pretty much made up my mind to build a log house somewhere on a good fishing lake near St. Louis. It's within a reasonable driving distance for both RJ and Rachel. As for Laura Lee and Diane, they have to fly to see me now anyway, so that's not going to be a problem for them, since there is little difference in the distance. My sisters and their families live in Springfield, which won't be a long drive for them either.

"As you know, the business agreement I signed prohibits me from working within a hundred mile radius of South Bend. I figured St. Louis would be a good market for me to find work should I decide to do so down the road." There was no need to tell Stan he already had a job at a St. Louis advertising agency waiting for him when, and if, he wanted it.

"I hope it works out for you, Richard. Our partnership has been a good one, and we have both prospered. If you need to take time away these next couple of months, don't worry about it. Go do what you have to do."

"Thanks, Stan. I appreciate it."

Stan closed Richard's door on his way out, leaving Richard to think about Stan's remark about their partnership. The two of them had built one of South Bend's most successful advertising agencies from the ground floor up. Strange how two personalities so different in temperament could forge a partnership that produced such a successful outcome. Now, when he was in the midst of making his exodus, he had no personal feelings one way or the other concerning its future.

CHAPTER TWENTY-SIX
Kate

After Kate got home from school, she decided to type her notes. Although it was late, she was not ready for sleep. She was sitting at the keyboard when she heard the phone ring in the kitchen at exactly 10:45 p.m. and hurried to pick it up, knowing it would be Richard calling.

"Hey, you sure are punctual," Kate said.

"That is just one of my many attributes," Richard said jokingly.

"Oh, you have attributes, do you? I can't wait to see what the others are."

"You're mocking me, aren't you?" Richard asked.

"No, I simply haven't had much interaction with artists, that's all. You know how it is."

"I don't know how it is, but you can bet I intend to find out," Richard countered. He remembered from the old days how much Kate liked to banter back and forth.

"No comment," she retorted playfully. "Back to business, Mr. Lawton. I came up with three places that fit your criteria. All of them have lakes and are within a short driving distance from St. Louis. Also, all of their offices are open on the weekend with representatives on hand to answers any questions. You'll be able to see all three before you have to head back home.

"I am taking off Friday from work and offering my services as a guide, so you don't have to deal with maps and the like. Will my going along be all right with you?" Kate asked.

"Of course. That was my intention all along, and I should have made that clear to you from the start. I hope I'm not imposing or interfering with your schedule. Are you sure it will be okay for you to take off Friday?" Richard asked.

"It's no problem, Richard. I'm taking a vacation day. It's fine, really."

"Great. Shall I meet you at your house or what?" he asked.

"I think the best thing is for me to meet you at the airport and after you rent a car you can then follow me to The Leland. We can grab something to eat and then see at least one or maybe two of the places Friday and the other one Saturday. Does that sound okay?"

"Fine. That will give us more than enough time to check out all three this weekend. If you're ready, give me the phone numbers. I'll try and set up some appointments."

Kate gave him the phone numbers of the people she had talked to regarding Richard's intentions, and he jotted them down. He then gave her his flight number and arrival time.

"I'll meet you at the gate," Kate said.

"Is it okay if I say I can hardly wait to see you?" Richard asked.

"Absolutely."

They talked a little while longer, neither one of them wanting to end the conversation. Eventually, after the small talk ran out, Richard broke the connection and said goodbye.

Kate turned off her computer, got into her nightgown and went to bed. She said her prayers and quietly laid there. She was more than ready for sleep, but all she could think about was this whole business concerning Richard Lawton. Why was he planning to relocate? Why the St. Louis area? Why involve me? What does he want from me? These unanswered questions played over and over again in her mind like a broken record.

Despite her feelings of sadness for Richard's martial state, he was not free, and since the annulment Mike had instigated had not been granted, in the eyes of the Catholic Church neither was she.

She turned out the light, rolled over and pulled the covers up to her chin as if protecting herself from her own vulnerability.

Friday morning the pealing of the alarm clock woke her. She turned it off and noticed from her bedroom window a light snow had fallen during the night. Grabbing her robe, she went to the window to get a better view. She was grateful there was not enough snow to be a problem but just enough to magically transform what she saw into a pleasant winter scene. However, it was definitely going to be a boot day.

Although she slept in later than usual, she would have plenty of time to get dressed, stop at the Donut Hole for her usual morning coffee and donut, and then drive to the airport. Richard's plane was scheduled for a 9 a.m. arrival. She hoped the morning traffic out to the airport would not be more than usual.

She made the bed, went into the bathroom and took a shower. It took her some time to decide what to wear. Not wanting to appear overdressed, she finally chose a wool skirt and sweater. She dressed, combed her hair and put on her coat. Her next stop was the Donut Hole and then the airport.

The sitting area at the gate where Richard would arrive was almost totally empty. Four other people were also waiting, and each person was sitting in a different row. Kate took an aisle seat in the fourth row, glancing at the clock on the wall. The airline attendant announced Flight 207 from South Bend would be landing in ten minutes.

She was nervous about seeing him, wondering what to say and do. How shall I greet him? Should I shake his hand or let him take the lead? Should I stand up or keep sitting down? And finally, she pondered why she was there in the first place.

Her eyes were glued to the arrival door. He entered the waiting area and looked around for her. Then she saw him. He was wearing a London Fog coat, a tweed hat and carried an attaché case. When he saw her, he smiled and walked toward her.

"Hi, Kate."

"Hi. Welcome to St. Louis," Kate said.

"Thank you. It's good of you to meet me, too. I've been here before, but never by plane."

"How was the flight?" she asked.

"Fine. Right on time, and the ride was smooth." He put his arm around her shoulder and propelled her into the stream of traffic going toward the main lobby of the airport, as if it was the most natural thing in the world for him to do, just like a husband might do, when he greeted his wife after returning from a business trip.

One of the things she remembered about Richard was his decisiveness. Once he made up his mind about his course of action, he directed all his energies toward the outcome.

As they walked toward the concourse, he asked, "So, what's the agenda for today, or do we have to make one?"

"Let's take care of the car rental thing first. I'll go with you to the rental counter. We'll go in your car to where I parked mine in the airport parking garage. You can follow me to my house where we'll drop off one of the cars. Then, we'll go to The Leland and get you settled. By that time, we should need nourishment of some kind, and if we want to see two areas this afternoon, let's aim for a light lunch, if that's all right with you," Kate said.

"Sounds good. By the way, did you make dinner reservations for tonight?" Richard asked.

"I hope you won't be disappointed, but I didn't make any reservations for tonight, only for tomorrow night. The company I work for has season tickets for many St. Louis events that are given to the salesmen in the Marketing Department for entertaining their clients. Sometimes if the tickets are not used, the salesmen offer them to others on the team," Kate explained.

"When I asked Mark Mahoney, one of the salesmen, about a good place to eat tomorrow night, he recommended McGuire's, one of St. Louis' finest restaurants. Since we are a pretty tight group, he wanted more details and asked me the reason for dining out. I briefly told him about you, and why you were coming to St. Louis. After I filled him in, he asked me what other plans had been made for the evening. Before I could respond, he offered me two tickets to the Lyric Theatre or the Blues hockey game for tonight, both of which start at 7 p.m. I hope I made the right decision, I said I would take the Lyric tickets. Are you a big hockey fan?" Kate asked, hoping he would say he wasn't.

"I like hockey and have been to a couple of games, but I don't follow any hockey team like I follow professional and college football, especially the Fighting Irish," Richard replied.

"I selected the one I would rather attend, only because I love going to the Lyric, and you cannot beat the box seats. The Lyric reminds me of the Alhambra Theatre back home. The downside to all of this is I know very little about the group that is performing at the Lyric," Kate said.

"What group is it?" he asked.

"Mannheim Steamroller," she responded.

"You're kidding me. We have box seats to their concert? I have quite a few of their CDs. Wow! I sure didn't expect a surprise like this. I am going to see a live performance of one of my favorite groups," Richard said.

"You're just saying that to make me feel better, aren't you?" Kate asked.

"Okay. I'll prove it to you. I just bought their latest CD, *Saving the Wildlife*, composed by Chip Davis. Now, do you believe me?"

"Already, all right. You've convinced me," Kate replied, waving her arms in the air.

As they approached the car rental booth, her fears began to melt away. She felt comfortable being with Richard, and it felt really good to have a man she knew, by her side, who made her feel wanted, despite the passage of time.

After lunch, Kate drove the rental car into the early, afternoon traffic and said, "Crystal Springs is the first place we are going to check out. We have about an hour drive in front of us."

She handed him the maps she brought. One was a city map, and the other one was the map of Missouri. "We are going south on 270. This highway is one of the busiest. It's brutal during morning rush hour and just as bad at the end of the work day with bumper-to-bumper traffic at both times."

"Is this the highway you take to work?" he asked.

"No. I usually stop at the Donut Hole before going to work. From there I take Highway 55, which is the closest. Before I hit the downtown area, I then switch over to Highway 44, which takes me to work in midtown. Actually, the drive isn't all that bad, and I'm use to it. It takes me about thirty-five minutes to get from the donut shop to the company parking garage. From there I have about a five-minute walk to the building, which is directly across from Union Station."

"So, you're a woman of the business world, I take it," Richard said.

"I see you haven't lost your vivid imagination. There is nothing glamorous about my job. But, it is a good one, and I can thank Ruth for getting me the job."

"I remember you telling me how your friend managed to get you through an interview, plus the trials and tribulations of your first day on the job, and you not having much computer knowledge."

"Being divorced and on your own is a perpetual condition of sink or swim. I've become a pretty good swimmer. Like I said, I've been very lucky," she replied.

As Kate drove, Richard looked out the window, taking in all of the sights along the way as if memorizing them for further reference.

Kate broke the silence and began telling him about Crystal Springs. "The area has three lakes, and all of them run into a creek that feeds into the Mississippi River. There are 454 homes on 2,500 acres of land plus a swimming pool, three parks, tennis, basketball and volleyball courts. Four-wheeler trails and back roads are everywhere. Most of the home owners are retired or elderly. Crystal Springs is considered a resort area. Many of the homes are only occupied part-time. All three areas we are going to visit have an association fee, too."

"You are amazing. Were you a real estate agent somewhere in your past?" Richard asked.

Kate laughed. "I knew you would be pressed for time. I tried to get as much information as I could on the places we are going to visit, so you could narrow down your search. As I said before, there are only three possibilities that cover your list of must haves and are within a reasonable driving distance to St. Louis. This one is the farthest.

"We'll do a quick drive today through two of them, and then tomorrow we can start out early to see the last one. After you have seen them all, there will be plenty of time to return to the one you like the best for another visit before we go to dinner, should you want to do so."

"Great. You've become so self-assured, Kate, and I mean that as a compliment."

"Being on your own and a breadwinner does that to you," she replied and winked at him.

After an extensive drive through Crystal Springs, Kate parked the car on a side road near the entrance and turned off the ignition. "Well, we've seen about all there is to see, so what's the verdict? Hit or miss?" Kate asked.

"Truthfully, it's a little too rustic for me. Many of the log houses are really more of a cabin than my idea of what a log house should be. Also, there are quite a few roads that are still unpaved. If I had to make a decision solely on what we have seen today, I vote no," Richard replied.

"Me, too. I had a feeling this would not be your cup of tea, but wanted you to see it for the sake of comparison. Let's get back on the highway and check out the second one on the list. It's a private, gated community called Rolling Hills. There are campgrounds, a picnic and swimming area and three lakes with public boat ramps. Unlike Crystal Springs, mobile homes are not allowed," Kate said.

Within a short time, they arrived at Rolling Hills. Two huge Roman columns had been erected on each side of the two lane road leading to the entrance. The columns were not straight and leaned toward each other. Kate passed through them and continued driving toward the guardhouse, which was a short distance away from the entrance. Although it was a gated community, there was no guard on duty.

"So much for security," Kate remarked, as she continued to drive pass the guardhouse.

They spent the next half hour checking out what Rolling Hills had to offer. They both noticed the homes were similar in construction and size to those at Crystal Springs, but there were not as many log houses.

As they drove pass the pool and picnic grounds, the Roman theme continued with statues and pedestals placed here and there. Many of the statues were broken and most of them needed to be repainted. As they continued to drive through Rolling Hills, Richard felt the overall feel of the place was not as rustic as Crystal Springs, but still gave the appearance it was a weekend retreat rather than one of permanency.

"I've seen enough, Kate," Richard said. "I don't think this is the one, either."

"Say no more. I've never been to Rolling Hills before today, so I didn't know what to expect. However, from what I've seen, including the Roman theme, Rolling Hills doesn't work for me, either. Let's call it a day," Kate said.

As they made their way to the exit, they once again passed under the leaning Roman columns. "I probably would have to buy a toga if I moved here," Richard said, and they both laughed at the absurdity of his comment, as Kate drove toward the highway.

She parked the rental car in front of her house, and both of them got out. "What time do you want me to pick you up tonight?" Richard asked, as he walked toward her.

"How about forty-five minutes from now? We would have enough time to shower, dress and have dinner at Miss Tillie's, which is five minutes from here. The food is good, although a little bland, and there is an excellent variety. Not the fanciest place or gourmet eating, but it would be quick," Kate said.

"Works for me," Richard replied, as they stood facing each other on the sidewalk leading up to Kate's front door, waiting for the other one to break away. She thought he was going to take her in his arms and kiss her right then and there, but he did not. Instead, he turned, walked toward his car and waved back at her and said, "I'll be back before you know it, ringing your doorbell."

CHAPTER TWENTY-SEVEN
Richard

They were in the line of cars parked behind the Lyric, waiting their turn to exit. He waited patiently for his turn to enter the traffic heading toward the highway.

"What a show! Never thought I would get to see a live performance of the Mannheim Steamroller, much less with Ms. Kate O'Connor. How about you? Did you enjoy it?" Richard asked.

"Oh, I did. I really did. The whole day has been wonderful despite not finding what you came looking for."

Richard corrected her silently. He definitely found what he had come looking for, and he had every intention of telling her that, when and if the opportunity presented itself. Every time he glanced in her direction, she took his breath away. His young Kate of the past had become quite a beautiful and remarkable woman.

On the ride home, Kate opened the subject about tomorrow's agenda. "I know you were disappointed in what we saw today, but I saved the best for last. I think you're going to be quite surprised when we visit Lieu des Lacs."

"Have you been there before?" Richard asked.

"Yes. When Ruth got divorced, she was awarded the lot she and her husband purchased at Lieu des Lacs earlier in their marriage. According to Ruth, they planned to start building a home there after her husband retired. Their lot is on the 9 hole golf course, but there is also an 18 hole PGA course where many golf tournaments are played. Are you a golfer?" Kate asked.

"No, not really. Now and then I play with clients. Tennis is my thing, and it was you who taught me to play the summer before I left for art school."

"As I remember, you didn't win very many games," Kate said with a big grin, teasing him.

"Well, the tables have turned, my dear Kate, and when tennis weather arrives, I'll be more than happy to take you on."

Kate made no reply to his last comment. Every time the future was mentioned, his intentions were becoming more and more clear to her in one way and problematic in another.

"Have you ever wanted to live in a log house?" he asked.

"That question brings back an old dream, Richard. When I first became divorced, I took Jackie with me to see some log houses. Matter of fact, the two models were right down the street from where you are staying. I fell in love with one of them.

"The floor plan of the one I liked had a living room with a fireplace, a dining area and kitchen on the first floor plus a bedroom and a bath. Stairs led to a loft and a second bedroom and another bath. It was all so homey. I really could see myself living there," Kate continued.

"There are restrictions in building a log house in the county where I live, but most importantly was the price. In the settlement I got the house we lived in while I was married to Mike plus $400 a month for two years, which helped to make the house payments. I figured if I couldn't get my act together in two years, I would never get it together. There was no insurance. Mike got the car and the debts he incurred while living at The Leland."

Richard interrupted her by asking, "Mike lived at The Leland?"

"Yes, for almost three months, then he found an apartment."

"I'm sorry I interrupted. Please, go on," Richard said.

"When I sold the house, I put the majority of the money toward the cost of my new one, leaving a few thousand dollars in the bank for emergencies. I ended up leasing a car and making small house payments. Not too long ago, the log house models were put up for auction. To answer your question, yes, I always wanted to live in a log house. It was once a dream of mine that is never going to happen," Kate said.

"Sometimes things change, and dreams come true," Richard remarked.

"Yes, that's true. But, I also believe one's oar needs to be rowed in the sea of reality, and I have become an expert at rowing," Kate said, justifying her position. "Turn left at the next stop light. Do you recognize where you are now?"

"Yes. One more block and your house is on the corner. Right?" Richard asked.

"You got it. Park in front. That way you will be facing the right direction when you go back to the motel."

As she instructed, he parked the car and turned off the ignition. He noticed she was sitting as far away from him as she had in high school when they were dating.

"I'll walk you to your door," Richard said, as he got out and walked over to her side of the car.

She was nervous, as they walked up to the front porch, not knowing what to say next, but felt she was expected to say something. It was late, and she didn't think it was appropriate to ask him to come in. She took a deep breath, faced Richard and said, "I had a great time today."

"I had a great time, too, Kate. What time do you want me to pick you up tomorrow?" he asked.

"Your call," Kate responded.

"How about 8 a.m.?" he asked. "Let's have breakfast before we hit the road and start the day together."

Kate nodded her head and said, "Fine."

"It's been a long time since I have been on a front porch with a girl, much less a woman, after an evening out and about. At our age is it still called dating?" Richard asked.

"Whatever it's called, I like it much better now than when we were teenagers. No father to answer to," and Kate laughed.

"Then there's nothing to fear," Richard said, as he took her in his arms and kissed her. Her body melted into his, lost in the moment of being wanted.

When they parted, he said, "Kate…"

"Yes."

"Will you go steady with me?" Richard asked, whispering softly in her ear.

"Absolutely," she said breathlessly and kissed him back.

CHAPTER TWENTY-EIGHT
Kate

When the alarm clock woke Kate the next morning, she rose with more energy than usual and was anxious for the day to begin. Richard would be picking her up soon for breakfast. She showered first, washed her hair and lingered under the hot water more than usual, while dosing her body with a perfumed body splash. Toweling off, she thought about what she would wear. Hoping that Richard would dress casually, she decided on jeans, a white turtle neck and a navy blue wool blazer.

As she was dressing, she thought about last night, especially what had happened on her front porch. His romancing had erased any doubts she might have had about his intentions toward her. He was playing for keeps and last night's embrace and kiss confirmed everything he had expressed in his previous letters to her.

The fact that she had returned his ardor, without much thought to the consequences, surprised and troubled her at the same time. Problems existed in both of their situations—problems that had no fast and ready solutions. If the relationship continued and they became more deeply involved, she knew guilt would be her companion.

The ringing of the doorbell ended the mental bout she was having between her emotions and her conscience. She opened the door, and Richard stepped into the foyer.

"Good morning, Kate."

"Good morning," she replied, as she closed the door.

"It's breezy out there this morning so I left the car running," Richard said.

"I'm ready to go," she replied, as she studied his face. The color of his eyes were blue and reminded her of the sky on a clear day. Then, she looked intently at his lips.

"Hungry?" he asked.

"Starving," she countered.

He reached for her, kissing her with an intensity that completely erased the previous mental battle she was having within herself.

"Starving for this or starving for food?" Richard asked playfully.

"No fair asking me a question like that on an empty stomach," she replied. "You have to feed me first, then I'll let you know the verdict."

She put on her coat and gathered her things. They went out the door arm-in-arm, grinning at each other all the way to the car.

CHAPTER TWENTY-NINE
Richard

"Let me drive, Richard. You can get a better feel for the way out to Lieu des Lacs if I drive," Kate said.

"Good idea. How far is Lieu des Lacs from your house?" Richard asked.

"About forty-five minutes max. Both highways to get there are four lanes, and traffic moves pretty good," Kate said.

Richard unfolded the map he had taken out of the glove compartment, marking it so he would remember the way. "Tell me about this place, Kate."

"Lieu des Lacs is a gated community, approximately thirty years old. There are sixteen lakes, some for fishing and some for boating, a clubhouse that serves three meals a day, a community swimming pool, tennis courts and two golf courses.

"The Valley course is a 9 hole course, and the Skyview course is a PGA 18 hole course. Many tournaments are held at Skyview," Kate continued.

"Other amenities are a basketball court, baseball field, playground and campground plus a picnic area with cooking facilities that butts up to Big River with stunning views. Lieu des Lacs has its own fire and police protection, a convenience grocery store that also offers pizza and a gas station. As you come into the complex, there is also a bank," Kate added.

"As I said before, I saved the best for last. I really think you're going to be impressed with what you are about to see," Kate said, hoping she would be right in her assumption.

While Kate was talking, Richard was looking out the window and said, "I had forgotten how beautiful the landscape of Missouri is, especially the outcroppings."

"The farther you go south, the better it gets," Kate replied. "Before you get to Lieu des Lacs, which is French for Place of Lakes, you pass a couple of small towns on the way. We get off at Belle Ville and from there it's about seven miles to the Lieu des Lacs guard house."

"What kind of town is Belle Ville?" Richard inquired.

"I've only been to Belle Ville and Lieu des Lacs twice. Belle Ville is French for beautiful town and noted for its rose garden around the square. I think I told you Ruth received a lot in Lieu des Lacs in her divorce settlement, and she drove me around to see both areas one Sunday afternoon," Kate said.

"Belle Ville is like a lot of small towns. It has a Catholic Church and school, a couple of decent places to eat and the other usual types of businesses on a smaller scale," Kate finished.

"Have you been inside the church?" Richard asked.

"Oh, yes. It's much like the church I attended while growing up on Seventh Street in Springfield—a main aisle and two side ones. The church may be old, but it has been kept up wonderfully, and the Stations of the Cross are as spectacular as some of the finest art work I have ever seen in an art museum," Kate said.

"And the school?" he asked.

"I don't know much about it except what I saw. It has a red double front door and a gold Cross on the roof, just like so many other Catholic elementary schools. If we have time I'll give you a tour of the town after we check out Lieu des Lacs," Kate said, as they headed down the highway, each anticipating the visit to Lieu des Lacs.

The entrance to the development was impressive. A boulevard stretched from the highway to the guard house with trees and rose bushes lining the outer sides of the road.

Kate stopped the car at the guard house, saying hello to the young female attendant.

"Welcome to Lieu des Lacs. What is the nature of your visit today?" the attendant asked.

"We're here to check out the area," Kate replied.

"No problem, but you'll need a visitor sticker, which you can obtain at the realty office. Drive up to the building on your right," the attendance said, as she pointed to it. "Frank Ambrose is on duty. He'll be glad to help you."

"Thank you," Kate said.

Turning to Richard, she said, "Having an attendant on duty is a big plus, not only for the welcoming aspect but for security. Neither one of the places we visited yesterday had an attendant."

"Yes, I did notice. Security seems to be much tighter here, and I like that," Richard replied.

Kate pulled up in front of the realty office and parked the car. "You go in, and I'll wait in the car. I'll be fine. I brought along a paper I need to edit for school." She wanted to give him space and privacy.

"You sure?" Richard asked.

"Yes. Take your time. We have all afternoon," Kate replied.

Richard opened the car door and waved back to her as he walked toward the realty office and climbed the steps to the front door. When he entered the room, a tall, thin man who had little hair and wore thick glasses greeted him with a warm smile.

"Welcome to Lieu des Lacs. My name is Frank Ambrose. You are?" Frank asked.

"Richard Lawton. I'm thinking about building a log house possibly in Lieu des Lacs."

"You've come to the right place. Will you be a permanent resident or a seasonal one?"

"Permanent. I'd like to build on one of the bigger lakes," Richard added.

"We have sixteen lakes and of those, three are very large. Come over to the map here, and I'll show you the locations of the various lakes," Frank said.

Richard followed Frank over to the map on the wall behind his desk.

"The red dots indicate lots for sale, and the blue ones indicate lots that have been sold. Lake Madeleine, the biggest lake, still has some lots available, but the prime lots are all gone, so I would recommend one of the other two, Lake Bordeaux or Lake Fontaine, which are both a little smaller than Lake Madeleine but still are pretty big lakes."

Richard looked at the map more closely. "So many of the streets have French names as well as some of the lakes. Why is that?" Richard asked.

"We're only seven miles from Belle Ville, which the French settled many years ago, as well as some of the other surrounding areas close by. When this development was originally built thirty years ago, the owners decided to stick with the French origin," Frank replied.

While Frank was talking, Richard was scanning the map. "Hey, there's a Notre Dame Drive on this map," Richard exclaimed.

"Yep. After crossing over the dam road, Notre Dame Drive is the first left, which takes you to Lake Fontaine. There is only one other house on Notre Dame Drive, and those people are not permanent residents."

"It looks like the lot on the point has already been sold," Richard said, noting the blue dot on the property.

"That particular lot is a beauty, being on the point and all. I sold it to a young couple, the Morrisons, about a year ago. Morrison had just earned a modest bonus check and used half of it toward the down payment on the lot. I remember him telling me they had no plans to build on it anytime soon with four kids' college education facing them in the future. We joked about another payment to add to their list of monthly bills. He told me he was buying the lot for their retirement years and would not be building on it until then," Frank said.

"We have other lake lots that I would like to show you, Richard. I suggest we check them out and maybe one of them will meet your requirements," Frank said.

"Works for me," Richard replied eagerly.

"Give me a minute to gather up the paperwork. I'll meet you in the parking lot," Frank said, taking several file folders from his desk and putting them into his briefcase.

Richard made fast tracks to the front door, taking the steps two at a time on the way down to the parking lot. By the time he reached Kate, he was out of breath and had a big smile on his face.

She saw him coming and rolled down the driver's front window, looking puzzled.

"This has to be it!" Richard exclaimed. "Can you believe there is a street named Notre Dame Drive? Grab your purse. We're going with Frank Ambrose, the realty salesman, in his car. He's going to show us what is available." He opened Kate's door, took her hand and pulled her out of the seat, as if she couldn't get out fast enough for him.

"You haven't changed a bit, Richard. Something or someone has rung those chimes of yours. During our time together in high school, I remember how you use to respond to situations with enormous enthusiasm when you knew you were on the right track."

"I think this might be another one of those times," Richard responded excitedly.

Richard and Kate got into Frank's car, and introductions were made. Frank gave Richard a map of the area, and he immediately began looking for Notre Dame Drive. When he found it, he pointed it out to Kate who smiled, as if she was confirming the reason for his exuberance.

"If your mind is made up about building on one of the big lakes, let's begin with Lake Madeleine first. You mentioned you want to build a log house. Presently, there are not more than five log houses in Lieu des Lacs. Most of the homes here were built when this development first began and now have passed on to another generation."

They drove around Lake Madeleine, and Frank pointed out the only two lots directly on the water that were for sale. Richard asked appropriate questions, but neither lot appealed to him. Frank pulled over to the side of the road and turned off the ignition, "What's your reaction to these two lots?" the salesman asked.

"I don't think so, Frank. I'm going to pass on both of them," Richard said and let it go at that without explaining why he was not interested.

"No problem. Next on the list is Lake Bordeaux. There are also two lots on this lake. However, one of them is also very much like the one we just looked at," Frank said.

"If it's at the end, no point in looking at it. I want something more in the middle," Richard replied.

The lot Frank showed Richard and Kate next was in the middle of the lake but there were houses already built on both sides of the lot as well as both sides on the road approaching it.

"As you can see, you have plenty of neighbors. Would this be a deal breaker?" Frank asked.

"Well, I am not against neighbors, but I prefer to be more secluded," Richard answered.

"Okay. Keep this one in mind though. It meets all your other requirements. There is one more to see on Lake Fontaine. Maybe this one will be the one," Frank said.

On the way to Lake Fontaine, they passed the clubhouse. Everything Richard saw increased his desire to see more. He was impressed with all of the various amenities he had seen so far.

As they passed by the clubhouse, Kate said, "If there is enough time, maybe we could have lunch at the clubhouse."

"Good idea," Richard replied. "Let's do that."

Frank broke into their conversation. "Notice that the swimming pool, tennis courts, play areas, PGA course and pro shop are located near the clubhouse. The fire house is down the way a bit. By the way, the police department is located in the building across the road from my office."

Soon they crossed the dam road where the vastness of Lake Fontaine could be seen from the car. "Frank, would you please pull over. I want to get out and look at something," Richard requested.

Frank did as he was asked. He had no idea what had captured Richard's attention.

"Frank, that lot over there that juts out into the water with all those big pine trees, is it for sale?" Richard asked.

"That's the one I was telling you about. Remember, it's been sold," Frank replied.

"I would like to see it anyway," Richard said, getting back into the car.

"Okay." Frank couldn't see the sense of it, but did as Richard asked, heading toward Notre Dame Drive.

When they reached the property, a wooden signboard on a post six feet high had been placed on the rear of the lot. Two words had been carved on the signboard, Settler's Cove.

Frank stayed in the car while Richard walked down to the edge of the property with Kate by his side. When he reached the shoreline, he looked out at the lake and remained motionless for some time. He turned and looked back and in his mind visualized waking up each morning, looking out the bedroom window at the lake with Kate nestled in his arms.

"What do you think, Kate?" Richard asked.

"It's appears to be exactly what you said you were looking for, but Frank said somebody already bought it," Kate replied.

"I remember what he said. After we have a leisurely lunch at the clubhouse, I want to talk to him about something before we head back to St. Louis," Richard said.

They walked back to the car where Frank was waiting for them, leaning against one of the doors. Richard noticed he was smoking a cigar.

"I see you have a habit just like mine," Richard commented.

"Tried to quit a couple of times, but lost that battle," Frank said with a sigh.

"I know exactly what you mean," Richard replied, recalling his own frustration in trying to break the habit.

Frank put out his cigar and got behind the wheel. "Well, there's one more to see not too far from here," Frank said, backing up the car and turning around. He was surprised, when Richard said, "I think I've seen enough. I know which one I want."

Richard had shown no real enthusiasm for any of the properties Frank had shown him except the one that was not for sale.

"I don't understand, Richard," Frank said, totally perplexed.

"I don't think I do either," Kate added.

"I never waste my time and effort going after something that is improbable, and my gut tells me I am in the right place at the right time. I have a plan," Richard said.

Many of Richard's past business transactions had been put together over a good smoke. He hoped Frank would be up for the one he was about to propose to him.

Frank drove them back to his office. Richard and Kate got in the rental car and headed toward the clubhouse for lunch. After they got seated, they looked over the menu as the waitress waited to take their order "What are you going to have, Kate?"

"I think I am going to have the Reuben and coffee, Richard."

Looking up at the waitress, Richard said, "I'll have the same," and handed the menus back to the waitress who smiled and departed.

"What do you think so far about the lots we've seen?" Richard asked.

"No to the first. The second would work but doesn't meet all your requirements. Of course, the one that is not available is the perfect one," Kate replied.

"I agree. Lieu des Lacs has so much more to offer than the other two places we visited, and the drive to St. Louis would not be all that bad either. According to the terms of the agreement I signed, I cannot work within a one hundred mile radius of South Bend. Which would more than take care of that point.

"If you don't mind, after we have lunch I'm going back to Frank's office. I want to get as much information as I can face-to-face before I leave rather than over the telephone. Do you mind?" Richard asked.

"Not at all. If I finish editing my paper, I brought along a book to read. I'll stay here. You can pick me up when you're finished with Frank," Kate replied.

"You're the best," and Richard squeezed her hand.

After they finished their lunch, Richard left Kate in the clubhouse lobby while he went to talk with Frank about a proposal concerning the lot he wanted—the one the Morrisons had purchased.

After Richard brought Frank up to speed regarding his intentions, he asked for Frank's opinion. "It's a long shot, Richard, but I'll be more than happy to present your offer to the Morrisons. You've certainly made an offer well worth considering. The price they paid for that lot is considerably lower than what you're offering. If money is a factor, it would be hard to pass up your offer. It just might work," Frank said.

"Let's hope they feel the same way. I have another question for you. Do you know of a reputable company that builds log houses? Should I get this property, I want to begin construction immediately. However, since I am not from these parts, I definitely want to check out the builder personally before I commit," Richard explained.

"I understand. I can help you with an experienced builder," Frank said. He relit his cigar, opened a file drawer in his desk and thumbed through his folders. Within a few minutes, he found what he was looking for and handed a brochure to Richard. "These guys are located in New Brunswick, which is about an hour's drive from here. I can vouch for their integrity, and as far as construction goes, I've seen several of the houses they have built, and they are all quality construction. It's a two-man ownership. A brother of one of the owners goes to my church," Frank said.

Richard liked what he was hearing. Looking at his watch he noticed most of the afternoon had slipped away. It was too late to try and visit New Brunswick today, thinking of the dinner with Kate that evening. "Would it be possible for me to use your phone and call them now? I'd like for them to send me their literature," Richard said.

Richard was moving ahead as if it was a done deal with the Morrisons, which confused Frank. If they refused, Richard might walk away, leaving Frank without a client. To put a brake on the situation, Frank replied, "Maybe we should wait until we hear if the Morrisons are interested in selling. If they aren't, you may want to consider that other lot," Frank suggested.

Richard smiled. He had been down this road before many times and had learned most people respond positively to a good profit, especially in this case. It appeared the Morrisons were a long way off from building. "I gather you don't think they will be interested in my offer?" Richard asked.

"I didn't say that, Richard. I've been in this business long enough to not make predictions. Your guess is as good as mine," Frank said. He thumbed through another folder and found what he was looking for and gave Richard the telephone number he requested.

"You can use the phone on that other desk to make your call while I try and contact the Morrisons," Frank offered.

Both men set about their tasks. Richard finished before Frank did and waited patiently until he finished. "Well, they didn't hang up on me after I told them your offer—a good sign I would say," Frank said. "They want to think about it over the weekend and said they would get back to me Monday. I'll call you as soon as I know something."

"Thanks, Frank. I'll be back in South Bend by then, and you can call me at my office," Richard said. He gave Frank his business card, shook his hand and went to pick up Kate at the clubhouse.

Driving back to St. Louis, Richard told Kate about his meeting with Frank. After she had heard all the particulars, she turned to him and said, "You amaze me, you really do. What makes you think the people who own that lot are willing to let it go just because you want to build on it yourself?" Kate asked incredulously.

"Haven't you ever heard of the saying, ask and you shall receive? Where's all that faith of yours?"

That one stopped her cold. She didn't know quite how to respond to his question and needed some time to think about it.

"I'm waiting," he said.

"I'm not sure that Biblical reference applies in this situation," was the best response she could come up with on the spur of the moment.

"In other words, you have doubts?" Richard asked.

"Absolutely," she replied.

"Ah, there's that word again. It seems when you feel strongly about something, you use that word to express yourself," Richard said.

"I've forgotten how very sharp you are," she replied, blushing.

His next comment really threw her for a loop. "Doubt comes first, faith follows."

For some unexplainable reason, she was embarrassed by what he said and remained silent.

He looked over at Kate, feeling her discomfort by the look on her face. "Trust me, Kate. I would never do anything that would ever cause you to doubt me," Richard said.

"I believe you," she replied in a tone so soft he had to strain to hear it.

They drove back to St. Louis, making small conversation that lightened the mood. When they reached Kate's house, Richard pulled in front and parked. "How about me coming back at 5:30 p.m.? Will that give us plenty of time?" Richard asked.

"Our reservation is for 7 p.m. It's about a twenty-minute drive to the restaurant. That's probably a little early," Kate replied.

"Obviously, you forgot to include 'necking' time," he said.

"Richard, Richard. I'll see you at 6:15 p.m., and I want you to know I am not a woman to be honked for," she said impishly. Without waiting for his reply, she picked up her purse, book and papers and headed toward the front door with key in hand.

As he pulled away from the curb, he sounded the car horn twice and saw Kate shake her head, as she walked up to her front door.

CHAPTER THIRTY
Kate

After taking a bubble bath, Kate toweled herself off while looking in the bathroom mirror. She felt good about herself and was anticipating the evening ahead with Richard. It had been a long time since she had been invited out on a Saturday night in the company of a man.

She brushed her hair dry and put on the lingerie she had been saving for a special occasion—a lacy black bra and matching panties and a half slip also trimmed in wide black lace around the bottom. Sitting on the chaise lounge in her bedroom, she slid sheer black hose carefully up each leg so they wouldn't snag. Then she leaned over to fasten the black suede ankle-strap high heels. On the bed was the dress she had bought on sale months ago, justifying the purchase in case she ever got an invite to go out on the town with a member of the opposite sex. Tonight, the dress and Kate were going to make an appearance, and both of them were more than ready.

The dress was a mid-length black sheath with a V-shaped neckline and three-quarter sleeves trimmed in tiny black beads on the cuffs. Taking it off the hanger, she slipped it on and adjusted it to her figure. From her jewelry box she selected silver earrings and a silver bracelet.

Returning to the bathroom, she applied lipstick and sprinkled herself with Giorgio, a birthday gift from her son Mike Jr. On her way to the living room, she paused to look at herself in the hall mirror. She was more nervous than she wanted to admit. Fifty-eight years old and jittery like a teenager on a first date. It's just a dinner, Kate, she told herself. All you're going to do is eat and with a little luck not spill anything or miss your mouth. Hearing the doorbell ring, she went to answer the door. She turned on the porch light and greeted Richard.

"Hi. Come on in. I'm ready. I'll just get my coat."

Richard stepped into the foyer and could not take his eyes off of her. They were close in the small area, and he smelled her perfume. Kate took her coat from the hall closet, and Richard helped her put it on. When she turned around, it was all he could do not to enfold her in his arms. Instead, he said, "You're beautiful, Kate. That dress was made for you."

She could feel her cheeks redden, once again being embarrassed by his reaction to her and not knowing what to say. Gathering her purse and gloves, she hurriedly said, "Let's go. You first. I'll be right behind you after I lock up."

Richard took her arm as they walked toward the car and opened the door for her. She liked being treated like a lady and watched him walk around to his side. All at once she felt the tension leave her body. It was going to be okay, just two people going out to dinner who liked each other's company and making new beginnings.

While driving to the restaurant they made small talk about the events of the day. When they arrived, Richard signaled to the valet to park the car. After entering McGuire's, a restaurant in St. Louis known for their delicious steaks, they checked their coats and were immediately seated. Within a short time, the maître d´ introduced himself, handed Kate and Richard menus and asked if they would like a cocktail.

"How about it, Kate?" Richard asked.

"Absolutely," Kate replied.

He laughed. "There you go again with that word. I guess that means yes."

She looked at the waiter and replied, "I'll have a glass of White Zinfandel."

"I'll have the same," Richard said to the waiter, who nodded and left to get their drinks.

"I'm not much of a drinker anymore or for that matter never was one to begin with. Over the years I've taken a liking to drinking wine. I don't go out for a fine dinner now except with clients. Louise, my housekeeper, fixes me dinner twice a week on the days she comes to clean and do the laundry. The rest of the time, I eat green boxes."

"What? You eat green boxes. I don't understand," Kate said.

"The brand of frozen dinners I eat have quite a lot of green in the design on the box they come packaged in, and I've come to think of them as green boxes. After awhile, they all seem to taste pretty much the same," Richard explained.

"I eat strange myself," Kate responded. "I have to be at school twice a week by 6 p.m., and I don't have time to grab something decent to eat before class begins. I sometimes get a package of crackers from the vending machine at school and eat at break time. On nights when I'm home, I have a bowl of canned chili or soup and a sandwich and eat while watching television. Saturday, Ruth and I go to 5 p.m. Mass and go out to eat after church at a restaurant that serves good food, is reasonable and close to home. Then, we usually catch a movie. Sunday, I go grocery shopping and try to cook something simple for dinner," she explained.

"Well, it appears we both need to indulge ourselves tonight. Would you like a shrimp cocktail?" Richard asked.

"Yes, I would. I remember you were the first one to introduce me to that wonderful pre-dinner treat. You probably don't remember, do you?" Kate asked.

"There is nothing I have forgotten about you or what we did together. I took you to The Plantation for a steak dinner right before I left for art school. I ordered shrimp cocktails for both of us," Richard said.

"You always did take me to nice places. By the way, I really like your tie. It brings out the blue in your eyes. It looks new," Kate remarked, hoping she was not getting too personal.

"No, I've had it awhile. I'm glad you like it." The tie was the one he bought for the reunion and didn't get to wear because he didn't go. He remembered Ken had made fun of him for buying a new tie, implying he bought it to impress Kate. He made a mental note to himself. It was going to be big payback time for Ken the next time he saw him. The tie thing had worked.

Looking around the restaurant, Richard noticed how handsomely it was decorated. A three-piece ensemble and a piano were playing soft jazz music in the far corner.

"What's the name of this place again?" Richard asked.

"McGuire's. The guys at work take clients here all the time for dinner. I asked one of them which steak house was the best. Hands down, they all agreed McGuire's is the best," Kate said.

After finishing their shrimp cocktail, the waiter returned to take their order. Kate went first. "I'll have the filet, a baked potato and broccoli. I'd like the filet cooked medium."

"What kind of salad dressing would you like on your salad?" the waiter inquired.

"Ranch," Kate answered.

Turning toward Richard, he asked, "And you sir?"

"I'll have the same," Richard said.

When the waiter left with their order, Kate said, "You didn't have to order the same as me, you know."

"I would have ordered the same had I gone first," Richard said.

"Okay. Let's talk about dessert. What's your favorite?" Kate asked.

"I never order dessert when I eat at a restaurant," he replied.

"Unbelievable. Neither do I," Kate responded.

"See how compatible we are? That's a big factor in a relationship, you know," Richard said.

"First the Steamrollers, now the wine and the food choices. You're beginning to make me wonder where all this compatibility is going," Kate flirted.

"Mine to know, yours to find out," Richard said, trying hard to be charming and mysterious at the same time.

Over dinner, Richard and Kate again talked about the day's happenings, oblivious of everyone else in the room. They ordered coffee and as the evening wore on, they lingered, neither of them wanting the evening to end.

Kate finally asked, "What time is your flight in the morning?"

"Early, 6:15 a.m. I have to take back the rental car, too," Richard said.

Looking at her watch, Kate said, "We better go."

Richard paid the bill and got their coats. They waited for Richard's car to be brought around to the front of the restaurant. The attendant opened the door for Kate this time. As she settled herself in the front seat, she wondered if she should invite Richard in to see her house. It was late, and he did have an early flight in the morning. There should be a manual written about dating after divorce she thought. Being out of the dating game for so long, she was unsure of what to do and how to act in certain situations, and this was another one of them.

Richard broke the silence and asked, "I'd like very much to see your house before I head back, Kate. Would it be all right if I came in for a few minutes? I'd like to leave with a mental picture of you at home until the next time I see you."

Not only had he come to her rescue, he indicated there would be a next time. "Of course, I think I can come with up with a little brandy to top off our evening," she replied.

Kate turned on the car radio. An old fifties pop song was playing. "Didn't we sing this song in choir when we were in high school?" Kate asked.

"We did indeed," Richard said and started singing along with the music. Kate joined in.

When the song was over, Richard turned to her and, with a grin on his face, said, "We still have it."

"Was there any doubt?" she asked.

The drive to Kate's house was spent talking about old times and reminiscing. Richard parked the car on Kate's driveway. He helped her out of the car. They walked to the side entrance of the house and entered the sun porch between the house and the garage. An old upright painted piano dominated the wall next to the back door, which opened into the kitchen. A navy blue couch was against the opposite wall that was finished in white wainscoting three-fourths of the way up. The upper section was wallpapered in a cabbage rose pattern against a blue background. At the end of this wall was a door leading to the garage.

While Kate was digging in her purse for her house keys, Richard looked around the sun porch. A small table was in front of the louvered door, which opened to the back yard. Obviously, this entrance was not used as such. On the table was a lamp, several books, a notebook and some pens.

As his gaze traveled upward, he instantly recognized a framed drawing on the wall. It was one he had done, an 11 x 14 chalk drawing on a black background. A cloud was crying and shedding tears on a cactus. He remembered what he had called the silly thing—*The Little White Cloud That Cried*. He had given it to Kate the summer they started dating.

Before he could ask about the drawing, Kate said, "I apologize for the wait. I have so many keys on this key ring it takes me awhile to find the right one." She opened the kitchen door and went in. Richard followed her into the kitchen, still thinking about the drawing on the wall.

The very first thing he noticed was the kitchen floor, which was carpeted in a dark blue geometric pattern. The fridge and stove were white as were the painted cabinets. A window was over the sink and, on the opposite wall, was a country kitchen table with two chairs and two benches. Over the table was a framed print.

"That print ties this room together perfectly," Richard said.

"Thank you. I think so, too. I bought it at an art gallery in France, when I went there with Ruth. It's a Monet print entitled *Nympheas at Giverny*," Kate said.

Kate remembered her manners and said, "Let me take your coat, Richard. We can sit in the living room and talk. If you don't mind, how about lighting a fire? Use those fake logs in the basket. Just throw a couple on and put a match to them and, in no time, we'll have a nice little fire. In the meantime, I'll hunt up the brandy," Kate said.

She hung up their coats in the hall closet and went in search of the brandy, while Richard started a fire.

After the fire got going, he again took in his surroundings. Kate's house was small and cozy. On each side of the fireplace were built-in bookcases filled to capacity with books. On the mantle framed pictures of her family were arranged from one end to the other. The furniture in both the living and dining rooms was comfortable and tasteful. Lovely accessories were placed here and there in both rooms. In her letters she told him she had traveled to several countries in Europe at one time or another. What he saw was probably some of the things she had brought back. The house was definitely Kate.

It was not long before she returned and handed Richard his brandy. They settled themselves next to each other on the couch. Turning toward Kate, he raised his brandy snifter and said, "Let's toast to a fantastic two days." She nodded and touched her snifter to his.

He broke the mood by asking, "I couldn't help but notice my drawing you have on the wall by the piano. I'm curious. What made you keep it all this time? I'm surprised you cared enough about the work to hang onto it. You also had it framed in a quality frame. And it wasn't framed when I gave it to you."

"You've found me out. I figured you might just one day become a famous artist, and I would then have an original. So, I decided to hold on to it, and I don't buy cheap frames," Kate explained.

"You know, Kate, being Irish you have just about enough baloney in you that might convince the weaker minded. I was hoping to hear you held on to it because of some sentiment," he said, trying hard to hide his disappointment.

"Well, did you hold onto anything I gave you out of sentiment?" she asked.

"That one is easy. No, I didn't, because you never gave me anything," he replied.

"I didn't? How very thoughtless of me," Kate said, and they both laughed.

Richard finished his brandy and looked at his watch. "I better get on my way." He went to get his coat from the closet. She got up and followed him.

"I'll walk you to the car," she murmured.

He helped her put on her coat and then put on his and followed her out to the driveway. Before he opened the car door, he turned to her and said, "These past two days have been two of the best days I've had in a very long time."

"Me, too," Kate said and moved closer to him.

He lifted her chin and kissed her tenderly. "I don't know when I'll be coming back, Kate."

"In that case, I think you better kiss me again," she said.

He took her in his arms and crushed his lips to hers. When they parted, he asked, "Hey, you're still my steady girl, aren't you?"

"Absolutely," Kate answered.

He opened the door to his car and got in. After backing out and turning the corner, he honked and waved to Kate. She waved back and did a little happy dance as she went back into the house.

CHAPTER THIRTY-ONE
Richard

When Richard woke up the next morning and looked out the window of the motel, the ground was already covered with several inches of snow. He hoped to make it home before the falling snow became a problem.

He showered, dressed and packed his bag, thinking of Kate and the time they had spent together. He wanted to call her before he left, but most probably she would still be sleeping. Picking up his bag, he took one last look around the room to see if he had missed anything, opened the door and took the elevator to the lobby.

On the drive to the airport, he planned his day. His first stop would be the nursing home to check on Betty. After spending some time with her, he would go home. He had to pay some bills and wanted to make files and organize all the material he had collected on Lieu des Lacs. Hopefully, Louise had stocked the pantry and fridge, so he wouldn't have to eat out.

Kate told him she was going to church in the morning and after lunch intended to spend the afternoon at the library working on a mid-term paper.

His thoughts and plans were full of her. She had led him to exactly the kind of place he wanted to start rebuilding his life, and spending the last two days with her confirmed his desire to pursue her, in the hope she would become a part of it.

The future he envisioned for them excited him and fueled him with an energy he hadn't experienced in a long while. Richard Lawton had become a man on a mission. He pulled into the rental area, turned in the car and boarded the service van to the airport.

South Bend had been hit with a good amount of snow, while he was gone. However, the roads were clear, and traffic moved at a good pace from the airport to his house. He pulled into the garage, parked the car and got his belongings from the trunk. He heard the telephone ring as he was hanging up his coat in the hall closet and hurried to answer it.

"Hey, buddy. It's Ken. Is this a bad time?" Ken asked from the other end of the line.

"Not at all. I just got home. How's it going?" Although Richard had talked to Ken at least twice a week to check on his progress since his accident, he hadn't seen him for awhile.

"Pretty good," Ken replied. "Legs are getting stronger each day. The doc says I can ditch the crutches soon and get by with a cane. Listen, you've probably got things to do. I won't keep you, but how about lunch tomorrow?"

"Sure. How about The Stadium at 11:30 a.m.?" Richard asked.

"Great. See you then," Ken said before hanging up.

Richard was glad Ken had called. He intended to call him later anyway. He picked up his bag and climbed the steps to the bedroom. After unpacking and sorting out the clean clothes from the soiled ones, he took a shower, shaved and dressed in sweats and sneakers. He then called all three of his daughters, giving them current information concerning their mother's condition, but he purposely did not tell any of them about his trip to St. Louis. There would be plenty of time for that when his plans became more solidified. No need to call RJ. He always phoned him Sunday evening, and Richard decided to wait for his call.

Sitting at his desk in his home office, Richard made files and a list of the people he wanted to contact tomorrow along with their phone number. First on his list was the florist. From the phone book in the motel room, he had written down the name and phone number of a florist, Sid Klein, in downtown St. Louis and the address of the company where Kate worked. Being in advertising, he was impressed by Klein's ad in the yellow pages, hoping his flower arrangements were as good as his ad.

In one of his letters, he told Kate he would come courting if there were sparks. After spending time with her the last two days, her response to him made him feel he was on the right track. On the paper with Sid Klein's number he made a notation—no roses, too predictable. Ask for something different.

After a late lunch he took a short nap and spent the rest of the afternoon and early evening reading the Sunday newspaper and watching television. As the evening wore on, he kept checking his watch, anticipating the time when he could call Kate and hear her voice again.

He could wait no longer. Patience was not one of his virtues, and he dialed her number. "Hi, are you busy?" he asked tentatively.

"No, not at all. I was sitting here in front of the fire proof-reading my paper for class."

"What's your week like, Kate?" he asked. During his visit, neither one of them had gone into much detail about their weekly activities. He wanted to know all about her and her life, even if it had to be by long distance for starters.

"Well, most mornings I go to the Donut Hole for coffee and a donut. Monday through Friday I go to work and attend evening classes after work Tuesday and Thursday until 10 p.m. Monday and Wednesday, after I come home and eat, I sometimes go to the library to do some research, because there are always papers to write every week. Friday after work, Ruth and I usually go out to dinner, which includes buying a lottery ticket for the big weekly lotto drawing. Saturday I do the household chores, work on the current home improvement project, and there always is one, and then attend 5 p.m. Mass with Ruth. We usually catch a movie after church. Sunday, the supposedly day of rest, I clean the house, do laundry, grocery shop, study and write papers for school, and now that the holidays are around the corner, squeeze in some time to get ready for Christmas," Kate finished, as she twirled the phone cord around her index finger.

"With a schedule like that, I feel badly because I took so much of your time last weekend," Richard said.

"Please, you didn't. I failed to mention my entire week is flexible except for three things: work, school and church," she replied.

"You sure? You're not just saying that to make me feel less guilty?"

"Believe me, if I don't want to do something, you'll hear plenty from me. How about your week?" she asked.

"Well, Monday through Friday, it's usually a nine-hour day, and sometimes later, if there is a deadline to meet. If I am working on a painting, I go home after work and eat whatever Louise has fixed for me, then return to the office to work some more," Richard said.

"What kind of painting do you do after hours?" Kate asked.

"I've done a lot of stuff for the Notre Dame Sports Department, such as posters, guidebook covers, game tickets, programs. Things like that," Richard said modestly.

Little did she know he was planning to do a pencil sketch of her as a Christmas gift. While he was taking pictures of the properties they had visited, he had also taken pictures of her.

"How about the weekend?" she asked.

"Sunday is my day for chores, too. I'm a big Notre Dame football fan and am glued to the television when they play. Same with NASCAR racing and the Red Birds. I assume you are also a Cardinal fan," Richard said.

"I am. Part of my job is to order the food goodies when the salesmen entertain clients at the baseball games. I get to go as a guest now and then. Sometimes Ruth gets to go, too. Seeing a game from a corporate box is a big treat for both of us. Otherwise, both of us would be watching the game on television, too," Kate said.

There was a lull in the conversation. Kate broke the silence by changing the subject and asked, "What will you do if the Morrisons do not accept your offer on the lot?"

"What I offered was a pretty good monetary incentive and according to Frank, since they have no immediate plans to build, I think I have a good shot at getting it," Richard said.

"I hope you get what you want," Kate said.

"I hope so, too," he replied. "Good night, Kate. I'll call you tomorrow."

"Good night, Richard. Sleep well," she replied and disconnected the call.

He wanted something far more important than a piece of real estate. He wanted her. With a little luck there was a good chance of getting both, and he was going for it.

CHAPTER THIRTY-TWO
Kate

Monday morning traffic was slower due to the snow that had fallen over the weekend. Kate left the donut shop, after having her coffee and donut earlier than usual, to make certain she would get to the office on time. Traffic could be a problem due to the unexpected snowfall. She waited as long as she could for Ruth. Most likely, she was also concerned about the traffic and had decided to skip their morning ritual.

Luckily, the parking garage was next to the building where Kate worked in mid-town St. Louis. It was a great area for shopping, too. Union Station, which was directly across the street, was filled with a good variety of restaurants and many upscale shops. A movie theatre complex, an ice skating arena and the main railroad terminal was located in the rear.

As soon as Kate entered her cubicle, the phone was ringing and two of the sales associates were waiting for her—just another typical Monday morning. By mid-morning, she had finished all of the work that had been in her basket and decided to take a break. This was rare, because her workload was always heavy due to the volume of work she received from the sales associates, the sales manager and the vice-president. Together, they formed a team, the nucleus of the Marketing Department. They were a great group, and many friendships had developed between them.

As she was leaving to go to the company cafeteria, the phone rang in her cubicle.

"Kate, this is Marge calling. There is a delivery for you waiting in the lobby. Would you please come and get it." The company rule was an employee had to pick up any delivery at the receiving desk in the lobby.

Kate was baffled. Who would be sending something to her?

"Okay, Marge. I'm on my way," Kate replied.

After getting some change from her purse for her coffee, she walked toward the elevator bank, which was a long walk from her cubicle that faced the windows and the street. As she passed the rows to the elevators where other employees were working, she said good morning to many of them.

When she exited the elevator, she saw a huge arrangement of the most extraordinary flowers she had ever seen at the receiving desk. She saw Marge waving to her and forgot all about getting coffee.

"Hi, Kate. These came for you. Honestly, I have never seen such a gorgeous arrangement. Whoever sent these must have paid a pretty penny," Marge said as she admired the flowers.

Kate, too, was overwhelmed by the flowers. She also noticed the vase that contained the flowers was a Waterford. She took the envelope that was inserted in the plastic card holder and opened it. The flowers were from Richard and on the card was a written message, *An awesome beginning. Thanks for all your help. Love, Richard.* She put the card back into the envelope and carefully picked up the bouquet, holding it in front of her, as if to shield herself from any onlookers, as she walked back toward the elevators.

When she got off the elevator, she felt conspicuous and had that long walk back to her desk. Some of her co-workers made comments, which she heard as she passed: *wow; awesome flowers; way to go, Kate; what's his name?*

When she finally reached her cubicle, her boss was standing nearby.

"Well, I've sent a lot of bouquets in my time, but that bouquet is more than beautiful; it's exquisite. I'm not going to lose you, am I?" he asked, looking directly at her.

Kate blushed and didn't respond to his question. Richard Lawton was causing quite a stir in her life.

CHAPTER THIRTY-THREE
Richard

Richard was leaving to go to an offsite meeting when Mrs. Joan Bradshaw, the company's receptionist, buzzed his office phone. He picked it up and said, "Richard Lawton."

"Good morning, Richard. It's Frank Ambrose. I'll be brief as you are probably busy. I have news from the Morrisons. They have accepted your offer."

"Super, Frank! That's great news! I'm on my way to a meeting. I'll give you a call later after my meeting is over. Thanks so much for making it happen."

"You're welcome, Richard. There's no rush to call me back. I just wanted to put your mind at ease. You now can go full steam ahead with your plans. Have a good day," Frank said.

Richard disconnected the call. All kinds of thoughts were running around in his head. For the first time in a long while, he asked his partner Stan to attend the meeting, and he agreed. With that out of the way, he closeted himself in his office and started making phone calls.

He made an appointment with New Brunswick Log Home Builders for the following Saturday morning and talked with one of the owners, Jake Davidson. Despite telling Frank he would call him later, he called him back and apologized, asking him to take care of any permits and other local necessary paperwork, and made arrangements to see him at his office late Saturday afternoon.

Lastly, he made reservations at The Leland. Tonight, he would call Kate and tell her the good news, hoping she would be free again this coming Friday and Saturday.

By the time he made all his calls, it was time to meet Ken for lunch. Hurriedly, he put on his coat and went out the door whistling. Today was a very good day despite the fact his car was covered in snow, and he had forgotten his boots. He was walking on air anyway and cheerfully brushed the snow from his windshield and windows while he continued to whistle.

Ken got a good parking spot in front of the restaurant and was waiting for him. When he saw Richard drive up, he got out of his car and walked toward him. "What a snow pile up, huh? I hate winter even when it doesn't snow," Ken said.

"You've got something up your sleeve, haven't you? I can always tell when you have something cooking. Your face is so easy to read," Ken added.

"You're right. I do have something cooking," Richard replied. "If you play your cards right, I might even tell you the latest news, you nosy so-and-so."

"I knew it, I knew it!" Ken said excitedly.

They entered the restaurant and checked their coats. Their usual booth was empty, and Vinita ushered them to it.

"Hi, guys. Where you been? I missed you all last week," Vinita said.

"Richard has been traveling the globe, and I have been on a diet but have thrown in the towel. Bring me the double cheeseburger with fries," Ken replied and pointed at Richard, "Him, too. Partners to the end and all that."

Vinita only shook her head and went to put in their order.

"Okay, friend. What's up? I know you went to see Kate, so let's have it," Ken said.

"There's much to tell," Richard said, as he began to fill Ken in on everything that happened and the news he just received.

When Richard was finished, Ken said, "I'm happy for you, Richard. But, what if the personal angle doesn't work out and you are stuck with living in Lieu des Lacs? Have you thought about that?"

"Yes, but here's the thing. In the contract I signed, I am not allowed to work within one hundred miles of South Bend. That rules out Chicago. There's an agency in St. Louis well over one hundred miles from here and is owned by a former business associate, who has offered me a part-time position with an open starting date, if I want it. His agency handles the Anheiser-Busch account. Plus, my sisters and their husbands still live in Springfield, Illinois, where all of us were raised. Laura Lee and Diane have to travel by plane to see me now, and I don't think the drive would be a problem for Rachel and RJ."

"By the way you are pitching your points, it sounds to me like you've already made the decision to move to Missouri," Ken said.

Before Ken could ask about Kate, Vinita brought their orders. After she left, he asked, "What about Kate?"

"She didn't throw me out. By the way, she made a comment about liking my tie. You know, the one I bought for the reunion. As I recall, you had such a good time making me feel like some schoolboy trying to impress his teacher. Remember?"

"Okay, okay. So she noticed your tie. Glad you made some points, but I really feel sorry for the woman," Ken said.

Several seconds passed before it dawned on him his friend was actually going to move away. He stopped eating and looked directly at Richard. "I feel sorry for me and Linda, too. Who will I eat lunch with, and what in the devil am I going to do Saturday mornings after you move? I'm going to miss you, ole buddy."

He looked at Ken, and their eyes locked. The moment was heavy with emotion. Richard broke the mood when he said jokingly, "For pity sakes, the log house I intend to build will have a guest room. If you can read a map, you and your charming wife are welcome to visit. Now, quit your whining, and pass me the ketchup."

After lunch, Richard went back to the office. He wanted to call Kate, but decided to wait until later.

That evening, he dialed Kate's number. She picked it up and said, "Hello."

"Hi. What are you doing?" he asked.

"Eating a bowl of chili. What is happening in your world?"

"I hope you're sitting down, because I have great news," Richard said. "Better yet if you're standing up, get ready to jump for joy. We got the lot. This calls for a celebration."

"That's wonderful," Kate replied, very much aware that he said *we* rather than *I* in reference to the lot.

"I was on the phone most of the morning after Frank called me. I didn't expect to come back to St. Louis this soon, but I want to check out the New Brunswick guy as soon as possible concerning log house construction. I want answers to the many questions I have before I sign a contract. I made an appointment Saturday morning around 10 a.m. to see him and want you to go with me. The weather forecast looks okay for driving.

"I intend to leave the office Friday right after lunch. I booked two nights at The Leland and will leave early Sunday morning. With the holidays coming up and the close of the year's business, this trip will most probably be the last one for me until January. How about it?" Say yes, Kate," he pleaded.

"You've got yourself a date," she said with enthusiasm. "I was planning to put up the Christmas tree and decorations this coming weekend, but I'll make time to do that next week."

"Wonderful. Here's the plan. We'll get a pizza Friday night and catch a movie. After we get back from New Brunswick, I'll treat you to a fine dinner at the Ambassador Hotel Saturday night. I picked up their brochure, when I was at The Leland. According to what I read, the Candlelight Room at the Ambassador has a dance band on the weekends. I would also be willing to bet the hotel and downtown area will be decorated for the holidays, too."

"I've never been to the Candlelight Room at the Ambassador Hotel, nor have I ever been inside the hotel, only driven by it many times. Thank you for asking me," Kate said.

"The pleasure is all mine," he replied.

"You might be interested to know I have been saving a dinner dress in case I ever got an invitation to go someplace really special. I think the tags are still attached to one of the sleeves. It's a short cocktail dress with three-quarter length sleeves in white wool trimmed in gold studs around a wide waistband and the neckline— the kind of dress that is well suited for a fine dinner, dancing and romancing."

"My kind of garment, especially that part about romancing," he replied.

"When I bought the dress, I also bought a pair of gold high-heel pumps to compliment it. I need to go shopping for a gold evening bag and silk hosiery to complete the outfit. I'll have plenty of time to do that before Friday," Kate said, already thinking ahead.

"Then, it's settled. In the meantime, I'll browse through my closet and see if I can come up with an outfit to match yours. How do you feel about me wearing a gold leather suit?" he asked.

"I wouldn't put it pass you. I'm still trying to get over the plaid dinner jacket," she said, teasing him.

"Before we get on another subject, thank you for the flowers, Richard. They are beyond beautiful. I have never seen so many unusual fresh flowers. I now have a lovely Waterford vase, too," Kate said.

"You're welcome," Richard replied.

Kate was in for quite a surprise. Little did she know Richard had made arrangements with Sid Klein Florist for her to receive a fresh bouquet every Monday morning.

"I'll be counting the days, Kate. When you get home after work Friday, call me at the motel, and we'll go from there. See you in four days," Richard said enthusiastically.

After he disconnected the call, he thought about the coming weekend. Come Saturday night, Richard Lawton and Kate O'Connor would be making their debut in the Candlelight Room, and he promised himself he would do everything possible to make the weekend memorable for both of them.

CHAPTER THIRTY-FOUR
Kate

Tuesday morning, when the alarm clock went off, Kate remembered she had set it an hour early. She wanted to look over her paper one more time in case it needed any last minute corrections before turning it in tonight at class. With Richard coming into town this weekend, she planned to get some of the Christmas stuff done during the week after work and also shop for a gold evening bag and hosiery. The past two weeks, the momentum of her life had accelerated. Between working, going to school, running her household and talking to Richard late into the night, the hours in the day were filled. She couldn't remember the last time she had talked to her sister or Ruth. She would call Jackie later tonight. As she was dialing Ruth's extension, she looked up. Ruth was walking toward her.

"It seems like ages since we have talked," Ruth said. "However, I did see those lovely flowers, when I dropped off some papers to your boss yesterday. You weren't at your desk. I assume the flowers are from Richard."

"They are," Kate replied.

"Pardon me for saying so, but his intentions are showing," Ruth said, eyes twinkling.

Kate said nothing.

"What's it like having a man in your life again?" Ruth asked nonchalantly.

Coming from anyone else, Kate might have been offended by Ruth's question, but the two women were more than good friends; they were like sisters, and both of them only wanted what was best for the other.

"It's certainly good for the old self-esteem, and it doesn't take a rocket scientist to figure out attention is the balm for rejection," Kate replied.

"I'm glad someone has come into your life. I'm truly happy for you, Kate."

Kate sensed Ruth was holding something back."Okay, okay, what is it? Do you want to add a postscript to those good wishes?" Kate asked.

Ruth cared about her friend and for that reason, she confronted her. "I'm reluctant to tell you what's on my mind, because it's really none of my business. But, I care about you, Kate. I'm going to cut right to the chase. Where do you think this relationship is going? This man is obviously in the process of making a big move, literally. Relocating, letters, phone calls, flowers, weekend visits and whatnot. Sounds to me like a serious suitor. Aren't you putting the cart before the horse? Have you heard anything regarding the annulment?"

"You know as well as I do that Father Steve said it would take about nine months," Kate answered somewhat irritably. She did not like being challenged by her friend.

"Have you shared any of this annulment thing with Richard?" Ruth asked, disregarding Kate's obvious reluctance to talk about the situation.

"No."

"Why not, Kate?"

"For one thing, he most probably wouldn't understand, because he's not Catholic. And, for another, he has mentioned nothing about marriage, Ruth."

"Kate, Kate. In for a penny, in for a pound. From what you've shared with me, I'd say his intentions are pretty apparent. When will you be seeing him again?" Ruth asked.

"This weekend. The couple, who own the lot he wanted, accepted his offer. We're going to check out New Brunswick Log Home Builders' operation Saturday. If he likes what he sees and hears, he is going to hire them and wants to get things going immediately. He's taking me to the Ambassador for dinner and dancing this Saturday," Kate said.

"Dinner and dancing. How romantic and at Christmas time to boot."

"Be happy for me, Ruth. Please."

"You know I am, Kate. I just don't want to see you get hurt or find yourself in a position where you have to choose," Ruth added.

"I don't understand. What do you mean?" Kate asked.

"If you get the annulment, fine and dandy. But, if you don't, you would be forced to choose between Richard and your church," Ruth said somberly.

Ruth's words hit Kate full force—a reality she did not want to address, much less face should that become the case. Right at that moment, she thought of Mike. Had he been granted his annulment, she would have been free, too. In his quest to get what he wanted at the time, Kate felt his answers reflected what he thought the powers that be wanted to hear. To her way of thinking, Mike had overplayed his hand, and they had seen right through him. Now, she wondered how much his responses would affect her chances of getting her annulment.

If the decision came back negative, Ruth was right. She would be forced to make a choice. All thoughts of the upcoming weekend and the Candlelight Room began to dim.

CHAPTER THIRTY-FIVE
Richard

Richard dialed RJ's phone, and he answered on the second ring, "Hi, Dad. I was just about to call you."

"Wanted you to know I'm going out of town again this weekend. I intended to call you yesterday, but time got away from me," Richard explained.

Richard proceeded to let RJ know what had transpired regarding last weekend's activities in St. Louis, but made no mention of Kate.

"That's great, Dad. I'm glad you got the lot you wanted. What now?" RJ asked.

"I'm going to New Brunswick to check out Jake Davidson's company, New Brunswick Log Home Builders, the company Frank Ambrose recommended. My company takeover is April 1, which gives me more than enough time before I close up shop here. The sooner the better, because winter weather could be a big factor in building, causing delays.

"I'm impressed so far, with what I've heard about Davidson and his company, and have even contacted a couple of people, who also hired him for log house construction, to get their input about his work," Richard said.

"I can tell by the sound of your voice you are excited about going. It's been a long time since you have made any plans for the future. For many years, you have simply been going through the motions. Living, yes, but enjoying little. More importantly, you have a desire to change things. I'm really happy for you, Dad.

"Ever since you attended your fortieth class reunion, you've changed and for the better. You are more energetic, outgoing and even lighthearted at times. Something has triggered that metamorphosis, but I haven't a clue as to the how, what and why of it. Regardless of what has incited this new vitality, I'm all for it."

His son's intuition surprised him, but he refrained from many any comment. Instead, he changed the subject and said, "I plan to leave Friday afternoon and will return sometime early Sunday afternoon. Are you planning to see your mother this weekend?" Richard asked.

"Yes. Don't worry about going to see her. Besides, you'll be bushed from driving. I'll give you a call at the office Monday and let you know the latest. I have to scoot. Good luck with Davidson," RJ said, disconnecting the call.

Richard hung up the phone and began hunting for the telephone directory. He thumbed through the yellow pages until he came to the jewelry section. Running his finger down the page, he copied the address and phone number for Taggert Jewelers, a store where he previously had made jewelry purchases for Betty and his daughters. He planned to visit the store later in the afternoon.

The entire week Richard was swamped at the office, bringing the company's business to an end for the year. Meetings with Stan often continued far beyond their normal business day.

He was excited about the coming weekend with Kate, which reminded him to send his suits to the cleaners. Playing the part of Romeo kept him on his toes. He couldn't make up his mind to wear his navy suit or the gray one this coming weekend and ended up sending both to the cleaners. Decisions, decisions.

Stops had to be made at the bank and arrangements made with Louise. He needed a haircut, and the car had to be washed, and so on and so on, with other countless trivial acts that only a person in love could concoct.

His last errand on his list was to stop by Taggert Jewelry and pick up his purchase, which he planned to do on the way out of town. He wanted this weekend to be perfect, and, since he was in charge of arrangements, he wanted to leave no margin for errors.

* * * * *

He pulled into The Leland's parking lot a little before 4:30 p.m. Friday afternoon. Getting his attaché case, suitcase and garment bag from the trunk, he walked into the lobby toward the registration desk. The desk clerk on duty recognized him and called him by name. "Good afternoon, Mr. Lawton. Good to see you again. Your reservation is for two nights. We are really booked this weekend. You're in room 329, which is on the end. Enjoy your stay."

Richard picked up the key and headed toward the elevator. After he opened the door to room 329, he immediately hung up his garment bag, unpacked his suitcase and put his shaving kit and other personal items on the counter in the bathroom.

Looking at his watch, he had at least thirty minutes or so before Kate would be home. He sat down in one of the two chairs in front of the window that looked out into the parking lot to wait for Kate's call and began reading *USA Today*. No sooner had he gotten settled, there was a knock on the door, and he got up to answer it.

"Mr. Lawton, this just came for you," the bellman said, as he handed Richard a single red rose in full bloom surrounded by baby's breath and ferns in a glass vase.

Richard thanked him and gave him a tip, took the vase and closed the door. The fragrance of the rose filled his nostrils. An envelope was in a plastic holder amid the arrangement, and he removed it. Inside the envelope was a card. The rose was from Kate. On the card she had written in her own handwriting, *I'm so thankful you're in my life.* He was filled with such joy over what she had written and was overwhelmed momentarily. Things were going along just as he had hoped. He was getting the hang of this courting thing and ready to move on to the next level.

After getting Kate's call, Richard changed into jeans and drove to Kate's house. She was waiting for him in the sun porch doorway and waved to him as he passed. He parked his car on her driveway, got out and could hardly keep from running to the doorway, where she stood.

"Hi. My day is just beginning," and greeted him with a kiss. When they parted, she said eagerly, "I need a repeat," and kissed him again.

"And, hello to you, too. Now, that is the way a woman should always greet her man," Richard said.

They went arm-in-arm into the kitchen and sat down at the kitchen table.

"I just got home. Give me a minute," Kate said. "It won't take me long to change into my jeans. There's Diet Coke in the fridge. Help yourself and look through the movie listings, while I change. Pick a good one. If you're hungry, we can eat first, then go to a movie or the other way around. Your call. We have the whole evening, so there's no rush." She left him on his own while she went to change her clothes.

Richard got a Diet Coke, picked up the paper and began looking at the movie listings. He couldn't remember the last time he had been to a movie. He always rented videos. As he looked at the listings, he saw exactly the movie he wanted to see with Kate—*Rudy*, a true story of Rudy Ruettiger, who dreams of attending Notre Dame University and playing on the Fighting Irish Football Team, despite many obstacles in his path.

"Hey, do you like sports stories, especially true ones?" he yelled.

"I like any true story about people," she replied.

"Have you seen *Rudy*?"

"No, I don't know anything about that movie," she replied.

"I've seen it, but would like to see it again. That's how much I enjoyed it."

"Are you sure?" she asked, as she rejoined him in the kitchen and sat across the table from him.

"Yeah, I'm sure." It took all of his control not to reach out for her.

"That's settled. Now, how about food? There's a really great pizza place about twenty minutes from here. We'd have more than enough time to eat leisurely and then catch the movie. By the way, did you bring any of the brochures and info with you from New Brunswick?" Kate asked.

"I did. They're at the motel. I thought if you weren't too tired after the movie, we could go back to the motel and jot down some things to ask Davidson tomorrow. I've started a list, and you probably have thought of some things, too. I really want to be prepared, when I speak to this guy. Talking in person is much better than talking over the phone," Richard said.

"Good idea, and I agree," Kate replied. "Better to be prepared rather than think on your feet and maybe miss out on some points."

They put on their jackets, locked the door and walked to Richard's car hand-in-hand.

When he opened the car door for her, he said, "Thank you for the rose. I'm glad you're in my life, too, Kate O'Connor."

As she slid into the seat and got comfortable, Richard thought about what she had written on the card. Had she thrown caution to the wind, using the rose as her way of announcing her feelings toward him? If that were the case, his intentions were proving to be reciprocated.

After the movie, while driving to The Leland, Kate said, "That was a great movie. Makes you think about dreams and how they come true sometimes, even against great odds."

He said nothing in reply, thinking about what she had just said.

"I probably wouldn't have chosen that movie, so thanks for sitting through it again, so I could see it," Kate added.

"You're welcome. I enjoyed seeing it over. Are you sure you're not too tired to get my act ready for tomorrow?" Richard asked.

"Not at all. You said your appointment with Davidson isn't until 10 a.m., so there's no big rush to get on the road early. Now both of us can sleep in," Kate replied.

Richard knew she was totally unaware her last remark conveyed a double meaning, but he picked up on it. If things went as he hoped, they would be sleeping in and waking up in each other's arms in the morning. He stepped on the gas and drove to The Leland.

They sat at the table in his motel room, jotting down questions for Jake Davidson, drinking White Zinfandel, which Richard had ordered from the bar. They had been at this task for over an hour.

Kate was having a hard time concentrating and said, "I've had it, Richard. It's almost midnight. You're probably beat, too. I think we better call it a night."

"You're right. I'm pretty bushed myself." He gathered up their notes, put them into his attaché case and rose to pull out her chair, so she could get up. When she did, she stumbled over her own shoes, which she had taken off earlier, and fell into his arms. He felt her breast graze his chest through his shirt as she righted herself. He pulled her closer to him and kissed her neck.

"Kate, I want to…"

She put her finger to his lips and said, "Yes."

They moved away from the table, kissing each other with every step, forgetting about their weariness they both had admitted to earlier. He unbuttoned her blouse as she unbuttoned his shirt, and they flung them aside. He then pulled his undershirt over his head, discarding it as she undid his belt and tugged at his jeans, which fell to the floor, leaving him standing only in his briefs and socks. She unfastened her jeans, pushed them downward around her ankles and stepped out of them, working off her anklets in the process, and stood in front of him in bra and panties. Taking off her last bit of clothing, she faced him unashamedly.

"You seem to be somewhat overdressed, Richard. Could you do something about that?" Kate asked as she pulled back the covers on the bed.

"Kate, it's been awhile, and I …"

"Me, too. We'll figure it out together. Make love to me, Richard."

"That's exactly what I had in mind to do," he said. He dropped his briefs and socks on the floor and got into the bed.

CHAPTER THIRTY-SIX
Kate

The sound of running water woke Kate. A few seconds passed before she realized she was not in her own bed. She looked around at her surroundings. Then, the reality of where she was surfaced. She smiled as she remembered the pleasure of their lovemaking the previous night.

Richard came into the room, fully dressed and said, "Hey, sleepyhead, good morning." He leaned down to kiss her cheek.

She felt self-conscious with the covers pulled up to her neck and not a stitch on underneath them, plus an unwashed face, uncombed hair and teeth that needed brushing. "Good morning to you. What time is it?" she asked.

"Almost 7 a.m. Here's the plan, Kate, if you agree. Get dressed, and I'll take you home so you can freshen up. While I wait for you, I'll go over the questions we worked on last night for Davidson, just in case we forgot something. We'll have a nice breakfast some place before we hit the road to New Brunswick. Of course, if you can figure out how we can squeeze another lovemaking session in between any of those stops, I would be more than willing."

His last suggestion caught her off guard and instantly triggered the memory of the pleasure he had given her last night.

"Why Kate O'Connor, I do believe you're blushing!"

The distance from the bed to the bathroom seemed like a mile to her. Nevertheless, she pulled up the sheet and wrapped it around her. She got up from the bed, with as much composure as she could muster, picked up her clothing from the floor and walked toward the bathroom.

He stood in her path, as if trying to put her at ease, and said, "You look regal even in a sheet."

She looked deep into his eyes and replied, "After I shower, if you behave yourself, I'll let you see my towel outfit." She turned and sashayed into the bathroom.

Within the hour, they were on their way to New Brunswick, giving Richard another opportunity to appreciate the beauty of Missouri. The landscape of the state in this particular locale was another reason for telling himself his decision to relocate in this part of Missouri was a good one.

A road sign indicated the next right turn would lead to New Brunswick Log Home Builders. He slowed down and drove less than a mile and turned into a graveled road.

"Look, Richard. There's New Brunswick's sign in front of that log house," Kate said.

"Yes, I see it. I guess that log house must be New Brunswick's offices," he replied.

He parked the car in front of the log house, and both of them got out of the car. A cobblestone path led to a long porch that stretched across the front of the log house. They climbed the steps and looked back over their shoulders. There were no houses for miles, only long stretches of black soil, waiting to be made ready for next season's planting.

Richard held the door open for Kate, and they entered a large room. A receptionist, who was seated at a desk, greeted them.

"Good morning. May I help you?" she asked.

"My name is Lawton. I have an appointment with..." Before he could finish his sentence, Jake Davidson walked across the room and introduced himself.

"Good morning, Richard. Any trouble in finding us?" Jake asked.

"No, none at all. Although I was surprised when I pulled up. I didn't expect your headquarters to be in a log house," Richard replied.

"Best way to advertise our kits," Davidson responded. "This particular one is probably the most popular one." Davidson's gaze turned toward Kate.

"Jake, this is Kate O'Connor," Richard said.

Davidson extended his hand as she did hers. "Nice to meet you, Ms. O'Connor."

"Please, it's Kate," she responded.

He nodded and turned back to Richard. "I know you are somewhat pressed for time, so let's get down to specifics. Would you folks like anything to drink before we begin?" Jake asked.

Richard answered for both of them. "No, thank you. We're good."

Davidson ushered them into his office and seated them on comfortable chairs at a round table. He then began explaining the details of log house construction, showed them the floor plans of the five models, discussed costs and financing and answered their questions.

"That's about it, Richard. According to what you have shared with me, I would recommend the three bedrooms with a loft, two baths and an open first floor concept. This model also comes with a carport included in the price. If you want a garage, the cost would be more." He spread the floor plans across the table and handed him a postcard size picture of the house. He also gave a picture to Kate. "There are also quite a few extras you might be interested in, such as skylights and a Jacuzzi tub," Jake said as he handed Richard a list of the upgrades and the cost.

Richard had written Davison previously for information on all the models. After reviewing all five, he had pretty much made up his mind which one he wanted to build. He was relieved when he heard Davidson agree with his choice, putting them on the same page.
Wanting Kate's input, too, Richard turned to her and asked, "What one do you like, Kate?"

She didn't really know how to respond, because Richard had never discussed this aspect with her. Was he thinking of buying a large house for his kids and grandkids so there would be plenty of room when they visited or one only for himself, which would probably be the smallest one, the Pioneer? Whatever one he decided upon, it would be his house, not hers. Therefore, what difference would it make what she thought one way or the other? Both Richard and Davidson were looking at her, waiting for her answer.

Instead of answering Richard's question, Kate asked one of Davidson, "Would your firm by any chance be the one that had some models on display on Summerset Boulevard near Berry Road in St. Louis some time ago?"

"Yes. New Brunswick was at that location. When our contract came up for renewal, my partners and I decided to auction off all the models there and combine everything here. We wanted to expand, and that location wasn't large enough to fit our needs. We had been thinking about relocating for some time. Several years ago we began building the log models you now see. Our eventual goal is to build all five models for display, and now we have plenty of land to do so," Davidson explained.

Kate couldn't believe what she just heard and asked, "Mr. Davidson, what is the name of the three bedroom home you are recommending?"

"It's called the Missourian."

Her heart missed a beat. Davidson was advising Richard to buy the very same model she looked at after her divorce and wanted—the one she had taken Jackie to see.

"Thanks for the giving of your time, Jake. I'll look over the five models and call you midweek with my decision," Richard said.

"No problem. Call me any time, either at my office or home. The phone numbers where you can reach me are on my business card, which is attached to one of the brochures," Jake said.

Richard began putting the papers Davidson had given him in his attaché case. Both of them had forgotten Richard's earlier question to Kate about which model she liked. They were startled when she stood up. "My choice is the Missourian. It's the one I like," Kate said, without giving any thought to her possible influence concerning Richard's choice.

"You heard the lady, Jake. Kate just saved me from making a phone call. Build us the Missourian," Richard said, looking at Kate happily.

"Done. I'll get in touch with your man down in Lieu des Lacs. Weather permitting, we'll begin as soon as possible," Jake replied.

They shook hands and Davidson showed them to the front door. Walking to the car, Kate remembered the remark Ruth had made to her earlier—*in for a penny, in for a pound*—and instantly recalled the *us* in Richard's last statement to Jake Davidson.

After lunch they drove to Lieu des Lacs to meet with Frank Ambrose, which took up the rest of the afternoon, discussing the particulars concerning the building of the log house. Frank assured them he would take care of all the initial incidentals and take pictures of the building process, as it went along, and send them to Richard.

They left Frank's office feeling like they had accomplished all they had started out to do. Richard turned to Kate and said, "Do we have time to run by and see the lot before we head back?"

"Sure. You said our dinner reservation wasn't until 7 p.m. We have plenty of time. Do you remember how to get there without looking at the map?" Kate asked.

"I think so," Richard replied and turned the car toward Rue de Rivoli, the main road in Lieu des Lacs. Frank told him most newcomers used this paved road as an identification point, since it led to the tennis courts, golf course and clubhouse.

At the corner of Rue de Rivoli, he turned left, and then took another left and knew he was headed in the right direction. Soon after they saw the lake ahead of them. Richard stopped the car on the dam road. He turned to Kate and said, "Our lot is the only one that juts out into the water."

There it was again, the *our* reference to the lot, but Kate did not make a point of it. Instead, she replied, "Yes, it is. I'm so happy for you, Richard. I mean getting the lot you wanted and all. Most people would have walked away after hearing it was not available."

Kate thought back to the time when she stopped writing to him years ago, her way of ending any future contact with him. He never wrote or called her, asking for an explanation. Life went on for both of them, and she assumed he had accepted the situation for what is was—the end of their relationship. Here she was, forty years later, sitting beside him, complimenting him on his determination.

CHAPTER THIRTY-SEVEN
Richard

They checked their coats and walked toward the maître d´. Richard gave him his name, and the maître d´ signaled for a waiter to lead them to their table, which was near the dance floor. Within minutes, another waiter appeared and asked them for their drink order.

"Since this is my first time at the Candlelight Room, how about celebrating, Kate? How about two champagne cocktails?" Richard asked.

"It's my first time here, too. I've never had a champagne cocktail."

"Then, tonight's the night," Richard said enthusiastically.

The waiter left with their order, and Kate began looking around the room. White wreaths trimmed in gold ornaments and ribbons were placed attractively on the walls, and two white Christmas trees heavily laden with gold balls and hundreds of sparkling lights were on each side of the bandstand. Each table's centerpiece was a miniature duplication of the larger Christmas trees.

"It's so very beautiful," Kate said, as she glanced around the dining area.

"You're the one who's beautiful," Richard replied. "Your dress and accessories match perfectly with the décor."

"And, I have the most handsome escort in this entire room," Kate replied.

"Is it okay for a man to blush?" Richard asked, and they both laughed.

The waiter returned with their drinks. Richard proposed a toast, "Here's to a memorable evening and Merry Christmas."

Kate touched her glass to his and replied, "Merry Christmas. Thank you for bringing me here, Richard."

"You're welcome. The pleasure is all mine," he replied.

After their dinner of steak and lobster and all the trimmings, the waiter cleared the table and asked if they wanted dessert. Before Richard had a chance to answer, Kate declined for both of them. The waiter nodded, refilled their coffee cups and left.

"Are you sure you don't want dessert?" Richard asked.

"Positive," Kate replied. "I remember you said you never ordered dessert in a restaurant. However, before you go home, I thought I would give you a taste of my culinary expertise. I had time this afternoon to make a chocolate cream pie for you."

"I can hardly wait, and I have something for you, too," Richard replied. He then reached into his suit pocket, took out a blue velvet box and placed it in front of Kate.

By the shape of the box, Kate knew it was a ring box and waited for him to say something. Seconds passed; he finally said, "Open it, Kate."

With trembling fingers she took the box in her hand and opened it. Inside was a marquise-cut blue sapphire ring surrounded by tiny diamonds, mounted in yellow gold.

"When a guy asks a girl to go steady, he usually gives her his class ring. I looked for mine and couldn't find it. I hope this one will do," Richard said.

She was totally surprised by his gift. Looking directly into his eyes she said, "I don't know what to say."

"You don't have to say anything." He reached across the table, took the ring out of the box and slid it over the fourth finger of her right hand.

"How did you know the sapphire is my birthstone?" Kate asked.

"I have a good memory, Kate," Richard said, as he squeezed her hand and kissed her fingertips. "How about a dance? They're playing one of my favorites."

Both of them pushed back their chairs and walked to the dance floor. He took her in his arms and held her tightly. She could smell his aftershave as he held her close.

As they danced, Richard softly sang the lyrics in Kate's ear, and when the song ended, he tilted her face to his and kissed her lips tenderly. "I love you, Kate O'Connor."

"And, I love you, Richard Lawton."

When they got to Kate's house, Richard parked the car along the curb in front of her house, got out of the car and opened Kate's door. They walked up to the front porch. Kate handed him her house key. He unlocked the door, stood aside to let her pass and then followed her into the foyer. They took off their coats, and Kate hung them both in the hall closet.

"Why don't you plug in the tree lights and light a fire? I'll make some coffee to go with the pie. It'll just take a minute. We can sit on the couch and have our dessert there," Kate said, as she turned and walked toward the kitchen.

After getting comfortable on the couch, he noticed a portable radio on the end table and turned the dial to a station playing music from the fifties.

A cozy fire, a Christmas tree, romantic music, chocolate cream pie and Kate. He smiled at his good fortune.

Within a short time, she came back into the living room, carrying a tray. She put it on the coffee table in front of him and handed him his pie and coffee. She sat down next to him but far enough away to give him plenty of room. After getting situated, she leaned over and served herself.

"Well, Richard, what's the verdict? Is this the best chocolate cream pie you've ever tasted or not?" Kate asked.

"How did you know chocolate cream pie is my favorite?" Richard asked.

"Before you left for art school, you took me to the Colonial Restaurant for pie after a date one night. Don't tell me you've forgotten that the Colonial was known for their homemade pies? You ordered chocolate cream and later told me it was your favorite," Kate said.

The more time he spent with her, memories of their past relationship kept surfacing. He couldn't help but think it was a good omen.

"Come over here," he said, after both of them had finished their pie and coffee. Instead of moving closer to him, she took his hand and led him to her bedroom.

As she pulled the spread down on the bed, he was thinking about having a life with a woman, who could not only make the best chocolate cream pie he had ever eaten, but also rang his chimes and had no reservations about him ringing hers.

CHAPTER THIRTY-EIGHT
Kate

When Kate woke up, Richard was gone. She put on her robe and went to the kitchen to make coffee. On the kitchen table she found a note Richard had left for her and laughed when she read it. *I really liked the pie, especially what followed after. Will call tonight. Love, Richard.* She remembered he had told her his son was having a Christmas Open House today, beginning at noon and had promised to attend, which required him to leave earlier than usual.

While she filled the coffee pot with water, she thought about all the things she intended to do that day. There was the grocery shopping to do plus reviewing for a final exam Tuesday. Thank goodness, Tuesday was the last day of class. She could then enjoy the holidays.

Her thoughts then drifted to what she planned to give Richard for Christmas. The idea had come to her when they had visited Jake Davidson at New Brunswick Log Home Builders. Jake had given her a colored picture of the Missourian. Kate planned to take it to Kinko's and have a black and white copy made. While Richard had been tied up with Jake, she had spent the time working on a poem to accompany the picture and finally, during off moments during the weekend, had gotten it to a point where she was satisfied.

Her idea was to have the poem engraved on a silver plate, centered underneath the picture of the Missourian and then have it framed. In her mind she visualized the gift double matted in azure and light blue in a walnut frame with a matching easel. In order to have all of this done and shipped to him in time for Christmas, she needed to act fast. Luckily, a store that did engraving was not far from her home and was open Sundays during the holiday season. Framing would not be a problem, either. One of her friends owned a framing shop. Kate knew she could count on her friend to do the matting and framing despite the lateness of the hour.

Glancing at the clock on the kitchen wall, she would have to hurry to make 8 a.m. Mass. Picking up her breakfast dishes, she put them in the sink and went to shower and dress. Confessions were heard fifteen minutes prior to the start of the Mass, and she needed to go.

CHAPTER THIRTY-NINE
Richard

It was all he could do to keep his eyes open, driving the last twenty miles to his house. It was going to be a long day. Richard was tired from driving, and he still had things to do when he got home plus attend his son's Christmas Open House.

He parked the car in the garage and took out his suitcase, garment bag and attaché case from the trunk, hoping that Louise had come while he was gone. When he opened the door, he gave a sigh of relief. On the kitchen counter were his shirts neatly folded from the laundry and hanging nearby, on the door, was his cleaning. On top of the mail, which she had also arranged neatly, was a note she had written: *Welcome back. Everything okay. Got out the Christmas decorations and put them in the living room. I tried all the tree lights and they work, but we need some extension cords. See you tomorrow.*

He realized he had forgotten to tell Louise he had decided not to decorate this year. His daughters weren't coming home for Christmas, and RJ and his family were going to Disneyland with Sarah and her parents over the holidays. He didn't see the sense of putting up a tree plus all the other decorations just for himself. Now, the front room floor was piled high with boxes.

He didn't want to hurt Louise's feelings, since she had taken the trouble to get the Christmas stuff out, but he also didn't want to be bothered with decorating. The decorating problem would have to wait, and he went upstairs to change his clothes. He would unpack later. The mail could wait, too.

Although he wanted to take a nap, he took a shower instead to revive himself and got dressed for his son's Christmas party, hoping he could get away from the party early.

The next morning, Louise found him asleep on the couch. The television was still on. She turned it off and let him sleep.

The noise from the kitchen woke Richard. He was disoriented for a minute until Louise came into the living room and said, "Good morning, Mr. L. Looks like you didn't make it to the second floor last night. You look like you could use a hot breakfast."

"That I could, Louise. When I got home from RJ's party, I guess I must have crashed on the couch. I'm famished. Give me twenty minutes." He got up, folded the afghan that had covered him and returned it to its rightful place on top of the couch, desperately wanting a cup of hot coffee. But, first things first, and he went upstairs to dress.

They sat together at the kitchen island, Richard eating his breakfast and Louise nursing her second cup of coffee. "When do you plan to get the Christmas tree?" she asked.

Before he could reply, she went on to say, "I know you told me the girls would not be coming home for the holidays this year and your son was also going away, but it's just not right, you being by yourself and without a Christmas tree," Louise said emphatically.

"Now, here's the plan, Mr. L. You go and get a tree, and no artificial one, either. Get a fresh one that smells nice. Not too big and not too small. My husband is going to his lodge meeting Wednesday night. I'll stay later Wednesday, and we'll decorate it together. In the meantime, I'll hang the door wreaths today, after I do my usual Monday chores," she added.

"It wouldn't hurt to pick up three or four poinsettia plants. In the past Mrs. Betty always had several of them in the foyer. Oh, I almost forgot. Pick up two white extension cords, too. Deal or no deal? And, if you choose no deal, you'll be walking on thin ice with me," Louise said.

"Well, if you put it that way—deal," Richard said, giving in to her demands.

"That's what I wanted to hear, Mr. L.," Louise said, clearing away his dishes.

Richard put on his overcoat, picked up his attaché case on the way out to the garage and got into his car, thinking of all the things he had to do today. While driving to work, he made a mental list of them. Food for the company Christmas party had to be ordered as well as fruit baskets for their clients and Vinita. Christmas bonuses for their staff also had to be discussed with Stan, so he could get the ball rolling. And, all the pending advertising jobs needed to be reviewed to ensure they would be completed before the office closed for the holidays. He also had to finish Kate's picture tonight, so he could take it to the framer's tomorrow. Between all the things on his to-do list, he now had to buy a Christmas tree. He also wanted to spend some time with Betty.

Later, when he walked into Betty's room, she was sleeping soundly, most probably heavily sedated. He put the large red poinsettia plant on the nightstand, so she could see it when she woke. The florist had wrapped the pot in gold foil and fastened a huge red bow around it.

He noticed someone had taped the Christmas cards she received around the dresser mirror. Although the cards and the poinsettia gave the room a hint of Christmas spirit, they failed to mask the reality that it was still a room occupied by a very sick person.

He didn't bother to take off his overcoat and sat in a chair next to her bed, looking at his wife, or rather, his ex-wife. He sat there in the silence, reflecting on their life together.

Their marriage had serious problems from the very start. They stayed married, not because they loved each other, but because both had reasons of their own for doing so. Somewhere along the line, he had made peace with their situation and often wondered if Betty's excessive drinking was her way of dealing with their marriage.

He was thankful for their four beautiful children, but all of them had seen and heard too much of their marital discord while growing up.

His thoughts drifted to Kate. There was a chance for happiness with her, and it appeared to be within his reach. What he felt at that moment was immense sadness. It was too late for Betty. Life had dealt her a bad hand, one she could not win. He covered his eyes with his hands and wept.

CHAPTER FORTY
Kate

Christmas Eve was only a day away. Despite her best efforts, Kate was among the many last minute shoppers. After driving around the shopping center's parking lot several times, she finally got lucky and found a spot close to Famous Barr, which is where she wanted to go.

The department store was packed with shoppers. She needed a suitable gift for Jackie and Cole and took the escalator to the upper level, thinking she might find something in the kitchen appliance department. Finally, she decided on an electric ice cream maker. Not too long ago, Jackie mentioned their ice cream maker had seen better days. Nearby was a gift basket of assorted toppings, which she also picked up. Not only were all the items on sale, but she also had a store coupon.

While she was waiting in line to pay for her purchases, she thought about the upcoming holiday and her family. Her two single sons, Andy and Sean, and her youngest son, Ryan, and his family, would be spending Christmas Eve at her house but not staying all night. The rest of Kate's married brood lived out of state and wouldn't be coming this year.

When she was married to Mike, Santa's gifts were always opened Christmas morning, and the tradition held, which made it difficult for the families who had kids. The Santa Claus thing required them to stay put on Christmas Eve and Christmas, and Kate understood. Although they sometimes came to see Kate during the Christmas holidays, they always visited after Santa Claus, and they went home before New Year's Eve.

Knowing Kate would be alone Christmas Day, Jackie had surprised her by asking her to dinner.

Kate's daydreaming was interrupted when the lady in back of her nudged her and said, "You're next."

She apologized, paid for her purchases and turned toward the escalator. The day had been a long one for her, and it wasn't over yet. She still had to make one more stop at the grocery store.

After finishing her grocery shopping, she headed home, parked her car in the garage and began unloading the car. Groceries first. She heard the telephone ringing in the kitchen, and hurriedly put down the two grocery bags on the sun porch floor.

"Hello," Kate said.

"You sound out of breath. Is this a bad time?" Richard asked.

"No, I rushed to get the phone, thinking it might be you," she replied.

"That kind of thinking makes me feel really good," he said and laughed.

"Hang on a minute. I need to get my groceries inside. I put them on the floor to open the kitchen door. It's wide open. Hold on." She let the phone dangle while bringing the bags inside and quickly put away the items that needed refrigeration. "Okay, I'm back."

"Did you get something from the florist today?" Richard asked.

"I did. After work I came home to change clothes before I went shopping. Apparently, the florist left the delivery at my neighbor's house next door. I guess she saw my car parked on the driveway, and she brought it over, shortly after I got home. I love the centerpiece, Richard. Thank you."

"You mentioned you were having some family over for Christmas Eve after church. I thought you might need something to spruce up your dining room table," Richard said.

"You are so good to me," Kate responded.

"That's because I love you. By the way, who's coming to dinner?" he asked.

"Only my kids, who live in St. Louis, are coming, but it really isn't a dinner. I'm making a big pot of chili, along with some finger food, and I ordered a Christmas cake from the bakery."

"Tell me the names of your children again, Kate. The other day I was trying to remember all of their names and where they lived, but knew I didn't have it right."

"Well, here goes from oldest to youngest. Mary Rose, Mike Jr., Andy, Abby, Patrick, Sean and Ryan. All of them are married except Andy and Sean. After you've master learning the names in this lineup, I'll tell you who is married to whom by name. There are also many grandchildren, too," Kate said.

"Thanks for your mercy. That is some roll call. Do you think I will ever get to meet them?" he asked.

"You will, but probably not all at once. It's hard to get my family together at one time in one place," she replied.

"I know what you mean. I have the same problem, but I am working on a plan for you to meet my daughters and son. The girls are planning to give RJ a surprise fortieth birthday party at his house in Indy. His birthday is coming up next month. I intend to send you an airline ticket. You can join the party and meet my family at the same time," Richard said.

His last remark hit home. To her way of thinking, an invitation to meet his family indicated a turning point in their relationship, upping the level of it.

"What do you say to that?" Richard asked.

"Thanks for asking me," she said, conveying her appreciation for the invite, but not committing herself and changed the subject. "Did you get my package, Richard?"

"Yes, I did, Kate. I put it under the tree."

"I thought you told me you weren't going to do any decorating or bother putting up a tree, because you were going to be by yourself," Kate said.

"Louise got on my case and brought out all the Christmas stuff, while I was away. I finally gave in," Richard admitted.

"Good for Louise."

"Did you get my package?" he asked.

"I did. It was on the front porch when I got home today," she answered.

"Did you open it?" he asked.

"No. When I got home from work I was in a hurry to get to the shopping center. I put it on the kitchen table before I left. I'm looking at it now," Kate replied.

"What do you say I give you a late call Christmas Eve? We can open our gifts together, while we talk on the phone," Richard suggested.

"That's a great idea. How about around midnight? By that time, everyone will have left," Kate replied.

They said their goodbyes. As Kate was putting away the gifts she had purchased, she thought about Richard's plan for her to meet his family. The relationship was taking on a more serious momentum, making her somewhat apprehensive. She was getting in deeper and deeper and had heard nothing from the Tribunal, concerning her petition for annulment.

CHAPTER FORTY-ONE
Richard

The conference room at Lawton and McBride had been turned into a dining area for the firm's Christmas party. Richard and Stan were standing in the doorway, as each employee entered the room, wishing them Merry Christmas.

"I think everyone is enjoying the luncheon, Richard," Stan said. "Choosing an Italian cuisine was a good choice."

"You can't beat Manetta's. Their food is always excellent," Richard replied.

"Yes, I think so, too. I'm glad we started doing this for our people years ago, Richard."

"They're a good crew, Stan. I don't think I've ever heard any of them complain when we had to ask them to stay overtime to complete a deadline on a job, either. There's nothing that works better in business than a mutual admiration society between the employer and the employees."

"I thought we would pass out the bonus checks after everyone gets through eating," Stan suggested.

"Fine with me. I am going to leave after that. I've got a couple of stops to make before I go home. Don't worry about the cleaning up. I've already taken care of that with the night crew," Richard said.

"Merry Christmas, Richard," Stan said. He grasped Richard's hand, giving him a firm handshake. "Our time together as partners is drawing to a close. This is our last Christmas party together. You're the best partner a man could have," Stan said in a voice that betrayed his emotion.

"Thank you and Merry Christmas," Richard replied. "We've had a good run, Stan."

"One of the best, and one I won't forget," Stan replied. "Let's give the group another ten minutes, then we'll pass out the checks. I'll hand you each envelope, and you can call out the name."

"Fine," Richard replied.

After the festivities ended and the bonus checks were distributed, Richard walked to his office, put on his coat and left to deliver the fruit basket to Vinita, his last stop of the day.

Richard spent the evening watching a rerun of an old Christmas movie and fell asleep.

The crackling of the fire awakened him. He looked at his watch. It was almost midnight. It was time to call Kate, and he dialed her number.

It rang several times before she picked it up and said, "Hello."

"Hope I haven't interrupted anything. Has everyone left?" Richard asked.

"Yes. I'm here by myself," Kate responded. "I was downstairs putting a load in the washer, when I heard the phone ring."

"How was the church service?" he asked.

"There wasn't an empty pew, Richard. It was so crowded people stood along the wall of both side aisles. Beautiful poinsettia plants were placed on the altar and side altars. Before the Mass the choir sang some of the traditional Christmas hymns, and during communion they sang *O Holy Night*. Christmas Eve Mass is so moving. When I left church, I felt my soul was at peace."

"I don't think I've ever attended a Christmas service in the Catholic Church," Richard said.

"If you had, you would have remembered it," Kate replied.

Richard thought about his own Methodist upbringing. During his years growing up, his family walked to church to attend the

Sunday service. After he was married, he traveled extensively. Often, his job required him to work Sunday mornings. When his children came along, he quit the traveling job and raised his children in the Methodist faith. He and his family became regular churchgoers.

When Betty became wheelchair bound, he bought a van with a lift. With his help, she was still able to attend church services and have a limited social life. When she entered the nursing home, he spent Sunday mornings visiting her. He did not stop believing; he simply stopped attending church services.

He stopped his woolgathering and asked, "How did the party go afterwards?"

"Everyone had a good time. They cleaned me out of food. I have a little chili left and a few pieces of cake. The finger food was a big hit, too. We opened packages later. All of them left about half an hour ago," Kate answered.

"Speaking of packages, where are you sitting?" he asked.

"I'm in bed. Your package is right beside me."

"You unwrap yours first," Richard said.

"I'm going to put the phone down so it may be a few minutes." She didn't wait for his reply and began opening the box he had sent. After tearing off the brown shipping paper, she found something in the box of considerable size wrapped in bubble wrap. Carefully removing the bubble wrap, she gasped when she saw the picture. It was a pencil sketch of her in a silver frame, double matted in azure blue and light blue. He had captured her in a side pose while driving. In the right-hand corner, he had written *To My Kate, at last. All my love, Richard.*

"Oh, Richard. This is really a surprise."

"Do you like it, Kate?"

"Yes, yes, I do. I never dreamed anyone would ever do a drawing of me."

"I took a picture of you the very first time we went to Lieu des Lacs to see Frank Ambrose and used the photo I took as reference. I caught you when you weren't looking, which explains the side view."

"Thank you so much. Frankly, I don't know how you found time to do it with all the many things going on in your life," Kate said, truly moved.

"You go to school in the evening, Kate; I paint in the evening. I'm glad you like it."

She put his gift down on the bed and asked, "Have you my package nearby?"

"I do," he replied.

"Time to open your gift," Kate said.

Richard put down the phone. She heard the sound of paper tearing. When he opened the box, he found a smaller one wrapped in Christmas paper. He picked up the phone and said, "Beautifully wrapped, Kate."

He then slipped off the ribbon and bow, tore the Christmas wrapping paper away and looked at his gift. Kate had framed a picture of the Missourian in a handsome walnut frame. Below the picture was an engraving on a silver plate which read, *On a lake, under God's blue sky, a log home calls to me. To come and paint and live my life, a dream that dares to be.*

She, too, had doubled matted his gift in azure blue and light blue. Also, in the box was a walnut easel. He took the easel from the box and put the picture to rest on it.

"You still there?" he asked.

"I'm here," she replied.

"Thank you, Kate. Now, I have something to look at every day to remind me of where my life is taking me."

"Did you notice both of us picked out the same color of mats?" she asked.

"Yes. We think alike in so many ways. Many times I know exactly what you are going to say before you say it, and when I ask you something, it usually mirrors my thoughts. You see, Kate, we are truly soul mates. We were meant to be together. Sleep well. I'll talk to you soon. I love you. Merry Christmas, Kate."

"I love you back. Merry Christmas, Richard."

He did not want to spoil the moment by telling her he would not be able to return to St. Louis for awhile. He would tell her that news later in a letter.

CHAPTER FORTY-TWO
Kate

Sleep eluded Kate after Richard's phone call. Her mind would not shut down. She knew Richard loved her and showed his love in so many ways. He listened to her, asked about her day, took an interest in her goals and dreams and supported them. He also appreciated her input even if he didn't always agree with it and treated her as an equal in every aspect of their relationship. Most importantly, he valued her.

Richard was definitely more open in expressing his feelings toward her while Mike was just the opposite. However, when she read the answers Mike had submitted to the Tribunal about their marriage, his answers shocked her, making it difficult for her to forget them. Occasionally, some little thing would trigger the memory of them, causing her great anguish one more time, just like now.

His answers to the Tribunal questions would always trouble her, mainly because she had difficulty in believing them. She again recalled his written responses to the Tribunal questions: He married her, because she was pregnant. Not because he loved her, but he was the father and had been brought up to do the right thing. If she hadn't been pregnant, there would have been no marriage. In his mind, it was never going to be a permanent situation.

It was the last one which troubled her the most.

Every time she thought about his responses, her self-esteem took another hit. It wasn't because she still had feelings for him, but she simply wanted to know the truth and after thirty years felt she deserved it.

Had he submitted those responses because he wanted an annulment to marry, telling the Tribunal what he thought they wanted to hear? Or, was he actually telling the truth?

Obviously, when he didn't get the annulment he applied for in order to marry in the Catholic Church, the marriage plans fell through. However, the lack of an annulment hadn't stopped him from eventually marrying a non-Catholic woman later, outside of the church. By that time, both of his parents had passed, and he didn't have to answer to anyone. His sister, who was younger and single, was still living but would never question any of his actions.

Kate yearned for valid and absolute closure from her marriage to Mike Flannigan. She needed to know if Mike's responses to the annulment questions were his true feelings. She wanted to move on emotionally and spiritually, knowing the truth would accomplish this, giving her peace of mind, even after all this passage of time.

When she discussed this with Father Steve some time ago, he told her she might never know the real feelings of her ex-husband and advised her not to dwell on the matter. It was an enigma, one she would have to learn to live with.

She turned off the light and said her prayers, tired from the exhaustion of again trying to figure out thirty years of living with a man she thought she knew.

* * * * *

Kate received Richard's letter several days after Christmas, informing her he wouldn't be able to attend Ruth's New Year's Eve party nor did he know when he would be coming back to St. Louis. Due to the upcoming takeover, he needed to spend time with Stan tying up loose ends and closing the books for the year. After reading his letter, Kate was disappointed, but understood the situation.

For the past couple of years, Ruth hosted a New Year's Eve party in her basement, which was perfect for entertaining. There was bar, a mini kitchen, a bathroom and a large room with a couch, comfortable chairs and a television. This year, Kate, her three sons, Andy, Sean and Ryan and his wife Christine, a couple of coworkers, who were friendly with both Kate and Ruth, and several neighbors were invited. Ruth's single son, David, who was visiting for the holidays this year, would also be there. Ruth supplied the sandwiches and beverages. The guests were asked to bring a covered dish.

They were a good group, and between charades and a game David brought called *Pictionary*, everybody had lots of laughs and a great time.

A tradition had been established over the years for everyone to bang a pot at the stroke of midnight to welcome in the New Year. Before the clock struck midnight, Ruth made sure everyone had a pot and a spoon or one of her baking utensils to carry out the ritual. Those newly invited thought the pot-banging was pretty silly, but went along with it. One minute to midnight, they all convened on Ruth's front lawn for the countdown. At the appointed time, they banged their pots amid lots of laughter. The ones who had been introduced to the ritual for the first time banged the loudest. Happy New Year wishes and hugs were exchanged.

Several porch lights came on. Some of Ruth's neighbors waved to the group. Over the past couple of years, her neighbors had gotten use to the way Ruth's friends brought in the New Year and made no effort to diminish its intensity and purpose.

Welcoming in the New Year was over, and the group went back inside the house. Within a short time, goodbyes were said. Kate's family was the last to leave. She hugged her friend and said, "Another great party, Ruth. Those beef sandwiches you made were wonderful as always."

"Thanks for bringing your bunch. They sure know how to liven up a party, especially Andy," Ruth said.

"Let me tell you something. If you're looking for a good time, Andy's number is the one you should dial."

"I'm lucky to have a friend like you, Kate," Ruth said.

"That admiration is returned tenfold," Kate replied.

They hugged and said goodbye. Ruth waited until they all got in their cars and then turned out the porch light.

When Kate arrived home, the light was flashing on her answering machine. She pressed the button and heard Richard's voice. "Hope you are having fun at Ruth's. I poured myself a glass of wine and toasted the New Year via the television and the dropping of the ball. I made a resolution. Here goes. I resolve to make every effort known to mankind to get us together forever, as soon as humanly possible. And, people have always said I am a man of my word. I love you. Happy New Year."

The one thought running through Kate's mind, as she deleted Richard's message, was the need to tell him about the pending annulment. She should have listened to Ruth and done so a long time ago.

The weeks after the New Year passed quickly for Kate. It was back to business as usual concerning work and classes. Richard's calls and letters kept her current on what was happening in his life, and her usual Friday and Saturday agenda resumed with Ruth.

Every Monday morning, Kate received flowers from Richard, which continued to attract the attention of her co-workers. He had to be spending a lot of money, sending a bouquet every week. A shiver of guilt went through her every time she thought about the bouquets. She was not looking forward to telling Richard about her marital status in the eyes of the Catholic Church and had only a short time before his visit this coming weekend to think about how she was going to do it.

* * * * *

Kate was standing over the sink looking out the window when she saw a car turn the corner and recognized Richard behind the wheel. He waved and honked several times and parked on her driveway. She opened the sun porch door and watched him walk up the stone path to the door.

"How's my steady gal?" he said, enfolding her in his arms.

"I'm improving by the minute," she replied, and they kissed, both reluctant to pull away.

"Now, that's what I've been missing," Richard said, as they broke apart.

"You've come to the right place," Kate said.

They went into the kitchen with arms around each other's waist. Richard took off his coat and sat down at the kitchen table.

"How about a cup of coffee?" Kate asked.

"Sounds good. I've already checked in at The Leland. I got a call from Jake Davidson. He thought it would be a good idea to pick out cabinets and tile for the kitchen and bathrooms the next time I was in town. I told him I was coming to St. Louis this weekend. If you've got nothing planned, we could drive down to his showroom and finish up this last piece of business. That leaves only the stone for the fireplace to decide upon later. Okay?" Richard asked.

"Sure. We've had incredible warm weather for January so far. The powers that be seem to know you are in the process of building a house and are giving you great temps. I assume work has been started."

"Yes, it has. I've already received some pictures from Frank."

"Can't fool me. Your excitement is showing. You want to see the site for yourself, don't you?" she asked.

"Yes, I do."

"Since we don't have anything planned for tonight, we can make both New Brunswick and Lieu des Lacs, too," Kate said.

She went into the closet and got her coat and boots.

Richard followed her and said, "Well, we do have someplace to go tonight. I got tickets for the hockey game. The Blues are favored to win; they're playing the Montreal Canadians. Have you ever been to a hockey game, Kate?"

"No, I haven't, but I've always wanted to go. Andy is a big hockey fan and goes when he can afford it. How did you get tickets at the last minute?"

"Magic, my dear, pure magic and a phone call to a St. Louis business buddy of mine whose next job at Lawton and McBride will be done at a big discount."

"Do you always get what you go after?" she asked.

"Only when the odds are in my favor," Richard replied.

They locked up the house, got into his car and began driving to New Brunswick.

The afternoon was spent taking care of business at New Brunswick and visiting the building site at Lieu des Lacs. In order to save time, they ate at Miss Tillie's before going to the hockey game. After the game they returned to Kate's house.

"What a contest," Richard said. "Did you enjoy it?"

"I think the players just like to fight," Kate said.

"There's always plenty of that," Richard said, as he put his arm around her.

They were curled up on the couch with a fire going, drinking wine. Richard put his wine glass down on the table and turned to her, taking her hands in his and said, "My letters and phone calls over the past months and our other times together should have erased any doubts as to why I am here, Kate. I came down to see if there were sparks between us after all these years. Your reaction to my advances tells me there are sparks on your part that match my own."

Kate said nothing to confirm or deny Richard's last statement. She was shaken by his seriousness and realized she was sitting next to a man who was carving out a new destiny for himself and wanted her to join him.

"I know my re-entry into your life has happened unexpectedly, but I made my intentions clear from the very beginning. And, they should not totally surprise you now. I want to begin a new life with you, Kate. We're both free to do so."

When Kate heard the word *free*, she moved away from him. "But, Richard..."

"Let me finish, Kate. I want to clear up some things that might be bothering you about my situation. Before Betty became really ill and with no hope of recovery, my lawyer advised me to divorce her. He told me the government would get a huge portion of my earnings, when she was confined to a nursing facility, which her doctors told me would be for the remainder of her life. I was advised to get a divorce to protect the assets I made—assets I would need, so I could pay for her care, the length of which is still unknown to her doctors. At the time of the divorce, Betty fully understood the reasoning behind it and agreed to it willingly. So you see, legally, I'm free."

Kate looked at him without responding to what he had just said. Instead, in the saddest of tones, she said, "But, I'm not."

"I don't understand. You're divorced like I am."

"Yes, but divorce is a little more complicated, Richard, when you're a Catholic."

When he heard the word Catholic, he drew in his breath. He always felt not being of the same faith as Kate when they were younger played a big part in her choosing someone of her own faith to marry back then.

"What do you mean by complicated?" he asked.

"I'll try to explain. In a nutshell, I have a legal divorce, but not a dissolution of my marriage to Mike, according to Catholic doctrine. Had Mike gotten his annulment, both of us would be free to marry. And, both of us could marry in the Catholic Church. Since he didn't get it, in the eyes of the Catholic Church, we are still married to each other."

Richard could hardly believe what he had just heard. It simply didn't make any sense to him.

Kate continued, "I didn't participate in the proceedings, because I didn't want to be blamed one way or the other. I decided to let the Tribunal make their judgment based on his responses concerning our marriage. He was the one who wanted an annulment to remarry, not me. He needed it to get married in the Catholic Church, probably because the woman he wanted as his wife was a Catholic with living parents. Two months later he withdrew his petition, and I thought that was the end of it. But, several months later, he approached the Tribunal to reopen the investigation. The Tribunal denied his annulment eventually, because he could not prove the nullity of our marriage.

"There was a time when I thought he might ask to come back, right after his annulment was denied. Had he asked, I might have taken him back. I would have done anything to have my family whole again.

"His leaving and divorcing me made me feel like a failure. It took me a long time to come to grips with that. Rejection isn't easy to handle, especially after thirty years of marriage. I felt if he couldn't love me, obviously no one else could either.

"I've walked a long and painful road, Richard, and so have our children because of the breakdown of our marriage and, consequently, our home.

"It took me quite awhile to get my head on straight and become the old Kate again. I finally accepted the fact Mike did not want to be married to me. I then went to see Father Steve, my parish priest. After I told him about the situation, he advised me to seek an annulment, which is in the works."

"How long does this annulment process take?" Richard asked.

"Anywhere from nine months to a year, sometimes longer."

"You said something about an annulment being in the works. What does that mean?"

"I have petitioned for one, and it is pending."

"Why didn't you tell me this before?"

"Everything has happened so fast between us. I guess I was caught up in being loved and loving you. I'm sorry, Richard."

"What happens if you don't get it?"

Her voice broke when she said, "I'd have to make a choice."

"Which would be what?"

"I could remarry, but not in the Catholic Church. If I did remarry outside the Catholic Church, I would not be able to receive communion."

"I've never understood the rules and rituals of the Catholic religion, Kate, and frankly, I'm glad I was not raised Catholic. Too much control and guilt to my way of thinking." From the tone of his voice, Kate realized how very upset he was. When he rose from the couch and began to pace back and forth, his actions confirmed this.

By the pained expression on her face, he knew she was holding something back. "What is it, Kate? There's more to this, isn't there?"

She was crying now and did not appear as if she was going to respond.

He was losing patience and asked her again, "What is it, Kate? Tell me."

Looking directly into his eyes, she said almost in a whisper, "I shouldn't be sleeping with you, either."

By this time, Richard was beside himself. The more Kate explained, the more angry he became. "Are you saying our lovemaking is sinful?"

"Oh, Richard. I knew you wouldn't understand. Maybe I've explained it poorly."

"No. You've explained it pretty well. I get it. Here I wanted to ease your mind over my situation, and now my mind is boggled by yours."

He went to the closet to get his coat. Kate got up and followed him, not knowing what to say or do. He put on his coat and turned to her and said, "I can't compete with your religion, Kate, and your guilt is too compelling for me right now."

He opened the door and left, leaving her standing in the foyer. She watched him drive away with tears streaming down her face. She had made a big mistake by not telling him sooner about the pending annulment.

Maybe she wouldn't have to make a choice after all. Apparently, Richard had already made it for her.

CHAPTER FORTY-THREE
Richard

All the way back to South Bend, Richard replayed last night's scene with Kate over and over in his head. He had checked out of The Leland earlier than he had told her, hoping to avoid seeing her had she shown up unexpectedly. The last thing he wanted to do was rehash the events of the previous evening. What happened in her living room last night was too raw and cut him to the bone. He wondered if she might have phoned him at the motel. And, if she had, what could she possibly say to him that would make any difference?

It was shortly after lunch when he pulled into his garage. He was exhausted, mentally and physically. He unpacked the car and brought his things into the house. The light on the kitchen phone was blinking. He put down his suitcase and pressed the button to retrieve his messages. Ken had called and so had Laura Lee. There was no message from Kate. He wanted to hear her voice, and he didn't. His emotions were like a roller coaster.

After checking the mailbox, he took the mail and his suitcase upstairs to his bedroom. He unpacked and took a hot shower. Dressed in sweats, he sat on the edge of the bed, intending to go through the mail, but his eyelids became heavy. He fell back on the bed pillow and surrendered to his tiredness. The mail slipped from his fingers and fell to the floor.

When he awoke, he looked at the clock on the bedside table. He had slept away most of the afternoon. After picking up the mail from the floor, he quickly dressed in casual clothes and went downstairs. He took a can of Diet Coke from the fridge, fixed himself a sandwich and put them on a table next to his chair in the living room, so he could watch television while he ate. When he finished eating, he looked at his watch. There was still time to check on Betty, before they served dinner at the nursing facility. Grabbing a jacket from the hall closet, he noticed there was no blinking light on the telephone in the kitchen on his way out, indicating no message.

Richard spent a restless night tossing and turning and decided to finally get up much earlier than usual. He couldn't wait to get to the office. The work that awaited him would more than occupy his mind and definitely keep him from thinking about his personal problems with Kate. He had some phone calls to make, including the florist in St. Louis.

Shortly after he sat down at his desk, his telephone rang, and he answered it.

"Hey, it's Ken. I called you over the weekend but didn't leave a message. I figured you were out of town."

"I was."

Although Richard was abrupt with him, Ken asked, "How about lunch?"

Richard hesitated, and Ken picked up on it.

"If you're swamped, I get it. Mondays are always a bear. If you don't want to go, I get that, too. We'll do lunch some other time. No big deal," Ken said.

"Sorry, Ken. I'm not in the best of moods. I didn't mean to be rude. Lunch is good, but let's not eat at The Stadium. I'm just not up to Vinita's sunny disposition today. How about we go somewhere else?"

"Fine, you name it."

"Let's meet at noon at Manetta's." Ken agreed, and Richard hung up the phone. He needed to talk to someone, and who better than

Ken? He was also a Catholic. Maybe Ken could help him understand the predicament he had gotten himself into.

Manetta's was busy. Richard entered the restaurant and looked around for his friend. All of the booths were taken, but he saw Ken waving. Richard gave him a nod and walked toward the table in the back where Ken was sitting. He took off his coat, laid it across one of the empty chairs and said nothing to Ken in the way of a greeting.

"Well, hello to you, too. Pardon me for saying so, but you don't look so good, even if it is Monday," Ken said.

"That's what I like about you most, Ken. You are one truthful son of a so-and-so."

Richard sat down without saying another word. Ken decided to let Richard open the conversation and waited for him to say something, but Richard just sat there. The waitress appeared and took their orders. After she left, the silence finally got on Ken's nerves and said, "All right, lay it on me. Something must be troubling you big time for you to stay quiet this long. Is it Betty?"

"No. I went to visit her late yesterday afternoon before dinner was served at the nursing home. She's the same. No change."

"Then, what's eating you?" Ken asked.

"Ken, you're a Catholic. I hope you can explain something to me that I simply cannot understand," and he told his friend about the disturbing discussion with Kate.

"I know you don't want to hear this, but she's right," his friend said. "She is divorced, according to state law, which makes her legally free, but not according to Catholic law. If her annulment is not granted, she can still marry, but the marriage would have to take place somewhere other than a Catholic Church."

"Kate would never do that, Ken," Richard said.

"How did you leave things?"

"I told her I didn't want to compete with her faith and walked out."

"Far be it from me to sit in judgment of your actions, Richard. You've obviously come to me for information, not a reprimand. Whether you want to acknowledge it or not, your future with Kate hangs in the balance of a Catholic Tribunal. They're going to base their decision on her answers to the questions they asked, concerning her Catholic marriage.

"Listen to me, Richard. The annulment process takes time. It's possible she will be granted the annulment. I read somewhere the Pope is granting more leniency to those seeking an annulment these days. If you love her, wouldn't it be better to wait until she finds out one way or the other?"

"I do love her, Ken, but I was burned badly by Kate before, when I was young, and she married someone else. I have no intention of putting myself through that emotional wringer again, especially at this stage of my life."

The waitress came with their food and served them.

"I'm sorry, Ken. I don't feel like eating." He got up, took out his wallet, laid some money on the table, faced his friend and said, "It has been made very clear to me that happiness with Kate is something I am not supposed to have." He put on his coat, turned and walked toward the exit.

Ken did nothing to stop him.

CHAPTER FORTY-FOUR
Kate

After Sunday Mass, Kate came directly home. She tried to study but could not concentrate, rehashing in her mind again the awful scene she had with Richard. The memory of it lingered. And, the worst part, she didn't know what to do about it. She thought about calling Ruth or her sister and telling them what had happened between her and Richard, but for what purpose? It isn't as if she needed advice; she wanted a solution. Maybe it was even too late for that, as far as Richard was concerned. He had been so angry when he left.

The afternoon turned into evening. Her telephone had yet to ring. Richard always called her around this time. She looked at her watch. There was no point in waiting. He wasn't going to call. She said her prayers and went to bed.

Monday morning began like all the others, and Kate was grateful to find her basket overloaded with work that would keep her mind from thinking about her personal problems with Richard. By mid-morning, she had accomplished a great deal, although the basket was far from empty. She looked up from her computer and saw Ruth.

"Here are the packets for this week's marketing meeting, Kate," Ruth said. "I'm sorry I am a little late in getting them to you. The copier broke down again. I had to go to another department to use one and wait my turn. Hey, where are the usual Monday morning flowers? They're always here before I make my drop offs."

"I doubt very much if there will be any more Monday morning flowers," Kate replied. Apparently, Richard wasted no time in contacting the florist to cancel his weekly order, but she was not going to let Ruth know how much this had hurt her. It had nothing to do with the absence of the flowers, but everything to do with the message it sent.

"From the expression on your face, Kate, something has happened. What's going on?" Ruth asked. She hadn't seen her friend over the weekend and did not have time this morning to stop at the donut shop.

"I can't talk now. Did you bring your lunch, Ruth?"

"Are you kidding? Today's Monday. I'm doing good to get myself here on time let alone pack a lunch."

"Can you meet me in the cafeteria?" Kate asked.

"Sure. What time?" Ruth asked.

"Let's go late, so we'll miss the crowd. I'll meet you at 1 p.m.," Kate replied.

When it was finally time to meet her friend, Kate hurried to the cafeteria. After they went through the serving line, they took a table in the far corner of the cafeteria dining room, so they would have privacy. They emptied their trays, and Ruth spoke first. "Can you give me a clue what this is all about?"

"My faith, Ruth. It's about my faith and Richard."

"I'm assuming things did not go well between you and Richard this past weekend," Ruth said hesitantly.

"That's an understatement," Kate said, and she told Ruth about the blowup between her and Richard. When she finished, she waited for some kind of a response from her friend, and, when Ruth said nothing, she called her on it. "Say something."

"Do you think the relationship is over? Is the door closed, or is there a chance to put the relationship back together?" Ruth asked.

"I don't know. I really don't know. When he left, he was very angry," Kate said.

"Look at the positive side first. If your annulment is granted, then you will be free—free to decide if marrying Richard is what you want. If it isn't granted, and Richard is still in the picture and asks you to marry him, you'll have to choose, Kate. Either marry him and get hitched elsewhere than a Catholic Church along with no communion or send him away. I hate to mention this, but sleeping with him, while you are waiting for a decision, is adding fuel to the fire, too."

"I know. How does one apologize for being human?" Kate asked.

"Do you know what your decision would be, if you don't get the annulment and he does ask you to marry him?" Ruth asked.

"I could never be anything but a Catholic. I know myself. Then, there's the other problem, the unspeakable one, if the annulment is granted. He has an ex-wife in a nursing home who is very, very sick with no chance of recovery. For me that situation would be every bit as hard to deal with every day as remarrying out of the church. I couldn't handle the guilt in either circumstance if I did marry him, which would eventually destroy the marriage anyway."

"You have nothing to do with his ex-wife's health problem, Kate."

"I know that, Ruth, but…"

Before Kate could explain, Ruth interrupted her. "Has he actually asked you to marry him?"

"No, not in so many words, but he's stated his intentions to me in his very first letter and was probably going to ask me to marry him this past weekend, until I opened my mouth about the annulment."

"Have you heard anything from the Tribunal?" Ruth asked.

"No. Father Steve told me there is no use in calling. I would only be told the case is pending. I wanted so badly to call Richard yesterday it hurt, but I didn't. What good would it have done? I would only be defending myself further and irritating him more." She sighed and said, "Being Catholic is not easy sometimes."

"No, it isn't," Ruth agreed.

Kate toyed with her food, pushing it around the plate and waited for Ruth to say something. When she didn't, she looked up and said, "Help me, Ruth. What should I do?"

"I love you like a sister, Kate, but only you can decide for yourself what to do. Maybe Richard will call, and you can mend the fences. If he doesn't and you're asking for my advice, do nothing. Wait until you hear from the Tribunal. You're trying to take control of the situation, and it's futile. In the meantime, put yourself in God's hands and pray."

CHAPTER FORTY-FIVE
Richard

Due to the impending takeover and the building of the log house, Richard's days were busy. Luckily, the couple, who were buying his home, were willing to give him ample time to vacate with a tentative closing date that fit everyone's plans. Each weekend, little by little, he began clearing out things he would not be taking with him. It occupied his mind and kept him from thinking about Kate, although not completely.

While sitting at his office desk, he thought again about his handling of what Kate had told him concerning her marital status in the eyes of her church. The florist order had been cancelled immediately, not to punish her, but to sever all romantic notions of courting her. He wrote no letters and made no phone calls to her, either. Pouring himself into his work had been his modus operandi for years. He returned to that safe haven, filling his mind every day with business and family matters.

Looking at his calendar, he had made an earlier note to himself to call Frank Ambrose sometime during the first week in February. Today was as good a day as any. He picked up the phone and dialed Frank's number.

"Lieu des Lacs Realty, Frank Ambrose speaking."

"Hi, Frank. It's Richard Lawton."

"Hi, Richard. I was going to call you later today. Our minds are running in the same direction."

"What's happening?" Richard asked.

"I think it's time for you to come down and look over some things. There's no problem. I just want to make certain we're all on the same page at this stage," Frank replied.

"Great. How about this coming weekend? I'll drive down Saturday and get there shortly after lunch."

"Works for me. See you then," Frank said.

Richard hung up the phone. He would have to stay all night unless he wanted to turn right around and drive back, which he didn't want to do. Maybe he would visit his sister. He hadn't talked to her in a long while. He could stay at her house Saturday night and drive back home Sunday morning, even though it would mean a longer drive for him. The last place he wanted to stay at was The Leland.

He dialed Connie's number.

It rang three times before she answered. "Hello."

"Hi, Connie. It's Richard."

"Richard. It's good to hear from you. How are things going, and how is Betty?"

"Things are going okay. As for Betty, nothing has changed. All they can do is to continue the medication which makes her comfortable."

"I'm sorry, Richard. I wish I could do something to help."

"You have, sis, by your caring thoughts and words," Richard said.

Connie changed the subject and said, "I hope you're calling to tell me you're coming this way. We haven't seen each other in a blue moon."

"As a matter of fact, I am. How about putting me up this Saturday night? I'm leaving early Saturday morning and driving down to Lieu des Lacs. I'm not particularly keen on turning right around and driving back home the same day after I finish my business there."

"You know better than to ask. Of course, you can stay. My darling husband is away this weekend, playing golf in Florida. We'll have time to catch up. I'll even make a nice dinner for the two of us. We'll light a fire and settle all the world's problems and maybe a few of our own over a good bottle of wine."

"Food and drink. You've said the magic words. See you soon and thanks," and he ended the call.

* * * * *

Frank heard footsteps on the porch and hurried to open the door for Richard. "Hello, again. You made good time. Have a seat."

"I got your latest pictures, Frank. Thanks for sending them. I intend to check on the building progress, after I finish my business with you. I can't believe the weather here. Every day I listen to the weather forecast for this area. According to what I've heard, a mild winter for the rest of February and March is predicted."

"We're definitely getting a break," Frank replied.

"I know you're anxious to be on your way so no more small talk. If we put our noses together, this won't take too long. I need your signature on two documents. After you sign them, I'll take both of them over to the Recorder's Office myself," Frank said.

Within a short time they finished their business. He saw Richard to the door, and they shook hands. "Thanks for coming down, Richard. You and your wife are sure lucky to be owners of such a fine home."

Richard made no effort to correct Frank's last statement nor did he smile or give him a nod to even acknowledge his remark. Richard saw a puzzled look on Frank's face and the shrugging of his shoulders before Frank closed the door. It was not like him to be rude, but it was too late. He knew he had hurt Frank's feelings.

On the drive to his sister's home, he stopped to buy a bottle of wine. When he arrived, Connie greeted him with a hug and said, "I'll chill this one for later. Wash up, dinner's almost ready. Since there is only the two of us, I thought we would eat in the kitchen."

"Wonderful. I hope you haven't gone to a great deal of trouble," he said.

"You're no trouble, Richard. I'm so happy you're here."

After having dinner, Connie suggested opening Richard's wine and having it in the living room.

"You're a good cook, Connie. The meal was great."

"You're welcome. I'm glad you enjoyed it. Now, tell me all the news."

They sat on Connie's couch in the living room. Richard brought her up-to-date on what was happening at his business and the log house but made no mention of his personal affairs.

"I bumped into Carolyn Martin at the library. Although Carolyn did not betray any confidences, I put two and two together. I gather you and Kate have had a falling out," Connie said.

There was no sense beating around the bush in Connie's mind, so she brought up a scene from the past and said, "I was in the kitchen washing dishes the night Mom told you that you would never marry Kate, because she is a Catholic."

"It appears she was right, Connie. Maybe I should be applauding Kate rather than criticizing her. She always stood firm in her beliefs when we were in high school. That was one of the many things that drew me to her. However, still being married to Mike Flannigan on paper is beyond me."

Connie replied, "And, what she wrote on paper, Richard, will decide whether she gets an annulment or not, according to what I understand."

"That may be true, Connie, but, as far as I'm concerned if her annulment is not granted, I am not going to volunteer for that kind of disappointment again. Been there, done that with Kate many, many years ago. You have no idea how hard, how very hard, it has been for me to walk away."

"You surprise me, Richard. I never thought my brother was a quitter. You're giving up before you know the outcome. That's so unlike you."

"Maybe, but think about it. If Kate doesn't get the annulment and really loves me, I have put her in a position of having to choose— marrying me outside of the Catholic Church and all the other negatives that decision would entail or walking away. Either way, it spells regret, but the latter would be much easier to live with for Kate. I've tried, and I've lost."

He put down his wine glass on the table and walked out of the room, leaving his sister alone to think about what he had just said.

CHAPTER FORTY-SIX
Kate

The routine of Kate's life before Richard entered it took hold again, and the days passed into weeks. Work and classes continued to fill her weekdays, and on the weekends she did things with Ruth. She missed Richard and was having a hard time of it. Every time she looked at the ring on her finger, it brought back the memories of him and their time together.

She came home from work, fixed herself something to eat and intended to spend the rest of the evening at her computer, typing up some notes for class. She was interrupted by the ringing of the telephone and went to answer it.

"Hello." She waited for the caller to say something.

"Hi, Kate. I hope I am not interrupting anything," Jackie said.

"No, you haven't interrupted anything. I needed a break anyway. I'm working on a paper for school, that's all. I'm sorry I haven't called, but...."

Jackie interrupted her sister and said, "It's okay, Kate. I understand, but I ran into Richard's sister Connie at the hairdresser's today. Connie gets her hair done at the same place I do. I sat next to her while both of us were waiting. We had some time to visit. Among other things, she told me Richard's wife or rather ex-wife, passed away last week."

Kate said nothing, and the silence lengthened. She had confided in Jackie concerning the situation between her and Richard shortly after they broke up. Jackie was well aware of the reasons for their parting.

"You still there?" Jackie asked.

"I'm here," Kate replied.

"I just thought you might want to know," Jackie added.

When her sister didn't make any effort to respond, Jackie changed the subject. "How's everybody at your end?"

"Everybody's fine," Kate said and filled her in on the latest news about the family.

The exchange of incidentals continued as if neither one of them wanted to broach the subject concerning the real reason Jackie had called her. Finally, when Jackie ran out of things to say she said, "Well, I better let you go. I'll talk to you soon. Take care of yourself."

"You, too," Kate replied, hanging up the phone. She thought about Richard's loss. Normally, when someone passed away Kate would send a sympathy card to the family. However, if she sent one to Richard after all the weeks of silence he might interpret it as something more than condolences—maybe the reopening of the door on her part.

She remembered the advice Ruth had given her about putting herself in God's hands and decided to heed it. Her intentions would be expressed in prayer instead. She resumed working on her paper, knowing she had made the right decision.

CHAPTER FORTY-SEVEN
Richard

After the funeral, Laura Lee, Diane, Rachel and RJ stayed through the weekend to help Richard clear out their mother's things from the nursing home and respond to the bereavement cards they received. Richard was thankful not only for their help, but for their company. It was a very sad time.

They watched old family movies, talked about the good times they shared as a family and told stories about their mother. They reminisced, they laughed and they cried. When they left Sunday night, the house once again became as it was before they arrived. Richard was alone again.

Tiredness had invaded Richard's soul as well as his body. The past months had not been easy for him. Coping with Betty's health, trying to decide what to do with his graphic art business and whether to sell or keep the big house had taken its toll. His finding of Kate only to lose her again had drained him emotionally. Even the smallest decision often depleted his energy. He was on his own again, and loneliness was his companion.

Richard knew in the depth of his heart God had a plan for him, and it was up to him to figure it out. Summoning the willpower to do so was the other side of the coin, often making him wonder if he had the inner strength to rise to the challenge.

Although he was not really hungry, for lack of something to do, he decided to eat. There was plenty of food in the fridge due to the thoughtfulness of his neighbors. He fixed himself a plate of leftovers and brought it into the living room. He sat down to watch a little television, before calling it a day. He was exhausted.

The last week had taken its toll on his body and mind. Sleep evaded him. His nights were spent tossing and turning in his bed. He hoped tonight he would be able to finally get a good night's sleep. He turned off the television, picked up his dirty dishes and went into the kitchen, putting them in the sink.

The following morning Louise heard her employer coming down the steps. When he entered the kitchen, he was still in his pajamas and bathrobe. "Good morning, Mr. L." Taking a better look at him, she said, "You don't look so good. Didn't you sleep well? How about a nice cup of coffee?"

"Coffee would be good," he replied and sat down at the kitchen table.

"You sure you're okay?" she asked.

"Sit down with me, Louise. Pour yourself a cup, too. I want to tell you about the strangest dream I had last night."

She did as she was asked, although this was most odd, and waited for him to continue.

"I went to bed early, after I had something to eat. I laid in bed thinking about the upcoming trip to Chicago to tie up the details with Epson, one of our clients. Over and over again I kept reworking Epson's advertising plan in my mind until I must have fallen asleep. What I'm about to tell you is bizarre, Louise, really bizarre," Richard said, looking directly into her eyes.

Louise nodded. He took her gesture as a sign she was ready to listen.

He pulled his chair closer to her, as if to shield Louise for what she was about to hear.

When I got into my car to go to work, a man was sitting in the front seat. He said good morning to me and told me to hurry, because according to his watch, I was running late. I asked him who he was and what he was doing in my car, but there was something about the man's demeanor that made me ask the question respectfully.

This man had fine, white hair that fell to his shoulders and was well dressed in a suit and topcoat, both of which looked rather new and in good taste. His eyes were his most compelling feature. They were very blue and looked at me with a depth and warmth that completely put me at ease.

He introduced himself and said his name was Spencer. He wanted to tag along with me today since I was going to Chicago, because he wanted to show me something, when I got there. He smiled and asked me to pick up the paper on the way out of the driveway and pointed out to me the paper was by the last honeysuckle bush on the lawn. How he knew it was a honeysuckle bush blew my mind. That bush looked like a bunch of sticks, but I did as I was asked.

He got into the front seat, saying he preferred sitting in the front rather than the back. While he was getting situated, he informed me no one else but me could see or hear him. His business was only with me.

Richard got up from the table to get himself another cup of coffee and also filled Louise's cup. He sat back down, cleared his voice and continued.

After parking the car at the train station, we settled down for the train ride to Chicago. I desperately needed to know why Spencer was now my new best friend. I asked him the real reason why he was here. According to him, where he comes from they like to keep things running smoothly. He told me their computer system is set up so that when the same prayer request comes through over and over again like mine had, it is followed up with immediate action called a Life Review, and he had been assigned to mine. He also said Life Reviews were taken very, very seriously by his superiors.

We got off the train, and I flagged a taxi, giving the cabby Epson's address. Within a short time the cab pulled up in front of the Meridian Building. Both of us stared up at the skyscraper complete with a penthouse. We went inside and got in one of the elevators, which was crowded. Eventually, we were the only two left in the elevator.

Everyone else had gotten off at other floors. However, the elevator passed Epson's floor and continued to climb.

Suddenly, the doors opened. Spencer and I got out. I was immediately blinded by the sunlight. Spencer took my arm and told me they were waiting for me. We walked toward a door. He rang the doorbell. The lock was released, and the door opened into a lush, green meadow with thick, sweet smelling grass. A soft breeze ruffled the leaves on the trees, and the sky was filled with drifting white clouds as the sun spilled its rays on the landscape below.

Louise couldn't help herself and blurted out, "Where did you think you were, Mr. L.?"

"I had no idea, but I did know I had never been there before in my life. It was so beautiful, Louise, and so very peaceful. I felt no fear, only an awareness of harmony and contentment."

Richard stopped speaking and gazed off into space, possibly recalling the feelings he had just described. Louise let him become lost in his thoughts for a few moments but wanted him to continue with his story. She interrupted his reverie and said, "Go on, Mr. L., with your dream."

Richard took a deep breath and picked up where he left off.

Spencer said we would have to walk a spell and hoped I wouldn't mind. We crossed the road into a meadow, which led to a gravel road, and started walking. After we walked a short while, I saw a lone figure in the distance coming toward us. I could see it was a man, but he was too far away for me to recognize. As he got closer, he waved. I stopped in my tracks. It was my brother Nick! He began running toward me.

By this time Richard had become emotional. His voice trembled. "Oh, Louise, I cried out Nick's name over and over again and gathered him into my arms when he reached me. You see, I lost my oldest brother to leukemia when I was fifteen years old. He was only twenty-four when he died. I miss him to this day."

"Was that the end of your dream, seeing your brother?" she asked.

Richard got hold of himself and said, "No, there's more."

Over Nick's shoulder, I saw another figure approaching. As the man got closer, I could see it was my father. We began running toward each other. He took me in his arms and hugged me tightly as I called out his name over and over again.

We stood in the middle of the road and rocked back and forth with our arms around each other in a dance of pure happiness. Both my brother and father looked the way they did when they were in perfect health and so very, very happy.

My father told me Betty had arrived last week. She was doing fine, settling in to the routine and had signed up for the physical fitness program.

After hearing the part about Mr. L's wife, Louise interrupted him and said, "This is really some dream, Mr. L."

"This next part is unbelievable, Louise."

We started down the road, my father, Nick and myself. Within a short time, we were standing in front of a mailbox. The family name, The Lawtons, was printed on the side of the mailbox in big red letters, and I asked my father if he lived there. He said he did not. He lived a distance from where we were.

"The log house we were standing in front of, Louise, was exactly like the one I am currently building, right down to the size of the logs, the two dormers on the roof and the same stone I just selected for the fireplace. There were lace curtains on all the windows. What's really strange, Louise, is that I was only thinking of getting lace curtains for the house yesterday and hadn't mentioned this to anyone or bought any."

Richard stared at Louise intently, assuming she would say something concerning the curtain thing. When she made no effort to comment, he started up again.

The door was opened, so we went in. Leaning over the loft was Spencer. When I turned around, my father and brother had left. Spencer told me they had duties to attend to.

I joined him in the loft, which was a replica of my art studio in South Bend. I opened the drawer of the red tool cabinet that stood against the wall, which was exactly like the red tool cabinet I have in my office. All of my brushes were arranged in rows, according to size, just like I have them at work. An easel and two tables were also there, again like the furniture in my office. Even the desk had the same damaged drawer front as the one I sit at every day.

Spencer then showed me the room facing the lake. It had the touches of a woman's hand. Fresh flowers were on the dresser. I could tell the quilt on the bed was handmade. The furniture was old but polished to a sheen. Next to the bed was a rocking chair that I remembered my grandmother sitting in when I visited her as a young boy.

I walked around to the other side of the bed. My eyes were drawn to a small object that was on the nightstand. I could hardly believe what I saw. It was a miniature Bible with a Cross on top just like the one I had given to Kate many years ago. I picked it up and pulled down the knob on top. Inside was a rosary, also just like the one I gave to Kate.

I turned around and asked Spencer why he had brought me here—the log house just like the one I was building, the loft fixed up like my office in South Bend, Nick and Pop and the rosary I held in my hand.

He told me every one has to find their way home. He had given me a glimpse of what might be in the hope it would help me in some way. However, he was very clear when he told me it was up to me to find my own answers.

He then asked me to close the bedroom curtains. I stepped in front of the windows that faced the lake. Great masses of clouds filled the sky and began moving in and around each other. Radiant beams of light filtered through the windows, blinding me. Feelings of love, peace and joy filled my body. I knew I was in the presence of holiness.

Spencer told me to draw the curtains, and I did as I was told. Before they closed completely, he reminded me again that Life Reviews were taken very seriously by his superiors. Then there was another blinding light, and he was gone.

I found myself in the elevator with a group of other people, and the elevator was descending. When I got out of the elevator on the main floor, a crowd of people were waiting for me to get out of their way so they could get on the elevator.

"Well, that's it, Louise. What do you make of it?"

Louise didn't answer Richard immediately. After a brief moment or two she said in the kindest way she could, "You've had a pretty full plate lately with everything that has happened, Mr. L. You've told me several times you haven't slept well. Maybe something has been on your mind that got you to thinking about all those things. Everybody dreams now and then. And Mr. L., it *was* only a dream. I wouldn't worry too much about it."

He looked at her like a small boy would, who was seeking some explanation to a problem he could not solve himself, and said, "Yeah, maybe you're right."

Richard got up from his chair and walked over to the kitchen window. Without turning, he asked Louise another question, "By any chance, Louise, have you ever come across somewhere in this house a tiny gold Bible like the one I just described to you?"

"No, Mr. L., I haven't. If you're looking for it, you've probably just misplaced it and stuck it somewhere and forgotten where you put it. I think something like that would probably be kept in a jewelry box or a drawer, and I don't do jewelry boxes or drawers. She picked up her coffee cup, put it in the dishwasher and gently patted Richard on his shoulder as she passed him. She had work to do.

CHAPTER FORTY-EIGHT
Kate

Kate worked the first three days of the week and took the rest of the week off to paint the basement walls, a job she had been putting off for months. After having coffee and a donut with Ruth at the Donut Hole, she came back and decided to tidy up first. She started in the living room. The Valentines she received on Valentine's Day, from all of her kids and grandchildren, were on display on the fireplace mantle. They had been there long after the holiday. She just hadn't taken the time to put them away. She especially liked the homemade ones her grandchildren had made for her.

Putting each one into a box that already contained cards from other holidays and special occasions, she realized she had not received a serious Valentine, serious meaning romantic, the kind of Valentine a woman might receive from a man who loved her. All of the ones she had received were funny Valentines. The simple acts of life, in this case the absence of a mushy Valentine from a significant other, made her more aware of her aloneness. She hastily put the cover on the box as if smothering her feelings, and returned it to the top shelf in her bedroom closet.

There were things she had to do today, and feeling sorry for herself was not one of them. She began polishing the table tops in the living room.

From the front room window, she saw the mailman coming up the walk to the front door and wondered why he hadn't put the mail in her box at the end of the driveway as he always did.

She put down her polishing cloth and went to open the door.

"Good morning," the mailman said, looking at her. "This parcel wouldn't fit in your mail box. I was going to leave it on the front porch, but good thing you were home," he explained, handing her the box along with the other mail. "Have a nice day," he said before he went down the steps and crossed over to the other side of the street to continue his route.

As she shut the door, she looked at the return address on the box. It was from JCPenney. She had ordered a shower curtain from Penney's catalog and had it mailed to her home rather than picking it up at the store. Putting the other mail on the dining room table, she tore off the wrappings, anxious to see her new shower curtain. She took it out of the box and immediately went to hang it, replacing the old one with the new one. When she stepped back to see if she liked it, she was happy with her purchase.

She then remembered she left the other mail on the dining room table and went to get it. There it was. The third letter in the pile. In the upper left hand corner was the return address of the Metropolitan Tribunal, Archdiocese of St. Louis, Missouri.

She got a knife from the kitchen drawer, sliced the envelope open and took out the letter with trembling fingers. The letter, typed on official stationary, did not take the form of the usual business letter. Instead, it began under the letterhead with the word Declaration typed in bold and underlined. Directly underneath was the case number, C-67; the petitioner's name, Mary Katherine O'Connor; the respondent's name, Michael Francis Flannigan; and the date of their marriage.

She began reading the body of the letter.

After carefully evaluating the evidence presented and after considering the laws of the Church concerning marriage, the

Tribunal has declared this marriage to be NULL. In accord with the requirements of the law of the Church, we hereby announce this decision to the parties and declare that it is effective immediately.

This ecclesiastical decision is based on evidence gathered and evaluated in the light of the laws of the Roman Catholic Church, for the purpose of determining certain rights with the Church. The decision is purely a religious matter and has no civil effects.

The letter was signed by the Judicial Vicar and the Ecclesiastical Notary.

In her hand she held documentation giving her marital freedom from Mike Flannigan. It was finally over, and the tears she shed were not only for herself but also for Mike. Her slate had been wiped clean of Mike's rejection, a failed marriage and the shame of divorce. She folded the letter and put it back into the envelope, hugging it tightly to her chest.

All kinds of thoughts were spinning around in her mind. She was free as a bird and no place to go. More importantly, no one to fly with her. Then the idea hit her, and she hoped she wasn't too late.

Painting the basement walls was forgotten. She went looking for her *Atlas*, found it in one of the kitchen drawers and thumbed through it until she found the map of Indiana. South Bend was at the top of the map. She had driven several times to Indianapolis before to visit Patrick without any problems. South Bend was farther, but, if she made it to Indy, she could make it to South Bend.

The next thing she did was to look for Richard's business card, knowing his office number would be on it. She rummaged through her desk drawer and found it among a pile of other business cards she had rubber banded together. Pulling it out from the others, she dialed his office. The receptionist answered, "Lawton and McBride Advertising. How may I help you?"

"Good morning. I'd like to make an appointment with Mr. Lawton for Thursday afternoon. Will he be in the office all day?" Kate asked.

"He's always here Thursday afternoons, but... May I have your name, please."

"Oh, I'm sorry, I'll have to call you back. Thank you."

Kate felt somewhat ashamed of herself for being devious, but she wanted to make certain Richard would not be out of town. She didn't want to drive that far only to find he was someplace else.

The afternoon was spent getting ready for her trip. She went to the bank, gassed up the car and packed an overnight bag. Finding his office would not be easy, either. Richard had once explained to her where his office was located. He had also given her the address and a picture of the building. She planned to buy a street guide or stop at a filling station for directions. She also looked in the paper to check the weather forecast for tomorrow. No inclement weather was predicted for Missouri or Indiana, only above average temps.

After packing the car, she ate dinner, watched television for awhile and went to bed early. As she rested in bed, she mentally kept reworking her plan concerning Richard. There had been no contact between them for several months. He would definitely be surprised to see her.

Maybe he would be angry or embarrassed by her unannounced appearance at his office. Maybe he had closed the door completely regarding any further contact with her. Maybe he had taken up with another woman. Then there was the biggest one of all—maybe he would reject her, before she had a chance to explain why she was there, and she wondered if she would be able to handle that.

She said her prayers and turned out the light.

Thursday morning Ruth was sitting at one of the tables near the front window at the Donut Hole drinking coffee and reading the newspaper. Kate pulled her car into the parking lot a little after 7 a.m. and parked. She locked her car and walked into the donut shop. There was a line of customers. When it was her turn, she ordered a coffee, brought it to Ruth's table and sat down across from her.

"Good morning, Ruth," Kate said.

"Hi, Kate. I didn't expect to see you today. How's the painting coming along?" Ruth asked her friend, putting down the newspaper.

"What painting? Oh, the basement painting. I haven't started. Something came up. I'm going on a little trip."

"Where to?"

"South Bend, Indiana," Kate replied.

Ruth immediately reacted. "What?"

Kate grabbed Ruth's hands in hers and said, "I got the annulment decision in the mail yesterday. I'm free, Ruth."

"Oh, Kate. I'm so happy for you," and she squeezed Kate's hands. "But... oh, now I get it. You're going to see Richard and tell him about the news, right?"

"I am," Kate said.

"How will you know where to find him?"

"I checked that out yesterday," and she told Ruth about what she had done.

"Are you sure this is what you want? What if his life has taken him down another path, since you haven't heard from him in awhile? Are you ready to accept that?"

"For the first time in a long while, I'm not going to listen to my head or do any analyzing. I'm going to listen to my heart, let the chips fall where they may. I love Richard Lawton, and, not too long ago, he said he loved me in more ways than I can remember. It won't be easy if he walks away from me, but I'm willing to take that chance. If I don't, I know I'll regret it the rest of my life."

"Then go, Kate. Drive carefully. Call me when you get back. In the meantime, you are in my prayers," Ruth said.

Kate got up, hugged her friend and walked out of the door toward her car. She got into her car and started the ignition, feeling good about herself without any reservations. She pulled out of the parking lot and started on her journey.

CHAPTER FORTY-NINE
Richard and Kate

Every Thursday afternoon at 3 p.m. a staff meeting was held in the conference room at Lawton and McBride. Richard liked to bring all of his employees together once a week at a specific time to go over any problems on existing jobs or address issues that needed answering and found a scheduled meeting time to be more efficient. He was the one who went out and got the work, but every now and then he also worked on a job to keep his skills sharp.

The large glassed-in conference room ran the entire length of the second floor. Entry was made through a door in the middle of the glass wall facing the corridor. A blackboard was mounted on the wall that faced the street between two windows. A conference table with chairs to accommodate twelve people was in the middle of the room. Richard's office was on the other side of the corridor plus a storage room and a washroom.

As the staff members began to take their places, Richard was at the blackboard, writing down the points he intended to make in his presentation.

Kate stopped at a drive-through for a hamburger and a Pepsi in order to save on the driving time. Twice she had to stop at filling stations to get directions. Although Richard lived in South Bend, his office was in Mishawaka on a street called Sadoris Way. She knew what the building looked like, because he had sent her pictures of it. After making another incorrect turn, she spotted the building and parked in front of it.

She looked at her watch and remembered she had lost an hour driving into Indiana from Missouri. Even at that, she had made good time, despite getting lost. It was a little after 3 p.m.

She combed her hair, put on fresh lipstick and walked toward the front double doors. The receptionist was sitting at her desk. Her plan was to simply walk past the receptionist as if she knew where she was going and hope for the best. Her outfit did not reflect business attire, either. She was dressed in jeans, boots, a parka and a Notre Dame scarf around her neck. Hopefully, the receptionist would consider her a local.

As luck would have it, the receptionist, a well-nourished lady named Joan Bradshaw, according to the nameplate on her desk, looked directly at her and asked, "May I help you?"

"I'm here to see Richard Lawton," Kate said.

The receptionist looked puzzled. She knew there were no appointments scheduled for her boss this afternoon due to the weekly staff meeting but did not wish to be rude.

"I'm sorry. Thursday afternoon is always reserved for a staff meeting in the conference room. Therefore, no appointments are made. There must be some mistake. May I book you for tomorrow at your convenience? What is your name?" she asked.

"He probably didn't tell you, that's all. He's expecting me. I know where the conference room is. I'll go on up," Kate said boldly and turned on her heels before climbing the steps two at a time. She heard footsteps behind her and assumed it was Ms. Bradshaw, but Kate had reached the landing well ahead of her pursuer. She turned her head and saw Richard through the glass. He was standing at the blackboard with his back to her. There were other people in the room, but Kate didn't care. She opened the door and said, "Good afternoon, Mr. Lawton. I am here to ask you two questions."

Upon hearing a voice that cut right through his being, Richard turned and blinked. Standing on the other side of the conference table was Kate O'Connor. Richard's staff members were dumbfounded, just like their boss.

Oblivious to those around her, Kate said assertively, "Here's the first question, Mr. Lawton. Am I still your steady girl?"

Richard could feel his face getting red and said nothing in reply.

"Come on, Mr. Lawton. It's rather a simple question. I'll repeat it for you." Slowly, she said, "Am...I...still...your...steady...girl?"

Richard said nothing, but nodded up and down, still not fully recovered from her being there.

"Good, we're making progress. Now, here's the big one. Will you marry me?" She started walking toward him, holding an envelope in both of her hands at chest level. As she got closer, he saw it was addressed to her and also noticed the return address—Metropolitan Tribunal, Archdiocese of St. Louis, Missouri. Her eyes were dancing. He knew then what the envelope contained.

He took her in his arms, and before he kissed her, said, "Absolutely." He heard her say very softly, "Right answer."

Had they not been lost in a world of their own, they would have heard the cheers and handclapping from the entire Lawton and McBride staff, including Ms. Bradshaw.

CHAPTER FIFTY
Kate

Richard and Kate made arrangements to be married Saturday, April 15, at 4 p.m., by Father Steve at his parish church, Ascension St. Paul in Normandy, a suburb of St. Louis. They asked Carolyn and Bob Martin to be their witnesses, and they said yes.

Kate picked the date and chose April 15, because it was the last day tax returns could be filed without a penalty. By choosing this date, she figured Richard would have a pretty good chance of remembering their future wedding anniversaries.

Kate went shopping for an appropriate outfit and other feminine things for her wedding, during the week after work. She was also determined to wear a hat, not just a small bridal one with a veil, but a big black hat.

She loved hats and was sorry when the Catholic Church no longer required women to wear a hat at services. She finally found a stunning royal blue suit at the boutique close to her house and just the right hat at Famous Barr, a black sheer wide brim one with a black rose attached to the satin black headband. While she was there, she also treated herself to new blue under things, a white matching gown and robe trimmed in floral embroidery.

After arriving home, she quickly unpacked her packages and held her own fashion show in front of the long hallway mirror to see if what she had chosen would be the look she wanted.

She heard the phone ring and rushed to answer it, knowing it was Richard.

"Were you out gallivanting with Ruth?" Richard asked.

"For your information, I do not gallivant."

Richard interrupted, "If you ever do, any gallivanting will only be done with me," and they both laughed.

"Actually, I went shopping for a wedding outfit and some other essentials."

"Like what?"

"Silly man. Do you think I am going to tell you? I want it to be a surprise, so you'll just have to wait until our wedding day. By the way, what color suit will you be wearing?"

"Orange."

"Very funny, but I wouldn't put it past you. I will never forget the plaid jacket you wore when you took me to the senior prom, the one your oldest sister made for you."

"It was something, wasn't it?"

"No comment," and she laughed again.

"I thought it was something. That jacket made me a man before my time. Not to change the subject, but what about our kids? Do you think we should invite them to the wedding or what?" Richard asked.

"I've been thinking about that, too," Kate said. "For my kids and yours, who have to take a plane, the expense might be somewhat of a burden. There is something else to consider, too. After we get married, we are going somewhere that night and the next day aren't we?"

"Yes, we are definitely going someplace that night and the next one, too. Remember I'm in charge of the honeymoon," Richard replied.

"We won't be here then. My kids, as well as yours, would have to get a motel," Kate said.

"You got any ideas?" Richard asked.

"I do. I know all my kids would want to come, but, if money is to be spent, I would much rather they come at a time when they could stay longer and all of us would be together."

"I agree. So, what's your idea?" Richard asked.

"Let's make some wedding announcements and mail them the day before we get married. In that way, all of them will get notification the first part of the following week. What do you think?" Kate asked.

"That'll work, and I agree about your kids and mine spending all that money to come and then we leave after the ceremony. I know I haven't met any of your bunch and you haven't met any of mine, but there will be plenty of time to do that later," Richard replied.

"Strange you should mention that plaid dinner jacket," Kate said. "I found a picture of the two of us someone took the night of the prom. Whoever took the picture must have given me one, and I kept it. We could buy some cream colored paper with matching envelopes and make cards. On the front put the prom picture of us and underneath it would be the first two lines of a verse I made up: *I wanted to marry my prom date, but Kate said, I'd rather wait.* When the card is opened, on the left side would be our wedding information. On the right side would be a recent picture of the two of us, and underneath our picture would be the rest of the verse: *It took awhile 'til she said yes. What's forty years more or less?*

"Very clever, Kate, very clever. And, that would work perfectly. Who would do all of the printing and such?"

"Kinko's. I've already made up a sample. I'll order some extras, and, if we decide to notify anyone else, we could use the card to send to them, too," Kate said.

"Another good idea. By the way, I called the photographer you recommended and made an appointment to have pictures taken," Richard said.

"How about the dinner after the ceremony? Did you make reservations at the Ritz Carlton for five people?" Kate asked.

"I did. Dinner for five off the menu at approximately 6 p.m.," Richard responded.

"How about the cake, Richard? I have to have a white cake with white icing."

"Yes, yes. I ordered the cake, too. What's the big fuss about the cake?" he asked.

"At my first wedding, I was married in the morning. There were six people in attendance: my mother, Mike's mother and father, the priest and the bride and groom. There was no cake at the luncheon after the ceremony. This time, there will be only five people present at our wedding: Carolyn and Bob, the priest and us. I am determined to have a cake, and a white cake with white icing is my big time favorite. Don't mess up, that's all I can say."

"Scout's honor. I've already seen to it," Richard said.

"Didn't you tell me you were thrown out of the Scouts because you took a bunch of boys in a rowboat over to the Girl Scout camp on the other side of the lake and got caught?" Kate asked.

"Okay, forget about the Scout's honor part. It's done. I promise you'll get your cake. I also made a reservation at The Leland for Friday night. We won't see each other until the next day. Bad luck and all that. I'm going to leave South Bend after work and will get in late, but I'll call you to let you know the groom has arrived.

"I'll pick you up at noon, and we'll go get the pictures taken and then go on to the church. After we have dinner, we can come back to your place and change clothes and start our wonderful life together.

"Remember, what I've planned is not going to be our real honeymoon, since you have to be at work Monday, and I need to be back in South Bend to finalize the closing deal. I promise we'll go someplace later for a real honeymoon," Richard said.

"How about giving me a clue as to where we are going after we are married?" Kate asked.

"Nope."

"Husbands and wives are supposed to share things," she added.

"True, but we aren't married yet. When we're married, then you can start with the rules. All I can say concerning our honeymoon is to prepare yourself for a very romantic encounter."

Richard said goodbye and hung up the phone. Kate O'Connor, soon to be Mrs. Richard Lawton, was in for a terrific surprise.

CHAPTER FIFTY-ONE
Richard and Kate

The day of Richard and Kate's wedding, the weather was perfect, with soft breezes and lots of sunshine. The tulips and forsythia bushes were in bloom, as well as the trees, announcing the rebirth of spring.

Kate looked out the kitchen window, taking in all the beauty of the upcoming season, and felt the same kind of rebirth in herself. Soon she would be Mrs. Richard Lawton and begin a new life, with a man she not only loved, but deeply respected and admired.

She showered, combed her hair and then began dressing for her wedding, first the new blue under things, then the sheer hosiery, and lastly, the suit and her black patent shoes. Then she went to her jewelry box and took out her mother's pearl earrings and the watch her father had given her when she graduated from high school and put them on, so their presence would be felt in memory.

She then applied lipstick, lightly sprayed Giorgio on her wrists and went to get her new hat. After she touched up her hair and was fully dressed, including her hat, she stood in front of the hall mirror and looked at her reflection. She was loved and the one thought that ran through her mind was how lucky she was to be given another chance at marital happiness.

The doorbell rang. She knew it was Richard and went to open the door. He took one look at her and said, "Wow! You look good enough to marry. I love the hat." He gave her a kiss on the cheek. "Here's something else to add to your wedding outfit," he said and handed her a white box.

When she opened the box, inside was a bouquet of white roses. "Oh, Richard. The roses are so lovely. Thank you."

"Every bride has to have flowers on her wedding day. I have a white rose for my suit lapel, too."

He looked at his watch and said, "We need to get going, Kate, or we're going to be late. We don't want to hold up the photographer. I got the stamps for the wedding announcements, too. While you're getting your things together, I'll put stamps on them. We can drop them at the post office on the way."

"The announcements are on the dining room table, Richard." She checked the kitchen door to see if it was locked and then went to get her purse and overnight bag.

They were standing in the foyer close together. He picked up her overnight bag, looked into her eyes and asked, "Ready to begin our life together?" Without missing a beat, she said, "Absolutely."

After the ceremony, Father Steve, Carolyn and Bob Martin and Mr. and Mrs. Richard Lawton drove in separate cars to the Ritz Carlton. The dining room was elegantly decorated in white tablecloths. A fresh flower arrangement was on every table, as well as a lighted candle. To add to the ambience, soft music could be heard in the background—memorable dining on a memorable day.

The group was shown to their table. Within minutes, a waiter appeared with champagne and filled their goblets. Father Steve gave the toast saying, "To Richard and Kate. May all your tomorrows be as happy as today. Hold tight to the love you share. God bless you both." Goblets were raised and touched.

The waiter reappeared and gave them each a menu. "Please order whatever you want," Richard said. "The only thing mandatory is the dessert. Kate insisted on a white cake with white icing, so I guess you're stuck."

Their dinner orders were placed. They chatted about the ceremony until they were served. During dinner, Bob asked, "Would I be out of line in asking if you're going on a honeymoon trip?"

Before Richard could reply, Kate said, "Richard is in charge of the honeymoon. Both of us have to be back on the job Monday morning, so I have no idea what he has planned for tonight and tomorrow. He did, however, tell me to pack outdoor attire and sensible shoes. For the life of me, I can't figure out where we are going."

Carolyn couldn't resist and said, "Maybe he is taking you on a hike or possibly some kind of work party. By now he probably knows how much you like to paint." Everyone broke into gales of laughter.

Being a practical man, Father Steve offered, "Honeymoons can be expensive. I couldn't help but notice the ring Richard put on your finger, Kate. Maybe his pockets are a little light right now, and he has to be somewhat innovative."

His comment triggered a look-see at Kate's wedding ring from Carolyn and Bob. Richard had chosen a wide yellow gold band with a large mounted diamond in the center with two smaller ones on each side and a plain wide yellow gold band for himself.

"What a beautiful ring, Kate. Did you design Kate's ring, Richard?" Carolyn asked.

"Yes. A friend of mine owns a jewelry store in South Bend. He took my design and made it happen."

While Richard was talking about the ring, Kate thought about her first wedding ring. Mike was in college and wrote her a letter before they were to be married, telling her to pick out a ring and mail the bill to him. Reimbursement would follow. Her family always traded at Stout's Jewelers in Springfield, so she went there alone and selected a narrow yellow gold band priced at $12. Mike never paid her the $12 for her wedding ring, although he had a job after school and on the weekends and had plenty of money to have a good time. She also did not have a bouquet or a wedding cake when they married, outward signs of how little he cared about her feelings on the most important day of her life.

As she recalled her wedding day with Mike and what led up to it, she felt enormously at peace. She now was married to a man, who she loved deeply, and knew in the depth of her soul she would be just as loved, if not more, in return. Richard Lawton was her husband, lover, soul mate and friend.

When everyone had finished eating, the waiter cleared their dishes and disappeared. Moments later, he wheeled in a round layer cake decorated in white icing and white roses on a serving cart and placed the cake at Kate's side.

"It's wonderful, Richard. I love it! A wedding without a white cake and white icing just isn't a traditional wedding in my book." She took the plates from the serving cart and began cutting a piece of cake for everyone, as the waiter filled their coffee cups.

When everyone was finished with dessert, they got up and hugged each other and promised to stay in touch and left to go their separate ways. Richard and Kate remained sitting at the table after the Martins and Father Steve left.

"It's been perfect, Richard. The picture taking, the wedding, the dinner and all the little things you did to make it so special. Thank you for making me feel so loved."

"You're welcome. I've never been so happy, and, for a very long time, I thought happiness would never be mine," he replied, kissing her fingertips.

"Now, it's time to move along, Mrs. Lawton. The day isn't over yet. Let's get the show on the road to bigger and better things."

Kate had no idea what he meant but made no comment. Gathering her things, she turned to him and said, "Do you think they'll let us take home the leftover cake? There's a tradition about saving what's left of the wedding cake for the first wedding anniversary."

"Oh, if that's the case, we better not take any chances concerning a tradition. I'll take care of it. If I have any trouble with the waiter when he comes back, I'll beat him silly until he sees it my way."

Kate gave him a big smile and said, "My hero!"

After leaving the Ritz Carlton, Richard drove to Kate's house, where they changed their dress clothes into casual attire. Kate kept wondering where they would spend the night but did not question Richard about their destination.

When Kate got into Richard's car, she noticed the back seat was piled with several quilts and two boxes. Richard got into the driver's seat and said, "Did you lock up everything good and tight? We won't be back until late tomorrow afternoon."

"I did. Richard, tomorrow is Sunday, and I have to go to Mass. Is this going to be possible where we are going? I really didn't pack any nice clothes, but…"

"Not to worry. I have that covered. Clean slacks and a jacket will be all you'll need. Now, no further questions. Okay?" He pulled away from the curb, and they began their honeymoon. Soon they were on Highway 55 going south with Kate watching all the exit signs trying to figure out where Richard was taking them.

They passed the town of Weldon. Kate thought he might be driving to Memphis since they were on the right highway. But, within a short time, he took another exit, and the direction signal on the dash indicated southwest. The night air and champagne took over, and she leaned her head back and closed her eyes. When she opened them, she began to recognize some things along the way. Then, she figured it out. They were going to Lieu des Lacs. But why? There was no motel there.

"Richard, I know where we are. What have you got up your sleeve?"

"Patience, wife. You'll find out soon enough."

Within a short time they passed the clubhouse in Lieu des Lacs. The lights from the homes were their lampposts, but the farther they traveled, the darker it became. Richard turned left after leaving the main road.

"We're going to the log house, aren't we?"

"Yes. It isn't finished, but I thought it might be romantic to spend our first married night together in our log home. The outside is all done, but there is still quite a bit of work to do inside."

Kate had not been to the site, since that fateful evening when they quarreled, and had no idea what to expect.

After turning on Notre Dame Road, Richard turned on his bright lights so they both could see better and pulled the car under the carport. He got out and walked over to Kate's side and opened the car door for her. He reached into the glove compartment and got out a flashlight and said, "Follow me."

They walked to the front door, and Richard opened it. Turning to Kate, he said, "Mrs. Lawton, I believe it's customary to carry the bride over the threshold," before he picked her up in his arms and carried her into their home. While still in his arms, he turned on the entry light. The great room was completely empty of furniture. Tools and other equipment were on the floor.

"Now, be a good girl and stay put. I have to unload the car. You can sit on that wooden bench over there and wait for me."

Kate did as she was told. While Richard went out to the car, she began looking around. In the great room, two big windows faced the lake. The floor was hardwood, and the ceiling was also finished in wood that reflected true craftsmanship.

Also in the great room was the kitchen with ample room for a table and chairs. The cabinetry, refrigerator, stove and dishwasher were already installed. She assumed the large space next to the kitchen was intended to be used for a sitting area. A staircase from the living room led to the loft. She couldn't see beyond the loft hallway and assumed there were other rooms upstairs.

Richard came back with their suitcases. She followed him down the hall. The master bedroom door was closed unlike the bathroom and the guest room.

"Let me turn on the light," Richard said, after opening the door to the master bedroom.

He walked into the room with Kate behind him and heard her intake of breath.

"It's the same furniture that was in the model house I saw with Jackie," Kate exclaimed.

"Yes, it is. I remembered you saying how much you liked the Amish bedroom set and decided to surprise you," Richard replied.

"How did you manage all this?" Kate asked.

"Jake Davidson checked his records and found the paperwork on the bedroom suite. He contacted his Amish supplier and was told the set was still available. I knew I couldn't be here when it was scheduled for delivery, so I called Frank Ambrose. I made arrangements with him to handle the delivery and mailed him a duplicate key to the house," Richard explained.

"I hope you like it. I arranged the bed against this wall so that when we wake up in the morning we will be able to see the lake. You have no idea of how many times I have dreamed of doing this with you nestled in my arms."

"I love it," Richard. "Especially the nestling part."

The master bedroom also faced the lake and had the same two sized windows as the living room. The unmade bed and nightstand were placed on the wall opposite the windows and at the end of the bed was a cedar chest. A dresser and a mirror, a chest of drawers and a rocking chair with a lamp table combo were placed in the far corner of the room.

"You can arrange the rest of the furniture any way you like tomorrow," he said. After you decide where the pieces should go, I'll hang the mirror."

He put down the quilt and pillows and said, "I hope you're not upset. I thought we could spend the first night of our marriage in our new home. I know it's bare bones, but I brought necessities."

She rushed into his arms. "It will be wonderful, Richard. She walked over to the window. "Look out at the lake. It's shimmering, and the sky is flooded with so many stars."

He joined her at the window and said, "Are you happy?"

"Yes, oh, yes. Kiss me, then let me help you get the rest of the stuff."

They embraced, clinging to each other in a moment of shared happiness.

"I'll be right back. Hold that feeling so we can take up where we left off," and he went out to get the boxes from the car.

Before long, the two of them had the room ready. Richard put a bottle of wine into a nearby empty bucket. He then went and got ice cubes from the fridge and filled the bucket with them to keep the wine cold.

Kate made the bed with the quilt and bed linens Richard brought and puffed up the pillows. She lighted several candles and placed them on the chest of drawers. She put their wine glasses on the nightstand as well as the leftover cake Richard had also brought.

"What a fine honeymoon suite," she said to Richard, looking around the room. "The only thing we are missing is some nice romantic music."

"Oh, contraire. I forgot to bring in the portable radio. Be back in a jiffy," he said and went to the car to get it. When he returned, he plugged in the radio and found a station playing romantic music to match their mood.

"You can undress in the bathroom. I forgot to bring light bulbs. Sorry. You'll have to use the flashlight. There's a cup in there and a fresh toothbrush and toothpaste in the medicine chest."

"I'll manage," Kate said. She picked up her overnight bag and went into the bathroom. In the meantime, Richard unpacked the other box, placed the coffeemaker on the kitchen counter and put away the food he had brought for tomorrow's breakfast.

When she came out of the bathroom and re-entered the bedroom, she was dressed in her new white gown and robe. "You look so beautiful, Kate. You take my breath away. I came so close to losing you for the second time, all because I didn't understand. Now, I do. Be patient with me. I love you so much," he whispered. He took her hand and led her to the bed. He undressed and got in bed beside her.

"Before I make love to you all night, there is something I have that belongs to you," and gave her a small box. "Go ahead. Open it."

She took the box from him and gently lifted the lid, expecting a piece of jewelry. It took only a second for Kate to realize what the box contained. It was the miniature Bible Richard had given her so long ago.

"You've kept this all these years?" she asked in a trembling voice.
"Yes."

She took the Bible out of the box, thinking of the time Richard had given it to her and the circumstances that made her return it to him. Pulling the knob downward on the top of the Bible, she took out the tiny delicate rosary. As if it were yesterday, she remembered asking him if he had the rosary blessed.

As she put the rosary back into its case, she noticed again what was metal-stamped in the bottom right hand corner of the case, Sydney Weston, New York Patent Pending. Under this bordered inscription and centered, three very small letters had also been engraved, YRF.

"I never noticed these three engraved letters before," Kate said. "Do you know what they mean, Richard?"

"Yes, I do," he said softly, looking at her lovingly.

Kate waited for him to say more, but he remained silent.

"What does YRF mean? Tell me, Richard."

"Those three letters have been there all this time, Kate. I had those letters engraved the day I bought the rosary for you forty some years ago. The letters stand for *Your Richard Forever.*"

With tears in her eyes, she turned toward him. She threw her arms around his neck, kissed him passionately and pressed her body against his.